FORTUNATE COOKIE

ASPEN GOLD SERIES BOOK 11

LIZZIE STARR

Cover & interior design by Cat & Doxie Author Services

This book is dedicated to
bakers, makers, and creators.
The world needs you.
Keep on doing what you do!

CHAPTER ONE

*C*ookie Lamont stood in the center of her immaculate store front and smiled with satisfaction. The bakery case sparkled, ready to show off the day's cupcake specials and local favorites. Behind the counter, the copper espresso machine gleamed under a strategically placed spotlight. She turned toward the front of the store and the tall, narrow paper mâché tree she decorated for the seasons. It was nearly Easter, so she really needed to add the colored eggs and fluffy bunny ornaments to honor the coming spring. Especially after last weekend's major blizzard. Tilting her head from one side to the other, she gave a final adjustment to the placement of a white twinkle light. Maybe she'd give up control and ask one of her baristas to decorate.

Cookie's Coffee & Cakes was ready to open for the day.

She raised the shade on the huge front window. A single body waiting on the sidewalk, hunched against the early morning chill, lifted a gloved hand in greeting. Cookie returned the wave and hurried to open the door. Winter business hadn't been the best in this tourist town, but with the warmer weather, things were looking up. She'd been in Spencer for nearly nine months and the locals had proved to be steady customers. Having the only fancy coffee service in this part of town hadn't hurt. Thank goodness she'd kept that expensive option in her business plan.

"Come on in, Mr. Kinsey. I'll get your coffee started."

Mr. Kinsey removed his coat dropped the jacket over the back of a chair. "Vernon," he said with a chuckle. "I'm here often enough to be on a first name basis with you."

"Vernon. I have some of those breakfast cupcakes you like. They're fresh from the oven. Can I get you one?"

"Sounds perfect, Cookie. You should branch out into pastries if you insist on opening so early. Not everyone can be convinced to try a cupcake first thing in the morning."

Cookie laughed. "I know. But cupcakes keep me busy enough. You'll have to go to the The Cooling Rack for your donut fix."

"No coffee at the bakery. And just plain stuff or tea..." He made a face. "Tea, at the bookstore. Although, Katie does have cinnamon rolls on Tuesday. Gotta be there early to get one of those."

Carefully delivering the steaming cup, Cookie sighed dramatically. "So that's why you're never here on Tuesday. I should have guessed." She and Kate Spencer, owner of the bookstore, had made a friendly agreement not that long ago. Cookie provided cupcakes for afternoon sales at the Rocky Mountain Bookstore twice a week and Kate directed serious coffee drinkers to Olde Town and Cookie's.

So business was good—even with the winter lull. Luckily, her online business took up any slack. In fact, she'd been surprised by a sudden influx of orders over the past two months. Word of mouth she suspected, since she hated doing any online marketing. She never would have imagined how popular erotic, anatomically correct, carved cakes would be. Especially her portrait cakes. She'd gotten over being embarrassed by the explicit cakes, but thank God she never had to meet any of those customers face to, uh, face.

"My cupcake?" Vernon interrupted her thoughts with a smile.

"Of course. Sorry, just lost in thought. Be right back."

❧

Anthony Burnham maneuvered his truck into a too small space in the parking area behind the Old Stone Church. Scaffolding and tarps covered the back façade of the old church, indicating there was some exterior work being done along with the interior redesign his mom had described in detail in one of her letters. It was about time someone rescued the beautiful old building. Who better than Willa Samuels, Spencer's renowned artist.

No, he'd forgotten. She was Willa Spencer now, married to Jakob Spencer, owner of the Aspen Gold Lodge. He stared into the dark, pre-dawn morning. Things, and people, certainly had changed since he'd last been home. He gave a soft snort. At least now he had plenty of time to hear all the stories.

He glanced across the street toward the area now known as Olde Town. The shops were dark, and he figured his moms wouldn't be up yet. In any case, right now he needed coffee. He no longer had an easy familiarity with the roads leading into town and driving those narrow mountain roads at night probably hadn't been the wisest choice. Especially with the high piles of snow left from clearing the pavement after the recent blizzard. But he was anxious to be home. He needed family.

He could head back to the edge of town and the 24-hour gas station, but no one would ever convince him that, despite the claims in commercials, the coffee was freshly brewed. At this time of the morning, there was a good chance it was yesterday's brew. He shuddered.

He'd wait until the first light came on in the apartment

over his family's store, then call from right outside the door. His moms had no idea he was coming. He looked forward to surprising the two women he loved more than anything in the world. Except maybe his sister, but she hadn't been home in longer than he'd stayed away. He should call her, convince her to come for a visit while he was here.

A wide yawn nearly cracked his jaw. With no hope of coffee, he needed to walk and let the cold wake him. So, he slipped from the warm truck cab, pocketed his keys and, with his collar turned up against the frigid wind off the mountains, he crossed the street.

He headed along the back sides of the buildings just across from the city park. His long strides brought him quickly to the far end of the block and the point where two sides of Olde Town made a triangle's point. Slightly more awake and shivering, he turned toward the center courtyard.

Bright light shining from a single store caught his attention. He knew most businesses opened later to serve the tourist trade. He shrugged. Maybe the lights were nothing more than a cleaning crew getting ready for the day.

Drawn like a moth to that bright light, he walked in a wide arch, studying the simple storefront. A cupcake store? Open at six? With a customer? Then he saw it. There, at the back of the store. A beacon of hope, warmth and comfort all wrapped in copper. An espresso machine. A good quality one, if he knew his machines.

And a blessing on this cold, Colorado morning.

He hesitated only a second then rushed to the entrance. He paused to check the hours listed on a small card near the door. Yep. Open. He tugged on the door and the aroma of dark, almost bitter roast coffee froze him in the doorway. He lifted his nose, inhaled and sighed.

"Hey, man, in or out. Just close the door." The customer sitting at a small, round wooden table gestured for Anthony to enter. "Mornin'. It's a pleasant change to see someone else out this early."

"Coffee," was all Anthony managed.

"I hear ya. Cookie had to go check her baking. She should be right back. She makes a mean latte. You a tourist?"

Dragging his focus from the coffee service, Tony shook his head. "No, used to live here. I'm just back to visit family."

"Have a seat." The man shoved out a chair with one foot. "I'm Vernon Kinsey."

"Anthony Burnham." He swung a leg over the chair and shrugging out of his coat, sat.

"Burnham? Like in Muffy Burnham?"

Anthony nodded. "My mother."

The older man screwed up his expression. "Anthony. Hmm. Your sister is Isabeau?"

Considering the older man, Tony paused before answering. "Yes."

"Don't look so concerned, young man. A long time ago I taught ballroom dancing here in town. Izzy was one of the most talented girls in class. Tell me, did she keep dancing?"

Yeah, she had. But not exactly the way the man meant. Last Tony had heard, she was an exotic dancer in Nebraska. "Off and on, I think. I really haven't talked to her for a while." At the man's disapproving frown, Tony continued, "But I'm hoping to talk her into coming home while I'm here. It'd be great to have the whole family together. It's been a few years. Too long."

Vernon lifted his cup. "There's truth in that, my boy. Ah, here's Cookie."

Coffee order hovering on his lips, Tony rose and moved toward the counter. A young woman had bent behind the clear display case, placing cupcakes in precise rows on a colorful tray. "Uh, excuse me?"

"Yikes." She jerked and stuck her thumb into the thick, creamy white icing on a dark cupcake. "Well, shi— shoot."

"I'm sorry, didn't mean to startle you. I, uh..." Words failed him when she straightened and looked at him with wide, chocolate-brown eyes. Dark hair, tucked up in a messy bun, highlighted her fair complexion. The contrast was a study in perfection. She lifted her hand as if to brush back a stray hair but stared instead at her frosting covered finger.

He had the insane desire to pull that finger into his mouth and lick off every bit of sweetness.

Seeming to pull herself together, she pasted on a perfect customer service smile and reached for a towel. "Hi, welcome to Cookie's Coffee & Cakes. What can I get for you?"

He couldn't look away. Her soft gaze held him in thrall. He wanted nothing, nothing but... "Coffee."

Her pasted-on smile softened to a true grin. "Plain or fancy?"

Regaining some semblance of composure, Tony gave his order in a well-practiced manner.

She turned without comment and started his drink. He hadn't specified a size, so was filled with relief when she grabbed the largest cup. Rooted in place, he watched her economical movements. When she placed the coffee on the counter, he pointed to the ruined cupcake. "Since I caused that, I'll take the cupcake, too."

"Oh, don't worry about it. One of the tribulations of baking. It's not the first time I've worn frosting. It won't be the last."

The suddenness of the vision filling his brain made him draw a sharp breath. This woman, wearing frosting. And nothing else. He gave his head a quick shake but couldn't dislodge the thought from his brain—or his uncomfortably interested body. He cleared his throat. "Still, in this case, I'd love that cupcake for breakfast."

❦

After the early morning coffee seekers had gone, Cookie blew out a long, slow breath trying to calm the fierce beating of her heart. Who was that man, that gorgeous man who left her befuddled, confused, and unwilling to resist the unusual attraction? She didn't need a man. Want a man. She had no time for a relationship, and definitely not for the needs of a man. Her father had distracted her mother from her dreams and Cookie was determined to stay far from that unhappy fate.

But, that one. She'd consider—maybe—a date or three. Or an evening in. She fanned her face with her hand. Even when her evenings started early and ended by eight there was plenty of time for possibilities.

She glanced down at the special order that had just come in from Kinky Kakes, her online baking business. Maybe she needed to stop making these erotic cakes. Especially if he was in town long. Hmm. Long.

No. She shook herself and sat back in her desk chair. Don't even go there. Shit, how could just one man with sandy blond hair and gray-blue eyes having coffee and a damn cupcake mess with her hard-won calm? Nope, she didn't need this in her life right now. Or ever.

Confident her barista was busy and had everything under control in the shop, she opened her secret business email and replied to a special order, confirming price, date and delivery.

In her mind she scheduled the baking for the next day the shop was closed. For now she needed to get back to that day's cupcakes.

And just in time. The rear door opened and her assistant baker entered. "Cookie, I need to talk to you."

"Sure. There's nothing going on right now. Come on into my office." Calling the corner where she had an old wooden desk with a computer her office was silly but made her feel good. Successful. Like she knew what she was doing.

The intrusion of her father's voice echoed through her thoughts. *You don't have the smarts to own a business, girl. Find yourself a good man. You'll be successful like your mother then.*

His idea of success was a woman at home, dinner on the table, a sweet smile and slim figure. The man lived in the 1950's and her mother went along on that time travel quest with him.

Cookie had seen the hurt in her mother's eyes when she hadn't performed up to the man's standards. Or the dead expression when he berated her mother's once successful career. When the man had thrown out the fabric samples and her mother's sewing machine, her mother had shut down and since then, been the happy Stepford wife he wanted.

Waiting until she was old enough to leave home meant hiding under her father's radar as much as possible. At least when she'd asked to take baking classes at the community college, she'd convinced him it was to improve her skills for her future husband.

The road to Spencer and her little cupcake shop had been long, hard and filled with unexpected curves. She didn't regret a moment of the hard work. Or the secret, online bakery that covered the mortgage payments for the building and supply deliveries the first few months. Once she'd added the coffee service, business had exploded.

Take that, Dad.

Maybe she should close the online bakery. She glanced at the old-fashioned ledger she kept along with her computerized spreadsheets. No. Not quite yet. Even with her concerns the town people might boycott her shop if they discovered her hidden business, emotionally she still needed that cushion to fall back on. But soon. At least by the end of the year.

"So, what's up," she asked the woman who perched on the edge of a chair facing her. Cookie smiled an encouragement.

The woman remained silent a few moments then blurted, "We just found out I'm pregnant."

"Congratulations."

"But my husband, well, he..."

Cookie knew the words the woman hesitated to say and took her hand. Her eyes held the same defeated dullness as her mother's had, despite her apparent joy at having a baby. "And your husband doesn't think you should be working outside the home."

A spark of surprise lit the woman's eyes then she shook her head. "He doesn't. But he also doesn't expect me just to quit and leave you with no help. He says I can have a month."

"Don't worry about me. But you'll be difficult to replace, you know."

"I will?"

The poor thing needed some encouragement. "Of course. You're one of the best bakers I've worked with. Oh, I know you didn't think you knew anything when you started. Remember how afraid you were of the big mixer?"

Finally relaxing, the woman chuckled. "It is a beast compared to the little one I have at home."

"You follow my recipes exactly so everything turns out perfectly every time."

"Except that time I forgot to turn on the timer after I set it. Whew, the smoke was horrible."

Cookie shrugged. "I think every baker's done that a time or two. Before long you'll be baking for your little one. Imagine the treats you'll be able to create now. I'm sure your husband will enjoy the sweet baked goods as well."

Relief filled the woman's eyes and washed over Cookie as well. She might not be able to change the world, or even the mind of this one man, but easing someone's concerns went a long way. "You've given me plenty of notice. Thanks for that. Hopefully I can get someone hired before you leave so you can help me train them."

"Help train?"

"Of course. You know the job, how I like things done. You'd be a great help to me. Like you always are. Now, those cupcakes aren't going to frost themselves. There's a tray of carrot cake that need cream cheese cinnamon icing. Go ahead and pipe a carrot on top for the decoration. Would you start with those, please?"

"Yes, yes of course, Cookie. And thanks."

"No, thank you. And congratulations on your future cupcake lover."

"If my sister throws a shower, I'm telling her she has to get cupcakes from here, not the grocery store."

"And I'll make them special just for you. Now get busy. I've got a little paperwork to finish."

Cookie watched her soon to be ex-employee for a minute then opened her ledger and made a note about the resignation. Despite the husband's obvious control over what his wife could or couldn't do, Cookie hoped they had a better relationship than Cookie's parents. Beyond hope there was little else Cookie could do. She fiddled with items on her desk to pass a couple minutes, then rose to do what she did best.

Lose herself in developing a new cupcake flavor.

CHAPTER TWO

The late spring morning sun brightened the center of the Olde Town triangle. Tony stood near the old pony express station turned tourist information center and studied the buildings. Not that long ago—before he'd left Spencer to pursue his dreams, the station had been a ramshackle mess barely held together by the efforts of the Historical Society. He remembered the school field trips when his grade school class walked over for a historical lesson, then ate sack lunches in the park.

Those were the days, he supposed.

Now refurbished to look old, the station offered information, tours, and tourist tchotchkes. Across the street stood an old one room schoolhouse the society had rescued and moved into town. While still under interior renovation, the building shone with a new coat of paint and freshly washed windows.

Two long rows of connected buildings formed two sides to the Olde Town triangle. Numerous statues, benches and an old-time soda fountain filled the space between. Tourism had been good to Spencer.

A light came on in the shop at one end of the row and the

shadow of someone unlocking the door made him smile. He took another sip of his cold, yet still delicious coffee. His moms were up and in the shop. Although anxious to surprise them, he continued to stand near the life-size bronze statue of a pony express rider. He wanted to see them, but not have to explain exactly why he was home. Or how he didn't know if he had anywhere to go after this visit.

He was in flux. And he didn't like it one bit.

Hosting a television show about building tree houses for the rich and famous was fine, and he'd had great fun with the unlimited budgets and ideas. But other than for entertainment value, what had that done for regular folks? There was little hope to replicate even the simplest of last season's designs with a limited budget.

He ached, physically ached with the desire to share the joy of spending time in the branches of a grand old tree with everyone. Rubbing his chest over his heart, Tony stared unseeing across Olde Towne. He barely understood this feeling himself so had been totally unsuccessful in conveying his new dream to the network executives.

His new dream. What exactly did he want?

That baker would be a good start.

Tony blinked his vision clear and turned to face the cupcake shop. Whoa. He wasn't looking for a relationship in Spencer. He hoped to find answers here in the calming presence of the women who raised him, and the acceptance and comfort of growing expanded family.

The 'Welcome to Spencer' sign maker wouldn't be able to keep up with the population count with so many of his cousins getting married. And having babies.

No. He wasn't going to be one of them. He drank the dregs of his coffee and crushed the cup in his fist. Tossing the cardboard ball into a waiting trash can, he crossed the triangle.

Time to surprise his moms.

He crossed the courtyard and entered S&B Pottery. The scents of damp clay and dried herbs transported him back to his high school days. His moms had always had an oddly eclectic shop, one matching their over-age hippie appearances and sensibilities. God, he'd forgotten how much he loved this place.

"Be right with you," a voice called from the back of the store.

"No hurry, Mom," he called back then grinned, spread his arms, and waited.

A shriek, followed by "Anthony?" broadened his smile. The two women burst through a beaded curtain and careened into each other as they rushed to be enfolded in his hug.

He stumbled back a step then held the two women tightly. He'd missed this. "I'm sorry."

His birth mom leaned back. "Sorry for what, dear?"

"Not coming home sooner."

"You're here now, that's what's important." Janelle, his mother's partner, stepped back then reached to brush at his shoulder. "You've been a busy boy."

He arched one eyebrow.

"Man. A busy man." Janelle laughed then grabbed him around the waist. "I'm so happy to see you."

"You, too, Ma." He kissed the top of his mother's head. "And Mom. I didn't realize how much I've missed our family."

His mother took one hand and tugged him toward the back of the shop. "Come on, tell us everything. How's work? I loved the last episode where you built the treehouse that cantilevered over the cliff. Who was your favorite celebrity? Any romance in your life?"

"Now Muffy, give our boy a break," Janelle said.

"Oh, of course. I'm sorry. When did you get in? Have you had breakfast?" Muffy eyed him and gave a satisfied nod and waggled her eyebrows. "At least you've been taking care of yourself. Lookin' good, son."

"Uh, thanks. I think."

"Muff, you'll embarrass the boy. Tony, sit. I can run upstairs and grab some coffee and—"

He held up one hand as he allowed her to push him onto a chair. "I just had coffee and a breakfast cupcake at the shop down the row. I'm good. For now."

Muffy leaned back and crossed her arms, and a satisfied grin filled her face. "So, you've met the baker? Is she nice? We don't know much about her. She keeps pretty much to herself and hasn't gotten involved with the Olde Town council. But then, she's only been here a few months. She seems to have weathered the winter well, though."

As a boy, he'd learned just to allow his mom to ramble. She always got to the point. Eventually. Sometimes he learned things that he'd never discover otherwise. He'd hoped one of his folks might have some insight about the baker. What they did or didn't know didn't matter. The way his prospects were looking right now, he'd be in town at long enough to get to know her himself.

Wait. What?

He'd also learned to keep track of his mother's rambling and answer appropriately. "Yes, I met her. Makes a damn good cupcake if the one I tasted is any indication. The shop looks successful, especially if it hasn't been open long."

Janelle sat across a scarred, paint and clay spattered table from him and glanced at Muffy for confirmation. "It's been, oh, about nine or ten months? She opened early last fall. But for now, that's enough about her. Isn't this usually the time for you to be working on next season's shows?"

The moment of truth. He'd barely acknowledged the situation to himself, let alone tried to explain it to anyone else. His moms had always been there for him, with love and support no matter what he'd done. Both good and bad.

They'd be sure to have suggestions to at least help focus his thoughts.

"I'm on a sort of hiatus."

"Sort of? What does that mean?" Muffy sat on a wooden crate she'd pulled next to the table.

Staring at the tabletop, he traced the edges of a glaze splatter with his finger.

Janelle stopped his restless movement. "Just tell us."

Tony took a deep breath and lifted his head to the concerned gazes of the women who raised him. "Do you know how much I love you?"

Muffy waved away his statement. "Of course we do, dear. Now, what is it that has you so conflicted? Don't give me that surprised look. Don't you think we can tell when something serious is bothering you? We've known you since you popped out of my womb, kiddo."

"Mom." Sometimes the things she said would embarrass a sailor. He fought the urge to duck his head like he had as an embarrassed kid.

She chuckled. "Get on with it, Tony. What's your trouble?"

"I'm tired of the show's format. Fed up with building tree-houses for those who want yet another status symbol. Of creating something that not everyone could have."

His mothers gave each other knowing glances. "See," Janelle said. "I knew he'd come around."

"Come around? Ma, what are you talking about?"

Muffy took his hand. "When the show began, you were happy. But as time and new seasons went on, we could tell you began to simply go through the motions. Oh, your work didn't suffer. No, not at all. And anyone who doesn't know you wouldn't have noticed anything different. But we did. Didn't say anything. This was for you to discover, dear. Now, what happened?"

Tony blinked and leaned back in his chair to study the

women. Guess it was true. You really didn't know or appreciate your parents until you got older. He took another deep breath. Even so, it wasn't easy to admit what in some respects felt like a professional failure.

"I pitched a new idea to the execs. I want to build treehouses using economical means and methods, so more people can experience the joy of being a part of the treetops. Instead of building and showing off, I want to take the viewer step by step through the process."

"So everyone can have a treehouse," Muffy agreed.

"If they have an appropriate tree," he confirmed. "But the execs didn't take kindly to the poor man's treehouse. I feel strongly enough about this that I refused to go back to the old format. We're at an impasse. I was accused of being a diva. Am I, Mom?"

Muffy chuckled. "Of course not, dear. You're standing up for what's right. For you. I think your idea sounds wonderful. And no, not just because I'm your mother. I'm sure you have building tips folks could use even if they're not building in the trees. Your viewers relate to you, and although I'm sure there are many who adore the rich and famous aspect, I'm also sure a majority of viewers would love their own treehouses. You know, common folks like me."

"You are far from common folks, Mom. Ma. The two of you are the best parents I could have hoped for. I'll get my situation figured out. Now how about you? How's the clay business?"

Tony tried to focus on their responses, and managed to acknowledge, be amazed, and consoling at the right times, although he was pretty sure he didn't fool his moms. He'd almost never been able to do that.

"And did you get an invitation?"

Tony blinked. He'd allowed his mind to wander too far afield. "Invitation?"

"To another of your cousin's weddings. It's next month."

Muffy rose and searched through a pile of envelopes and papers on the nearby desk. "It's a lovely invitation. The bride makes her own paper for cards and journals so she made the invitations herself. Ours just came yesterday so yours should be somewhere. Did you have your mail forwarded?"

He shrugged. "I don't remember. Let's see, I know Mandy, both Heath and Hunter, and oh, yeah, Jack, the newest Spencer are now all deep in wedded bliss."

Janelle shook her finger at him. "Don't make fun."

Chagrinned, he offered an honest apology. "Sorry. Who's next?"

"Ryder."

❧

"I'm glad you called me this morning," Cookie said, glancing around at the other women gathered at the table. "It's been way too long since I've been able to get away for a girl's night."

"More like a girl's late afternoon." Kate Spencer, owner of the bookstore said. She rubbed her rounded belly. "I have to go to bed early with this little one. And I don't dare eat too close to that time. But I was so craving some Chinese food. I'm glad you all could make it."

That afternoon's group included Kate, Vianna Harrison, a local artist and Ruby Lawe, another relative newcomer to town. Vianna chuckled. "Good thing Jack and Ryder are busy with construction at the ranch this afternoon, or we'd never have gotten away. Jack's a little protective."

Kate shook her head in mock sadness. "A little? Well, he missed out on my pregnancy with Madison, so I think he's trying to make up for it with this one. Oh, I'm not complaining. Much."

Ruby leaned her forearms on the table. "Try living with the police chief. Talk about protective. By the time I'm as far along as you, Kate, he'll probably have cocooned me in bubble wrap." She shook her head and gazed at the ceiling. "I can't wait."

Her deadpan comment made the others laugh. Ruby lifted one of her index fingers and pointed at Vianna, then Cookie. "Don't laugh, you two, Just wait until it's your turn."

Cookie gestured toward Vianna. "She's the one to watch. She's getting married soon. Me? I don't even have any prospects."

The vision of the man who'd become too much of a distraction filled her thoughts. She hadn't seen him since that first morning. Perhaps he'd only been in town that one day.

What a shame.

The waitress paused by their table with another small pot of tea, interrupting Cookie's daydream. She shook her head. She didn't really care for tea but sipped at one tiny cup just to say she'd been a part of the experience. Oddly enough, she didn't like coffee either. Just the aroma of freshly ground beans. At least she didn't drink any of her profits from the coffee bar in her shop.

"No matter when we get together, it's always fun," Cookie said. "I've been so busy for so long trying to get my business solvent, sometimes I think I've forgotten how to have fun."

"I hear you there, sister," Kate said. "I felt I'd finally become successful when I was able to hire a second part-time employee. Thank goodness she's worked out and is able to go full-time now. Madison was a toddler when I opened the store and that was tough. I have no desire to do that again."

The waitress returned and set a red rectangular try in the center of the table. "Ah," Ruby said, "Our fortune cookies."

The four women stared at the tiny tray with four wrapped cookies. "You first," Vianna prompted Ruby.

"Oh no, it should be you, or Kate."

Cookie shook her head. They'd done this every time. And

every time, she offered the same solution. "Everyone at once. Right? One. Two. Three."

Laughing, the woman reached for the fortune cookies, and with remarkably few bumps and tangled fingers, each sat back with their cookie. "Who's first?"

Three pairs of eyes focused on Cookie. Again, it was always the same. They claimed it was because of her name. She grumbled and tore open the wrapper. Taking her time to position the cookie just right, she grinned at her friends and snapped the crisp treat in two to expose the fortune. Everyone leaned toward the center of the table and Cookie lowered her voice.

"An agreeable romance will brighten your future."

"...in bed," the other three said softly.

After a moment, Ruby laughed. "Whoever came up with this was a genius.

"A long-time tradition, upheld in Chinese restaurants across America," Vianna said. "I've heard it just about everywhere I've been. Or some variation. I think there's one that's 'in pants'."

"That's not as much fun," Kate mused. "Now yours, Vianna."

As they went around the table reading their fortunes, Cookie's mind wandered. Her fortune had been a traditional 'you will meet someone'. In bed. She had sort of met someone earlier that week. Someone she really wouldn't mind finding in her bed. But a tourist's typical stay didn't generally allow for that kind of encounters.

Unless that's all they were looking for.

She wasn't.

Truthfully, he didn't appear to be just out looking for a good time. There was something settled about him, something familiar. Like she might have seen him before. Not in Spencer though. She definitely would have remembered.

"Cookie? Cookie? Earth to Cookie."

Uh oh, caught daydreaming. "Sorry, just, umm, thinking about a new cupcake flavor."

Kate wrinkled her nose. "Sure you were. Must be some special cupcake. You're blushing."

"Am not." But she was. She felt the heat at her cheeks.

"So, what kind of cupcake makes you blush."

This would be the perfect opportunity to tell them about her side business, but she wanted that to remain secret. At least until she was sure she wouldn't be run out of town or anything. She was being silly. Who really cared what she did in her miniscule time off?

Ruby's phone chimed, thankfully ending the attention focused on Cookie. "It's Hunter. I've got to go before he gets too anxious." Ruby dug through her purse and tossed money on the table. "If that doesn't cover mine and some tip, let me know. Sorry to cut this short."

Kate stretched. "It's time anyway. I need to move before my poor body freezes into one position. Now remember, we've got Vianna's wedding shower coming up in a couple weeks. Wait until you see the cake I just ordered. Oh, sorry, Cookie. But I wanted something different than cupcakes. Besides this way you can just come enjoy the fun without having to worry about anything."

Vianna stared at her folded hands in her lap. "You really don't need—"

Kate touched her arm. "Yes, yes I do. As matron of honor, it's my duty to make sure all the wedding traditions are properly upheld."

"But you didn't have a shower."

"Which is why yours is going to be extra fun. I'll more than make do with all the baby showers coming up." Kate winked at Ruby. "Both mine and everyone else's."

Once Ruby left the table, the others finished dividing the bill and said their good-byes. Vianna walked with Cookie to their cars. "You are coming to my shower, aren't you? Even without bringing cupcakes?"

Cookie chuckled. Vianna had arrived in Spencer not long after she had, and Cookie understood how overwhelming the tight knit community could be. Even though she'd seldom stepped out into community activities herself. "Yes, of course. I wouldn't miss your party for the world. I want you to know I'm still working to perfect my cinnamon roll cupcake. I'm sure it will never measure up to your rolls, but I keep trying."

"I do have a secret ingredient."

"That you won't tell." Cookie knew there had to be something she'd been missing in her batter, but nothing she'd tried had tasted right.

"No, I'll tell anyone who wants to know. I'm just not sure how it will fit into a cupcake."

Cookie stopped and planted her fists at her waist. If all she needed was this secret ingredient, she wanted to know. Right now. Then tomorrow...

Vianna chuckled. "You're ready to go right to the bakery and try it out, aren't you? I can see it in your face."

"Actually, I was thinking about tomorrow. So, secret ingredient?"

Shrugging, Vianna opened the door to the ancient Blazer she drove. "Sweet potatoes."

CHAPTER THREE

*I*nstead of working on the cinnamon roll cupcake the next morning, Cookie stood in the middle of the bakery's small kitchen, making her plan for the day. The bakery wasn't open on Monday, so she had the space to herself to work on two special order cakes. One was a simple penis shaped cake. She could do those in her sleep. Although when she'd started her online business, she'd been embarrassed while trying to carve a life-like body part.

The second... she moved to her desk to double check the order that had come in late Saturday. She'd replied automatically, confirming the cake and the date without looking past the basics of the order. Now she needed to check where the cake needed to be shipped to so she could plan her time.

She glanced at the email address and frowned. Her frown deepened at the name of the person who'd ordered, and the delivery address. She'd been busy and trying to keep her employees from seeing the computer screen, but still, how could she have missed all this important information.

Kate Spencer. Whimzy Pleasure Chest. Spencer Colorado.

Cookie closed her laptop and leaned her forehead against

the desktop. She couldn't turn around and cancel the order. She could drive the cake to Denver and ship it from there, but that would be a stupid waste of time she didn't have the luxury of wasting. Since her friend had ordered the cake, there was a good possibility Kate, and the others, wouldn't look down on her for being the baker.

Would they?

Cookie hadn't experienced many happy outcomes after she'd been 'caught' doing something others thought inappropriate. Her father's harsh face flashed into her mind's eye, the disapproval tightening his eyes and the flat line of his lips was too familiar.

Rebellion flared in her chest. She wouldn't be dictated to by the past. She'd made her decisions for good or bad. So, if she was going to make her erotic cake debut in Spencer, she'd damn well make it a memorable one.

She paused for a moment then pulled a small sketchbook from her tote bag. Kate had ordered a cake topped by a couple in the act. Other than hair colors and a long belt of blue wrapped around the bodies, there were no other specifics. The basic design was simple. She'd done couples before, both in cake and in modeling chocolate. They took longer to carve, but since she didn't have to figure in shipping, she had plenty of time to do an extra special job.

What would make this cake even better? Cake decorating competition shows were popular and she'd watched more than a few. At one time she'd even considered applying to be a contestant. What trick could she adapt from one of those shows?

She doodled a bit on the page before finally sketching the basic cake outline. This design needed something spectacular. Something no one would think of. She tapped her pencil against the desk then used the eraser end to push paperclips into a pile.

A slow smile stretched her lips. Movement. That's what it

needed. The cake needed some sort of mechanical special effect. Then she chuckled. If she could get the man's hips to move...

Electronics had never been anything she'd thought she'd need as a baker, but maybe she could figure out a way. Wait. Hadn't her employee, Ethan told her he competed in robot building and fighting? That was a thing? She shook her head. But maybe he could design a way for part of her cake to move. Without telling him exactly how she planned to use the mechanism.

She made a note, closed her sketchbook with a snap and rose. She'd get the cakes baked, cooled and the penis carving done today. Talk to Ethan tomorrow, then hopefully end up with a really special cake for Vianna's wedding shower. Plan set, she tied an apron around her waist and began.

Once her day's work was completed and the cakes covered and hidden in the back of the freezer Cookie exited the bakery through the front door into a bright mountain afternoon.

"Hey, Cookie."

The tenor voice froze her in place for a moment, then she sighed, tossed her keys into her tote and turned.

"Good afternoon, Mr. Hartwood."

A thorn in her side, the determined man smiled and strutted toward her. "I noticed you were working today and I hoped to catch you when you left."

No doubt he'd positioned himself so he could see her shop and waited. Like too often in the past, this was no chance encounter. Had he been someone else, like the blond who continually stepped into her thoughts as easily as he'd stepped into her building, she wouldn't be so irritated, and yes, a little creeped out. The man standing before her now had sleezebag written all over him.

And lucky her, he'd chosen her to pursue.

"Is there anything I can help you with?" She attempted to

keep a cool tone to her words while glancing around the triangle. A fair number of tourists wandered Olde Town providing a measure of safety. Hartwood wouldn't do anything to damage his public image.

"I assume you've been working, so wondered if you'd care to join me for a late lunch."

Care to join him? Not in this lifetime. She'd taken an instant dislike to the man from the moment he'd first introduced himself when she opened the shop. Now that he'd been elected as a trustee to the town board, he was even more insufferable. Like that title made him something special. There always seemed to be some underlying current, something he wanted. "I'm not—"

"Sorry I'm late, Cookie."

Startled, Cookie stared at the man who joined them. He brushed sandy blond hair from his forehead and smiled. "I got caught up with a project Mom wanted help with." He flattened his grin and nodded to Cale. "Hartwood."

"Burnham. So, you're back in town."

"Yep." The grin returned. "And I've got a lunch date with this lovely lady. Thank you for keeping her company while she waited." He cocked his head to one side and stared expectantly at Hartwood.

"She didn't say anything about a date," Cale muttered.

Taking advantage of the moment, Cookie said, "I was just about to. Have a nice day, Mr. Hartwood."

"Cale," he said automatically then after a narrow-eyed glare at them, turned on his heel and stomped across the Olde Town triangle.

"I hope you don't mind," her rescuer said. "But Mom noticed him hanging around before he approached you. Says he's been a nuisance. Maybe I took him down a peg."

"I don't mind at all. He doesn't take no very well."

"Never has. And has some grudge against just about

everyone he went to high school with. I'm proud to be on that list."

So, her blond went to school here? Said his mom... "You're from Spencer? I thought you were a tourist."

He gave a soft snort. "In some ways I could be. Except for a short visit about four years ago, I haven't really been back home for what, oh maybe ten, eleven years. I'm sure Mom could tell you the exact number of days."

"You said your mom saw him. Does she work here in Olde Town?"

"My folks own S & B Pottery there on the corner."

"I'm sure I met them when the other business owners welcomed me to Spencer. But I haven't gotten involved with the council or much anything else. I wanted to make sure my cupcakes were a success before I settled in and did anything like that."

Casually, he glanced around. She followed his gaze to where Hartwood hovered at the edge of a building as though hiding, but not quite. She shivered.

"He's watching. Guess that means I get to take you to lunch."

"You don't have to." Although getting to know this man now that she knew he wasn't a tourist could be interesting. "I was just on my way home anyway."

"Nope. We've got to make a proper show of this if we're to discourage our friend. If you don't mind, I'll take that bag from you and offer my arm."

She grinned at his exuberant play-acting, handed him her tote and linked elbows with him. "Where are we headed for lunch?"

"Pearl's okay? I haven't had one of Marty's hot beef sandwiches in forever."

"Sounds good. But, first, you know who I am. Shouldn't I know my escort's name?"

He stopped short, considered her a moment then nodded. "Probably a good idea. I'm Anthony Burnham. Tony to most folks. Tone to family and a special few. At your service, Cookie."

⸎

Once Tony had Cookie settled in a corner booth at Pearl's, he sat across from her watching the door. He didn't trust Hartwood not to show up and barge his way into their conversation. While Tony was a couple years younger than Hartwood, he hadn't escaped the angry teenager's notice. Family. Hartwood's irrational ire was completely based on family. If anyone had any relationship at all to the Spencer clan, they were shit in Hartwood's book. Being a younger cousin put him in line for direct conflict.

Especially when Hartwood had focused his attentions on Isabeau. Tony had stood up for his sister and received more than a few beatings from Hartwood and his gang.

Today when his mom pointed out Hartwood hanging over Cookie, the past had rushed up to slam him in the chest. It hadn't taken much encouragement from Mom to step into the fray. And while he didn't think Hartwood had a goon squad working for him anymore, he really couldn't be sure.

He wasn't willing to take any chances with Cookie's safety. The dark-haired woman drew him closer. Pulled at hope and longing deep in his chest, much like his career had when he'd first begun filming his shows. No. He rubbed his palms against his thighs. That wasn't right. That was... and this was... hell, he didn't know what this was.

"So, do you often go around rescuing women from Hartwood?"

The question caught him unaware. But once he relaxed against the booth's padded back, it was easy enough to answer. "Actually, this is only the second time. He thought my sister had a thing for him back in high school. His personality wasn't much different back then. But his power base is different now."

"Your sister? She was a lucky girl to have someone looking out for her,"

That statement had many layers he wasn't willing to examine right now. Maybe never.

"Has the pri— Uh, Hartwood been bothering you long?"

"I had a couple months of peace once I opened. Then somehow I gained his notice. Probably when he came around campaigning for the town board. He's gotten more insistent the last few weeks though."

A woman as beautiful as the baker was would garner any man's attention the moment he laid eyes on her. That surge of extra-ordinary awareness flowed over him again but he bit back the compliments hovering on his lips. This wasn't the time. Yet. "As long as I'm in town, if he bothers you, don't hesitate to let me know."

The sparkle in her dark eyes faded and he longed to discover the way to return the dancing light. Maybe she didn't want anyone to look out for her? His sister hadn't appreciated his constant hovering. Or had the change in Cookie's expression come when he mentioned leaving town?

Thankfully, the waitress hovering by the table for their order focused him in another direction. He was starved.

As they ate, he learned a little about her life once she'd opened her business in Spencer. She was easy to talk to, and had strong insights and opinions she wasn't fearful of voicing. He liked a woman who knew her own mind. He liked Cookie. More than he dared to admit.

Cookie turned down dessert, telling her rescuer she'd had enough sweet that morning while baking. She sat with Tony while he devoured a thick slice of cherry pie. Lunch had been a delightful adventure, and true to his word, the hot beef sandwich had been excellent. Lingering over his dessert extended the moments she wished would never end.

They'd spent most of the time talking about inconsequential things, the town of Spencer. And her. She didn't learn much about him other than how he'd grown up in this small Rocky Mountain town. And she couldn't shake that 'knowing' him feeling but had hesitated to ask him if he might feel the same or offer some explanation.

When they finally parted, she strode quickly to her car. Instead of driving the short distance to her apartment, she took the highway out of town toward Rocky Mountain National Park. She'd never traveled the entire route to end up on the other side of the mountains in Estes Park. Someday, when the roads were open and clear of snow, she promised herself she'd go on that adventure. Today the need to spend some time outside called to her.

She knew just the place, a tiny turn-off overlooking a mountain stream. When Kate and Vianna had taken her to a similar spot on the Saint Georges river, and made her step into the cold water as a rite of passage, she'd scoffed at the idea. But now, she loved dipping her toes in the cold snow melt and seeing how long she could remain motionless. Despite the fairly warm day, the snow was still melting in the mountains after the late March blizzard and the stream was sure to be frigid.

Perhaps the cold would shock some sense back into her. She hadn't mooned over a man since her sophomore year in high school when her father had hollered 'hey she likes you' out the car window at a senior lounging on his front porch. How her father had known she had a crush on the boy still amazed her. His actions had not. Even now.

She pulled off the highway then stood leaning against her vehicle for a long moment watching the clear water dance over rounded rocks and crash against boulders and fallen tree trunks. Even with the occasional roar of a vehicle passing on the highway, this was a beautiful, peaceful spot.

Someday she'd have to venture further into the mountains and find a more private place for her meditations.

She snorted. Meditations? That was too grand a word for the jumbled mess of her thoughts as they tumbled over each other, much like the river raced over the stones to create tiny rapids. Besides, her life was in order now. Her shop successful. Her online business as well. She was happy with her circle of girlfriends. There wasn't anything more she needed.

Certainly not the complications a man could bring to her contentment. She'd worked damn hard to find her place and she would not lose that place because of a man.

She sighed. Not every man was like her father or some of the bakers she'd studied under. Just one meal together and she already knew Tony was different. It hadn't really even taken the time spent at the café—rescuing her from Hartwood told her so much. The differences in him called to her heart, demanding more. She had no clue what that more might be, only that she wanted it with an odd desperation.

Climbing back into her vehicle, she tried to categorize her thoughts and feelings. A wealth of possibilities with Tony spread before her. Should she choose one and pursue the outcome or simply allow life and—a relationship—to happen naturally?

Now she was being silly. If a relationship with Tony, or any man, were in her future, she'd be amazed. Delighted, but amazed. Willing, but amazed.

She folded her arms and stared out the windshield. Under no circumstances would a man get in the way of her contentment and success.

Even if that man was amazing.

CHAPTER FOUR

*T*ony braked his truck at the entrance to the Michaels' ranch to study the arch of metal and wood. A hand painted sign stood to one side declaring the Stick Pony Equine Rehabilitation Center would open in a few months. Spencer and the surrounding area had both changed and remained the same.

Driving forward, Tony glanced around. This section of the ranch didn't look any different, but he'd been told there'd been a lot of construction happening in two separate locations on the property. His cousins had discovered their dreams and found a way to make them happen. Made him happy for them but it underscored the lack he currently felt in his life and direction. Maybe this visit would help clear his mind.

He parked near the old barn and exited his truck. The homestead didn't look much different, although a new addition expanded the house. Kate and Jackson were expecting a second child. Very cool. For them. More astonishing was how easily Jack seemed to have accepted the role of a Spencer grandson. In high school Jack had been pretty damn vocal about his dislike for Jakob Spencer.

Tony shrugged. Times changed and people changed. He hoped time hadn't changed Jack or Ryder.

"Tony!" The deep shout drew his attention past the barn to where a new building stood, clean and proud next to an expanded corral. The two figures waved him over and after a round of one-arm guy hugs and back slapping, he mounted the corral fence to sit with Jack and Ryder, looking out over the rolling pasture.

"So, what brings you back to Spencer?" Jack asked.

Ryder chuckled and elbowed Tony's side. "My wedding, of course. You've missed a bunch."

Tony shook his head. "Nope, didn't know about your upcoming nuptials until Mom told me."

"You should have gotten an invite."

"Probably came after I left New York. I'm here for a while, though."

"Hiatus from the show?" Ryder leaned forward with his forearms against his thighs and cast Tony an odd look. "How's the star doing?"

Tony shrugged then matched the pose. A cool breeze from the mountains tossed his hair and he thought absently it had been awhile since he'd been to the stylist. He took a deep breath and relished the fresh scents of pine, snow, and early spring grasses. This felt more like home than anywhere he'd traveled.

Home. He hadn't thought of anywhere as home for a long time. The shooting of his television show had kept him on the move for years. Maybe a sense of permanence was what was missing.

"The star? Huh. Can't really say, man. You know how it is, Ryder. Studio execs want one thing, talent another. This talent obviously doesn't have enough pull."

"I find that surprising. Just the other day I caught a rerun from your first season. That's what, six years ago? If they didn't like you, they wouldn't keep you on the air."

"I'm not so sure. Reruns may be all I'm good for now."

Jack jumped to the ground. "Let's ride. Knock that downer attitude right out of ya. Besides, I need the stretch. We'll head over to Ryder's site. I'll give you the grand tour of the surgical center later."

"It's been awhile since you've been on horseback," Jack observed a few minutes later while Tony struggled to saddle his mount.

"Hopefully riding will come back easier than dealing with this mess of tack has." Tony laughed. It felt good to laugh. To let his cares and confusion fade in the company of friends and family.

Once settled in the saddle, he listened intently as Jack and Ryder explained their vision for Stick Pony. The two halves, equine rehabilitation and a riding camp for the differently-abled, meshed well. There was plenty of land available on the ranch to expand even further should Jack and Ryder grow their ideas. Tony ignored the prickle of jealousy. He'd discover his next path. Eventually.

At Ryder's build site, concrete pads had been laid for a central building for offices and dining hall, as well as for a handful of cabins. An impressive layout with plenty of room for planned expansion.

Ryder pointed to an area of disturbed earth edged with stacks of logs. "Had to remove trees, but that's where the indoor riding ring will go. It'll be a safe environment for any of our campers to experience riding. Outdoors ring and exercise areas will be behind the building. I'm hoping to lay a few trails around the area so our campers can test their skills as they learn and become comfortable on their mounts. Took a long time just to get to this point and unfortunately we can't go any faster. The rules and regs for accessibility and safety are stringent. Don't get me wrong, I wouldn't want it any other way, but all the applications and inspections take time."

Jack swung one leg over his pommel and patted his mount's neck. "Not quite so many limitations for my buildings. Except those I put in place. I've already got one patient. Doing great on her rehab, too."

"We're hoping to have some of my campers help with the rehabilitating horses, too. If they're interested. From my limited experience with a couple of riding camps in California, the kids are excited to do anything and everything with and for their horses."

"You've thought this out well. I'm impressed. What are the cabins going to be like?" If construction started soon, Tony could volunteer to help build at least one cabin. The long weeks since his last job were wearing on him. Maybe that was what was missing. He needed to work.

"I know that look." Ryder shaded his eyes with one hand and grinned at Tony.

"What look?"

"The one that says you're bored and need something to do."

Tony shrugged. "How soon will you be starting construction on the cabins? I could lend a hand."

"We'll take all the help we can get. It was you that put the porch on the shack, wasn't it?"

The shack. He hadn't thought of that place in years. "Yeah, when I was last back in Spencer, oh about four years ago. So, the shack's still standing?"

Jack snorted. "Standing and occasionally still in use. Although not always for how we enjoyed it. I'll tell you some stories over a beer some evening."

"Kate lets you out of her sight to go out with the guys?"

"Hell, sometimes she kicks me out. Says I'm hovering or some such nonsense. I'm just watching out for her and our kids."

Ryder side stepped his horse closer to Tony's. "He's a total helicopter. I'm waiting for Kate to smash a vase or over his head. But... I understand. I have no idea how I'll react when Vianna is pregnant. I might be worse."

"At least you're facing the truth about yourself, dude." Jack laughed.

Tony left his cousins loudly discussing the merits of being over-protective idiots and rode past the completed cement pads. If he remembered right, there was something he wanted to check out. Once over a slight rise, he stopped and sighed.

A small copse of trees stood surrounded by rolling pasture land. Four huge douglas firs formed a ragged square, thick trunks stretching toward the bright blue sky. Wide-spread branches created a living link between the trees. He'd always loved these trees and suspected that love may have been a factor in his career choice.

He squinted and let his imagination soar. Then pulled out his phone and peered at them through the camera lens. He snapped a couple of shots. Yes, those trees would be the perfect supports for a huge tree house. But who would care with it stuck back here on Stick Pony land?

Stick Pony. That was it. Excitement rose in his chest, transferring to his mount. The horse side-stepped and tossed its head until Tony gained control. He guided the horse back and forth, peering at the trees, the spacing, the arch of branches. Additional supports would be needed to comply with regulations, but he could do it.

Soft hoofbeats sounded behind him and he turned, waiting until Jack and Ryder stopped their horses next to his. "I have an idea."

Over beers at the Wild Card, Tony explained the germ of his idea to his cousins. "I'm tired of building treehouses for the famous. The network doesn't agree with my desire, no, my need to do something different. I'm still under contract, but my agent is working on it so I don't think it will be long until we part ways."

"Here's to new starts." Ryder lifted his beer in salute. "I felt the same when I left California. I only knew I needed to be home."

"I don't know about the being home bit," Tony said. "But I want to do more, help more people find the joy of a tree-house. So, what I want to do is build a treehouse for Stick Pony."

Ryder paused with his beer half-way to his lips. "Uh, you know most of our campers wouldn't be able to climb a ladder or steps to get into a treehouse."

Tony waved away the comment with a hot wing from the platter they shared. "Yes, yes. I know. That's the beauty. I want to create a totally accessible treehouse. I see multiple levels. Ramps. Maybe some sort of an elevator."

"Whoa there, Tone. That's ambitious. A fantastic idea, but ambitious. I'm not sure we can get the funding with so much other building going on. We don't want to delay our opening date from mid-September."

"Pardon me, but I couldn't help but overhear."

Cale Hartwood stood at the end of their table, the attempt of an honest grin on his face. Tony sat straighter and pointed his finger at the man. "Go away."

Ryder slid his chair back but otherwise remained in a loose-limbed slouch. Jack rolled his gaze to the ceiling.

Hartwood backed up a step and lifted his hands, palms facing outward in a placating manner. "Gentlemen, please. I don't mean to intrude."

Jack snorted then cast Hartwood an innocent glance.

Hartwood stepped forward again. "Yes. But I may have a solution to your problem."

"No problem around here, except you," Ryder said,

Tony bit back a chuckle. Hartwood hadn't changed and

still had the same effect on these two he always had. It was good to know what to watch out for.

"You see...gentlemen... as a city trustee, I have many opportunities to help guide and direct the future of our lovely town. As part of my pledge to do so, I'm forming a commission to actively seek out opportunities with film and television production companies."

"Yeah," Ryder said dryly. "That worked so well for you last time."

"I had nothing to do with those pretenders, other than showing them the area. As they requested. No, my new commission will create promotional materials and provide opportunities for these companies to explore our community."

"So, what does this have to do with you eavesdropping?" Jack asked.

"I wasn't. I merely overheard an overly loud conversation as I sat enjoying a late afternoon beverage. As to how I can help you, my assistant and I have begun putting together an extensive list of producers and other executives in the film industry."

Ryder straightened. Restrained anger vibrated from him and Tony was relieved he wasn't the focus of that anger. "Forget your canned speech, Hartwood. Spill it and get gone."

"I could arrange for the construction of the treehouse to be filmed. A benefit to both your operation and the town."

Tony lifted one hand. "Nope. Won't work. I'm still under contract. Can't do any tv work without express permission. And I ain't askin'."

"But if you'll give me a chance to—"

Ryder rose. Silent, he stared at Hartwood until the man turned and stomped from the bar.

Once Ryder sat and downed half his beer, Tony asked, "So asshat up to the same old shit?"

Ryder and Jack shared a frown that told Tony all he needed to know.

Jack cradled his bottle between his hands. "Still trying to manipulate everything for his twisted purposes. Heard some talk from nearby towns that he's making himself a nuisance by aggressively hitting on women. Nobody's complained. He's been a good boy here in Spencer, though."

A deep chuckle from Ryder did little to ease the rise of trepidation in Tony's chest. "He's like a dog. Won't shit where he eats. Wouldn't trust him even as far as I could throw him after what happened with Izzy."

That attack in their senior year had changed Tony's sister, changed him. For a brief moment he wondered if she'd ever told anyone the secret they'd kept since that day.

Ryder stared at his half empty bottle then set it on the table with a dull thunk. "Enough of him. He's ruined my beer. I'll get a fresh round." When he returned, he leaned over the table and nodded. "I like your idea, Tone. We'll find a way. You'll be okay building as long as it's not being filmed?"

At Tony's nod, Ryder returned to his seat and lifted his beer. "Then here's to a new adventure. The Stick Pony Treehouse."

CHAPTER FIVE

On her assistant baker's last day in the bakery, Cookie surprised the young woman with a set of professional baking pans as a thank you for her hard work. Cookie would miss her, especially now that there was no one to cover the shift except herself. She was accustomed to the early hours but wasn't sure how to balance both what she needed to do as the owner of the shop with the frequent baking needing to be done to keep the cupcake display full.

Once the impromptu party was over and most of the afternoon's customers had left the store, Cookie brought a tall glass of soda and the remains of a ruined cupcake to one of the front tables. She looked around the room, trying for the millionth time since she'd opened to see the space as her customers did. She loved her little shop. The wall behind the display case was covered in a patchwork of soft turquoise, pink and white squares. The bright shine of the coffee station.

The door opened and one of her regulars entered. Darryl Townsend had recently retired from a local country western band and she sensed he was having difficulty navigating his new life and the lack of being continually busy. He ordered at the counter then turned, noticed her and wandered over.

"How's it going, Cookie? Today was your assistant's last day, wasn't it?"

"Pull up a chair. Yeah, she just left. I'm going to miss her. Her shoes will be tough to fill. Not many want such early hours."

"Hmm. Thanks," he said to the barista who delivered his coffee and a mini-cupcake. He turned a serious expression to Cookie. "About that."

"What? Something wrong with your order?"

He glanced down. "Nope just what I wanted. I've been contemplating your job vacancy."

She leaned forward. "Do you know someone who might be interested?"

"Yep." He thumped his chest. "Me."

"You? You just retired."

"Well, here's the thing. Life with a band can be hectic and after all these years, I was worn out. Performing like that is a job for the younger folks."

"Don't say that to someone like Mick Jagger."

Darryl chuckled. "Got me there. But for me it was time for me to be able to spend quality time with my wife and our kids and grandkids."

"So then why would you want to get another job?"

"For one thing, working here would require no out of town travel. At least I'm assuming that to be so."

Cookie grinned. "Oh, maybe only to deliver some cupcakes to the Aspen Gold Lodge or something like that."

"Do you sell cupcakes up at the lodge?"

Now wouldn't that be a dream come true? "I wish. I don't think their events are casual enough for cupcakes. I've seen photos of some of the cakes their pastry chef does. I couldn't compete."

"I don't believe that." Darryl stuffed his mini cupcake into his mouth and sighed around the bite. Once he swallowed, he continued, "Back to the job. You're probably wondering if I could actually do early mornings since I've been accustomed to late night performances."

"It crossed my mind."

"I'm a bit of an insomniac, so the late hours never bothered me. And I was often still up when my wife got off her shift at the hospital. Elaine works nights, you know. Now I've gotten in the habit of sleeping at night, and doing a good job of it. So, when she gets home, I'm up and ready to go. That's not working well when she likes to crawl into bed shortly after she gets home. She does most of her sleeping in the morning."

"I get it. You need to be out of the house while your wife sleeps."

He stared at his shoes. "Yeah. I try to keep quiet, but I guess that's just not in my nature. With the hours here, I'd be out of the house before she got home, so she can do her thing and get to bed. I'd be coming home about the time she'll be waking up. That will give us plenty of good, quality time together before she goes back to work."

"You've talked this over with her."

He grinned. "More like she talked it over with me. But I agree. I could check out some retail places, or the 24-hour gas stations. But I'm not sure that work would suit me."

She liked Darryl and he got along well with her part-time staff. Everyone in town knew him, so that could be a customer draw. He'd be a hard and conscientious worker. But... "Can you bake?"

"Worked in a mess hall during my stint in the army. I may not have as much experience with fancy cupcakes as I do with cooking for a thousand men, but I can follow a recipe. Been known to improve on a couple in my time as well. I might need extra training on that fancy coffee set up you've got here, though. I have a hard time even managing those little pod thingies at home." He shook his head in mock sadness. "Elaine says I'm hopeless."

Hiring Darryl would solve her staffing problems, and she enjoyed starting from scratch with any employee, so that was no problem. She didn't usually make such spur of the moment decisions, but this one felt right. Comfortable. She nodded.

"I can't hire you without an application, so let me grab the official paperwork. Fill them out and bring it back tomorrow morning. We'll start you off at six, but if it works out you could come in as early as five. Wear clean, comfortable clothes and close-toed shoes. I'll order you our official tee shirts after your trial period. How's that sound?"

Darryl leaned back in his chair. "Didn't think it would be that easy. Thought you might need a little convincing."

"It usually isn't. But I think we can work well together. We'll give it a try at least."

He stood and clicked his heels together, his athletic shoes making a muffled thump. "Yes, ma'am."

Laughing, Cookie stood as well. "And none of that ma'am stuff. We're pretty casual around here. I'll get that application."

She found the applications she'd printed out a few days ago under a stack of invoices. She really needed to get back to her precise and timely record keeping. What had gotten into her?

※

Early the next morning, Cookie checked off the invoices as the truck driver wheeled in her delivery of ingredients and shop necessities. She'd almost run out of lids for her largest coffee cups. That would have been a tragedy in her customer's eyes. She chuckled to herself. But with two full cases on the invoice, she'd be covering coffee cups for a long while.

After she signed the invoice and told the driver she'd see him next week, she turned and planted her hands at her hips to stare at the stacks of boxes and bags of flour and sugar.

"Good morning, Cookie."

The smooth voice tightened her shoulders and she closed her eyes in resignation. Today should have been a good day. It was supposed to be a good day. But not with him in her shop even before it opened. She turned.

"Mr. Hartwood. The store isn't open yet. You'll have to leave."

"Now, Cookie. I saw the delivery driver off and slipped in to say good morning. And see how everything is going for you. As a town trustee, it's my business to be concerned with our town's businesses." He snickered at his attempt at a joke.

"And as a trustee, you should know that customers aren't allowed in the bakery area of this shop. Please leave."

"I merely wished to ask if you'd care to have dinner with me tonight."

Care to have dinner with him? Somehow, she held back a shudder. Being in the same room, sometimes even the same town with the man was more than she could handle. She shook her head. "As I've said before, no. Thank you, but I don't care to have dinner, lunch, coffee, breakfast, a snack, anything with you."

While his smile never faltered, his eyes turned cold and hard. "I see. Ms. Lamont, I also see that you have items here that are required to be stored at least six inches above the floor. This is considered a violation of the Colorado food code. I would hate to have an inspector show up unexpected."

He was threatening her? Just because she wouldn't go out with him? Cookie took a deep breath and fisted her hands at her hips. The invoice crinkled so she lifted that hand and shook it at the man. "These items were just delivered. You saw the driver. There hasn't been any time to get anything put away properly."

"Ah, excuses. That might not be how the inspector sees it."

"Don't you threaten me, Mr. Hartwood."

"I don't threaten, Ms. Lamont. But should you change your mind about dinner..." He offered an ingratiating smile and spread his hands.

"Sorry I'm late, Cookie."

She turned to the door where Darryl Townsend stood watching the scene before him. He took a few steps into the bakery. "I'll get right on putting away the order." He held the door open. "Mr. Hartwood, you were just leaving?"

After giving the older man a murderous glare, Hartwood stomped from the bakery and slammed the heavy door behind him. Cookie collapsed onto her desk chair. "Thanks."

"Don't mention it. That guy's always been a creep. Probably has been since he learned to walk. Head's too big for that scrawny body. Don't let him push you around. If he tries again, just call me."

"Sooner or later he's got to get a clue that I don't want anything to do with him, doesn't he?"

Darryl shrugged.

"Then to threaten my business because I said no. Enough. I don't want to think about Cale Hartwood any more today. Or ever. So, ready for your first day?"

"Just tell me what you need done. First, I'll get this pile of stuff put away. No, just relax. If I can't figure out where something goes, I'll let you know. This bakery's not that big."

❦

Tony stood behind the counter in S&B Pottery watching the shop for his moms who were busy cleaning the neighboring store. They owned the entire building and had rented out the second shop for years. Their tenants retired to Arizona and his folks had decided to expand their business. Luckily there was already a door between the two shops, making it easier to widen the opening.

He'd offered to help with the demolition, but they'd waved him away stating they'd already hired a crew. Once they had the display cases and furnishings moved a safe distance from the doorway, the demolition would begin. They wouldn't even let him crate up the pottery that needed to be moved away from this side of the wall.

All in all, he was feeling pretty helpless and at a loss. He hated those feelings. So, he grabbed his laptop and began researching the requirements for an American Disabilities Act build. Ah, design standards. Exactly what he needed.

Ryder and Jack had steered him to their new cousin-in-law, Miranda's husband, who had done the architectural drawings for Stick Pony. Declan was almost as excited about the treehouse and Tony knew they'd make a good team. But he didn't want to rely on the other man's extensive knowledge. Tony wanted to know first-hand what kinds of building challenges he was up against. There were sure to be many.

Sketching a preliminary design on a scrap of paper, he matched angles and rises to the required standards. This would be a huge treehouse with lengthy ramps needed to enter even the lowest levels. The joy he imagined on a camper's face made all the minute planning worthwhile.

Involved in his research, he didn't hear the door open or recognize there was another person in the store until a throat cleared. He glanced up. Shit. "Hartwood. What do you want?"

"Relegated back to shopkeeper? I must say, you do appear in your natural habitat here."

"I repeat. What do you want?"

Hartwood glanced around the store, took a few steps in

one direction, then returned to the counter. "Expanding the shop, I see."

"Mom and Janelle are excited to showcase more of their work. And expand their working space as well. But you knew that, didn't you? As a 'trustee', you keep your finger on the pulse of Spencer business."

Hartwood gave him a flat smile. "What are you doing here?"

"Minding the shop while the owners are working next door."

"No. What are you doing in Spencer? Oh, I know what I overheard the other day at the Card. What's the real reason?"

"That is none of your business."

"I think it is when you try to poach my girl."

Poach his girl? What the hell? Then it registered. Cookie. Tony stifled his laugh with a cough, earning another dirty look.

"You stay away from her, Burnham. Or there will be consequences."

"Nothin' you can do to me that'll make an impression, dude."

Hartwood tapped his chin then grinned. "No, but surprise visits from the building code inspector can certainly slow down or even halt a remodel."

Anger burned through Tony. Taming the heat, he stood and moved from behind the counter. Just as Hartwood had in high school, this scumbag had the knack of finding his way around an issue to get what he wanted. Not this time.

Hartwood took a quick step back, but his grin never faded. He lifted his chin, his expression filled with challenge. And satisfaction.

Tony wouldn't give the asshat any satisfaction. Not today in his family's store. Too many breakables. Tony ambled to a shelf, took down a pot and brought it back to the counter. He grabbed a stack of tissue to wrap the item in pretense of readying it for shipment. The action was enough to temper his anger, so when he lifted his gaze to Hartwood, Tony was calm.

"Shouldn't be a problem. I've looked over the paperwork and plans and everything is in order. There's not a huge amount of construction involved, and I know Dagleish Construction does excellent, and proper work."

Hartwood returned to the counter and jabbed his finger toward Tony's face. "Leave Cookie Lamont alone." He stomped from the store.

Tony watched the prick's angry strides across the courtyard. "No, *you* leave Cookie alone."

Later that evening Tony joined a group of family and friends at the sports bar addition to the Wild Card. He was impressed Ace had gone with the times and expanded to the building next door, creating an outdoor patio area between. The sports bar had the same old west decorating theme, but with the addition of banks of televisions. Now most were tuned to a Denver Nuggets game.

Not a fan of watching televised basketball, Tony nursed a craft beer, ate far more hot wings than he should, and enjoyed the pure male company.

Ryder cheered an excellent cross court shot that increased the home team's lead. He perched on a stool and turned to Tony with a grin. "Remember when we executed one like that in high school?"

Tony snorted. "Sure. And then there was the time we tried, and Hartwood thought he was the star and tried to catch the ball to make the shot."

"You're in a foul mood."

"Not really. Just having Hartwood problems."

"Again? Want us to beat him up?"

Joe Cavanaugh, the local sheriff, joined them at the tall table. "Don't go beatin' up folks on my watch."

Tony reached across the tall, round table to shake Joe's hand. "Hey, good to see ya."

"You, too, Tone. Back in town for long?"

He shrugged and grabbed an over-piled nacho from the plate that had just landed on the table. "I'm really not sure. I'm gonna be helping with construction out at Stick Pony for a while."

Ryder clasped his shoulder. "He's building us a treehouse."

Tony shrugged again. "It's what I do."

Joe fixed him with a mock serious expression. "And who do you want beat up?"

"The family nemesis. Hartwood."

Joe sighed. "Don't doubt it. Now that he's a trustee, he's been insufferable. I haven't gotten too many complaints, but I know Hunter has over at the police department. Unfortunately, it's nothing we can take action on, other than record the incidents as possible harassment. He didn't take long to latch onto you. What's his beef this time?"

"Other than he hates me because of this family? He warned me to stay away from his 'girl'."

Ryder snorted. "His girl? Women around here are wise to his moves. He ain't got nobody. Probably why he's cranky all the time."

"He's claiming Cookie is his property." Just saying the words brought a rise of anger in Tony's chest. Again. He munched on another nacho then washed down an especially hot jalapeño with his beer.

"Cookie? The baker?" Ryder asked. "She seems like a smart cookie—pardon the pun. She wouldn't fall for Hartwood's line, would she? I'll ask Vianna to have a chat with her."

"Thanks, but no need. She's got his number. I helped her escape the dude's clutches the other day. I simply stepped in and took his place when he tried to ambush her for a lunch date. Now, he's threatening to sic the building inspectors on the expansion of Mom's shop."

Joe nodded. "I've heard similar complaints from others. In Olde Town, the downtown businesses, even some businesses further out. He doesn't appear to be bothering folks who've been in business here for a long time. But, if you say he's targeting S&B Pottery, I could be wrong. I'll check with Hunter. We need to coordinate knowledge and efforts. It's a sad day when we have to protect our citizens from a city trustee."

A wild cheer rose from the bar as the final seconds of the game counted down and the Nuggets scored another win.

"Thanks." Tony drained his glass and stood. "I should get going. Ryder, I'll be out to the site in the morning with the preliminary plans for the treehouse. Then my building skills are yours." He grinned. "It will be good to get back to work."

CHAPTER SIX

*L*ifting a hairbrush, Cookie stared at herself in the full-length mirror that covered the back of her bedroom door. How long had it been since she'd been on a date? A real date? Since before moving to Spencer, that's for sure. She wasn't sure she remembered how to date. Wasn't that a sad state of reality? Not that she probably ever really knew how to date. Before she left home, her father had orchestrated all of her interactions with boys. Then, later, she just didn't have the time.

She fussed with her hair and finally pulled it back into a low ponytail. Was this really a date? A movie night at the Old Stone Church with the Olde Town business owners would hardly be a romantic evening. Tony said casual, so she'd be casual. At least she had the right kind of clothes for casual.

She'd take whatever moments with Tony she could. He'd never been far from her thoughts since the moment he'd first entered her store. Then he'd played knight in shining armor and saved her from Hartwood's unwelcome advances.

While the town trustee continued to haunt her steps, Cookie hadn't seen enough of Tony in the past couple of weeks. He'd been in for coffee a few times, mumbled something about being busy and left without saying much more. She'd seen him in the central courtyard of Olde Town, a sketchbook on his lap, a pencil flying over the page. But he'd never remained there long enough for her find a quiet moment to leave her shop to talk to him.

Then out of the blue, he'd handed her a flyer and invited her to the potluck movie night.

She grinned at her reflection and touched the simple wire-wrapped rose quartz crystal hanging from a simple chain. In the dead of winter, she'd visited other shops in the triangle, providing cupcake samples for the owners. Ron Enbach, the proprietor of the Prospector Rock Shop, had insisted she take the small stone, saying it was perfect for her. She'd never given the power of stone much thought, but wearing the necklace made her happy.

Besides, it looked perfect with this outfit.

A knock sounded at her door startling her from her thoughts. It wasn't time for Tony to be here yet, was it? A quick glance at the clock on her stove told her it was time. She centered the stone drop in the neckline of her v-necked top and opened the door.

Dressed in jeans and a chambray work shirt, Tony stood before her. His wide grin made her smile in response. "You look great," he said. With a bow he handed her a small bouquet of spring flowers.

Finally taking the flowers when he pressed them against her palm she asked, "Why did you do this?"

"I thought bringing flowers was the polite thing to do."

She lifted the tissue paper wrapped blossoms to her nose to hide her concern. Her father had brought flowers to her mother, but only after a particularly vicious fight. Was Tony preparing for a confrontation, making a gesture before the fact? "Let me put these in water. Come on in."

She turned away before he'd even stepped over the threshold and busied herself at the kitchen sink. Just because no man had ever given her flowers didn't mean this one expected... expected what? A fight? Sex?

Sex with Tony. She clutched the edge of the counter and blew out a short breath. She'd thought about the possibility. Besides, what else would he want?

"You have a nice place here. I didn't realize these apartments had been redone."

With his back to her, he stood at the far end of the kitchen peninsula as he scanned her small living room. "Very homey."

"Thanks. I'm comfortable here. There's an apartment above the shop, but I needed separation between work and home. Right now I'm just using the space for storage. I suppose I should fix it up and rent it out."

"Would it take much? That apartment, I mean?"

"I have no idea. I do know the plumbing and electrical haven't been updated since, well, probably since they were first installed."

"Hmm." He turned with a grin. "Ready to go?"

She hurried to place the unarranged flowers in the vase. "Yep. You're sure cupcakes are enough to take to the potluck?"

"Positive. Mom said she'd be disappointed, especially since no one else is planning on bringing dessert."

On the short walk to the event, Cookie regretted how she'd packed the cupcakes for transport. Her date needed both hands to carry the large box. The odd tingle in her fingers made her long to hold his hand. She'd plan better next time. If there was a next time.

Unburdened, Cookie held the outer door open for others carrying their food offerings. Tony stayed at her side, chatting amicably with the growing crowd.

With time for only a quick glance at the lobby and display areas, Cookie followed Tony to the basement and set out her cupcakes at the end of a long, cloth covered table.

After a few minutes, the president of the Olde Town council shouted for attention. A round of thank yous followed then he called for the dishes to be uncovered and the meal to begin. Somehow Tony managed to find a tiny round table in a corner where they had a modicum of privacy. At the grins cast their way from the others, their somewhat alone time was approved.

The variety of bites on her plate were delightful, but even better was the company. She asked, and Tony told her about leaving Spencer after high school and attending the New York Film Academy. Then he'd gotten a low-level job working with a network specializing in how-to shows.

"After a few years of working behind the scenes, I pitched an idea to one of the executive producers and the network thought it was great. We did a pilot and now I've shot seven seasons of shows."

Cookie leaned back and shook her head. She should have recognized him. "You're the celebrity tree house guy."

He stood and bowed. "At your service. Didn't you know that?"

Ducking her head, she played with the last bit of vegetable salad on her plate. "You looked familiar. But I haven't been able to figure out why. I watched the first couple of seasons."

"The first couple?"

Offering him a smile to offset any hurt her statement may have caused, Cookie continued, "Yeah. Then coming up with a business plan and saving for the equipment I needed took up my time. And honestly, once I moved to Spencer, I haven't taken much time to watch television."

"Your business keeps you that busy?" A spark of honest interest danced in his eyes.

"Yes, it did. Maybe not so much now. I've got responsible and trustworthy employees. I suppose I don't need to spend all my time at the shop. But I don't have anything else to do. So, that's where I am."

"If you had some other interest, might you spend a little more time away from the shop."

She thought for a long moment while he carried their plates to a trashcan then gave him an honest answer. "I really don't know. I've never been given that choice. I've been so focused on making my shop a success, I haven't planned beyond that."

"You consider your shop successful?"

"Yes, I do. Even with a low number of tourists during the winter, I stayed in the black every month." She wasn't going to tell him about how the supplemental income from her online bakery had carried the shop on occasion. It was all still hers and counted as positive income.

"What would you like to do with free time?"

She chuckled. "I really don't know. It's been so long."

They fell silent. As the rest of the diners cleared their tables and covered the small amount of leftover food, Tony's mother moved to the front of the room and lowered a huge screen.

She turned to the gathering. "I'm delighted so many of you were able to make it tonight. It's been awhile since we've had a movie night. To welcome our son Anthony home, we knew no other movie would be so perfect."

Tony groaned. They wouldn't. At his mother's wide grin, he knew they would. And had.

Cookie touched his arm. "What's wrong?"

"Wait."

Muffy paused when Tony gave her the evil eye, then laughed and continued as he knew she would. "When Janelle and I were pregnant, there was one movie we watched over and over. How many VHS tapes did we wear out, hon?" She looked at Janelle whose shrug was tempered by a huge smile.

"In fact, our daughter was named after one of the characters."

"Don't do it," Tony mumbled. "Don't."

"But that's a whole 'nother story. Tonight, let's all relax as we hope you'll enjoy our fantasy favorite, *Ladyhawke.*"

The lights dimmed until the only glows were from the exit signs and the screen. Tony blew out a frustrated breath. He liked the move okay but hoped he could convince Cookie to sneak away. As the opening scene unfolded, she scooted her chair closer.

"I guess you've seen this a million times," she whispered.

He nodded. "At least."

"I've seen it, and it's good, but I'd rather do something where we can keep talking."

Pleased her thoughts mirrored his, Tony angled to face her. "Wanna play hooky?"

When she grinned, he took her hand and as silently as they could, made their way to the stairs and out of the building. Standing on the church's steps, he drew in a rejuvenating breath of the cool, fresh air.

Cookie chuckled. "Does your sister get tired of the movie, too? Or having her mom brag how she's named after a character?" She reached up to straighten his jacket collar. "You lucked out."

"Kind of. I thank God Mom has some sense. Navarre would be a horrible name to saddle a kid with. Or she could have named me after the Broderick character."

"Mouse?"

"Ha ha. No, his name was Gaston. Imagine how fun that would have been. Especially after the Disney movie came out." He gave a fake shudder at the thought.

"What did you mean by 'kind of'?"

"I rarely use my middle name. Just the initial. My whole, legal name, is Anthony Navarre Burnham."

She patted his shoulder. "That's not too bad. So where are we going?"

Tony had no idea if his plan was a good one or not. But Cookie needed to take time to relax and have fun. He'd thought bringing her the bright bouquet for no reason other than because the flowers were beautiful and reminded him of her was fun, but her reaction had surprised him. Hadn't anyone given her flowers before?

He would take time to figure out this woman, if she gave him the chance. He planned to stay in Spencer, at least as long as it took to complete the tree house for Stick Pony. And help with the cabins as well. He approved of his cousins' ideas and wanted to be a part of something that really could bring a positive change into someone's life.

Building extravagant tree houses for those who hardly needed another extravagance in their lives didn't really make a difference.

That's what he wanted in a nutshell. To make a difference.

He took her hand and led her across the street. "To the pottery shop."

"But it's closed."

"You forget, I have a special pass to be in the building after hours. Okay, so it's a key."

They entered the darkened store and he escorted her to the back room. On the off chance the evening flowed in this direction, he'd asked his moms to prepare the area for him. Everything he needed was set out. Including a few candles. He rolled his gaze to the ceiling. Candles might be a bit much tonight, considering Cookie's earlier reaction to flowers.

"This is where Mom makes most of her pots. There's a number of ways to build a piece of ceramics. Coils or slabs are the easiest. So we're not going to start with those."

"Not going to?" She tugged her hand from his and stepped back, crossing her arms. "What are you talking about?"

"Okay, okay. I thought it might be fun to create a bowl or container or something together."

"With clay? I've never done anything like that. I don't know if I can."

"Anyone can, Cookie. The main thing to remember is that perfection is a fallacy."

She gave him an odd look. "Says the man who I once saw take a tiny chisel to a joint in a treehouse because it wasn't a 'perfect' match."

Tony chuckled. "Caught me. There is a time for perfection and a time to just have fun. Now is the fun time. You in for it?"

"Uh, okay. Sure."

He handed her a clean smock. "Don't want you to get too messy."

The cute way she wrinkled her nose at the oversized shirt made his heart skip a beat. He rubbed his chest. This woman did odd things to him. Shoving the implications to the back of his brain, he waited until she'd donned the protective clothing then took her hand again.

He liked holding her hand. Soft. Her long fingers fit so well with his. Blinking, he cleared his throat. "Okay, to throw a pot, an artist uses a pottery wheel."

"I'm no artist."

"Really? I've eaten more than a few of your cupcakes. The flavors combinations, icing swirls and decorations are pure artistry. Don't limit your definition of an artist to classical terms. What makes a painter any more of an artist than a baker?"

"Or someone who builds treehouses?" she fired back at him

He had to admit he'd had trouble with this question. Setting together wood and metal, forming walls to support a roof, making sure a floor was smooth and splinter free, were art to him now. That need was a part of him now, of who he was. And something that the network had attempted to minimize in order to show off the extremes and expensive overindulgences of his builds.

There must be some way to convey that artistic side to viewers without all the glamorous trappings of rich folks. Beauty in simplicity. The art of simplicity.

"Are you still here, Tony?" Cookie touched his arm and he jerked back to the reality of the woman beside him.

"Thanks. Wool gathering. Ready to create some art?"

"I guess." The hesitancy in her tone made him grin. She shook her head and sighed. "Okay, let's do this so you can see I'm not so artistic."

Within a few minutes he'd centered a lump of wet clay on the potter's wheel for her and demonstrated a simple technique for forming the sides of a piece. Although she tried to convince him she was more than happy just to watch him work, he rose from the wheel and encouraged her to take his place.

"This is dirty work," she mumbled and pressed her cupped palms around the rotating clay.

"Dirty, yet satisfying. You're doing great."

"If you say so."

She struggled with forming the lump of clay then glanced up at him, her dark eyes pleading. "I don't think I'm getting the hang of this."

"It can take time. Here, let me help." He leaned over her shoulder to cup his hands around hers. The fragrance of her hair surrounded him, and he inhaled deeply. A slight floral tinge with strong vanilla and cinnamon undertones. Perfect for a baker. Perfect for her.

"Oh my God," Cookie said and lifted her hands. "I know what you're doing."

"Uh, you do?" Was sniffing her hair a bad thing?

"Yeah. Look at us at this potter's wheel. Your hands over mine. You're reenacting that stupid movie scene."

"Movie scene?"

"Don't act dumb. That scene from another eighties movie. One that was supposed to be so sensual and romantic. I really disliked that movie."

It took a few moments for his brain to catch up. He straightened. "Shit. Uh, sorry. I didn't even think about that." He moved to the side to face her. "I would never attempt to seduce you like that."

The flare of interest in her eyes at the word seduce gave him pause. Did she want him to seduce her? It wouldn't take much to get in that mood. Hell, just feeling the warmth of her body and the scent of her hair had him half-way there already. Then she ducked her head and the moment was gone.

He crouched beside her and stopped the wheel. "Really, Cookie. I didn't even think about that. Ever since I was little, I've enjoyed making pots. Not that I'm very good at it either. Sometime I'll show you the first one I made. Mom still has the misshaped lump displayed on a shelf."

Cookie reached out one hand as though to touch him but drew back her clay-covered fingers. "I understand. It's just that I always thought that movie was vastly overrated. Lots of folks love it. That's their choice. Thank you for sharing this part of you. But can we stop? I really want to wash my hands."

"You don't want to finish? Have a souvenir of our evening?" He hoped to lighten the suddenly serious mood. "A memento of something?"

Her smile grew slowly and she shook her head. "I've got flowers. Those will do. I don't feel comfortable with all this spinning clay. You said there were other ways to build a pot, so could I try one of those another day?"

The tension in his shoulders faded. She wasn't totally rejecting his idea. Or him. "Of course. The sink is back around the corner. I'll take care of the clay and we can leave."

She touched the tip of his nose with a clay-covered finger.

"Hey." He snatched at her hand, but she danced away.

"I've had a really good time this evening. Maybe, well, maybe next time I'll teach you how to bake."

Next time? She planned on a next time? Hope soared through him and he felt as though his feet lifted from the ground. But baking? "I'm afraid my kitchen skills, whether baking or just cooking a meal are pretty non-existent."

"Then we'll be even." She turned and found the sink.

Tony covered the clay with a sheet of plastic knowing his mom would find an early morning creative temptation in the damp clay. Maybe he'd give Cookie that pot. He penned a quick note and stuck it to the plastic with a bit of clay.

"I think I'm clean." Cookie held up her hands for inspection.

Taking both of her hands in his, Tony leaned closer. He needed to kiss this woman.

She stepped back and laughed. "You still have clay on your nose."

CHAPTER SEVEN

"*B*et there'd be lots of folks interested in this project," Jack said as he, Ryder and Tony stood on a slight rise overlooking the treehouse site. "I hate to say it, but Hartwood was right. About that. Have you considered talking to the network?"

Tony stuffed his hands into his jean pockets and rocked back on his heels. "Called this morning. Barely made it past the receptionist. And then had only about five minutes before they shut me down. They're insistent on continuing with the current successful format. They've sucked me dry, man. Dry."

He hadn't realized how much of his soul had been overwhelmed by network demands until he'd returned to the high country and his hometown. Tiniest bits of renewal filled his spirit each day he was here, especially when he was close to the mountains. Or with Cookie.

"What're you going to do?" Ryder asked.

"Done it," Tony said. "I had one year left on my contract and my attorney and agent have begun negotiations to terminate the contract. Unfortunately, one part of the termination clause is that I can't do any television of any kind for that year. Not a bad thing, but the clause also includes any media production like posting to video sites. The attorney is working on that. Being blocked from potential viewers could effectively end my career."

"Sucks, man." Jack clasped his shoulder.

"Not as much as I thought it might. I don't have to stop building treehouses. Just need to find a different way to share my knowledge. I've got enough saved to carry me through that year, and maybe longer if I'm careful." Tony shrugged. "I just need to figure out where to start."

"I've got a couple ideas," Jack offered. "You know my wife owns a bookstore."

"I noticed, dude. So?"

"She'd tell you that there's a good market for books on making things. Or those big books filled with pictures you keep on your coffee table to impress visitors." He chuckled. "Anyway, she'd say 'write a book, dumb ass'."

"Doubt she'd say 'dumb ass'."

"I added that part. Think about it, Tone. You could record the build, do close-ups of how-tos and give your expertise to everyone. Shame about video blog possibilities. Bet you'd get a few thousand followers if you did daily or weekly updates to show off your stuff."

Tony thought for a moment. "I'd never thought about writing a book. As long as I don't reference any of my past work, that might fly under the network's conditions. I'll get my agent to push back on a vlog. He's good. Should be able to work something out."

"Glad to help." Jack turned and shuddered. "I've got to get back to the clinic. I'm seeing Rollie's snake again today. Stupid thing keeps eating rocks."

Watching Jack stride away, Tony chuckled. "Still doesn't deal well with snakes, huh?"

"Nope." Ryder turned back toward the poured concrete pads where the main building and first set of cabins were planned. "I think best when I'm busy. Join me in pounding a few nails?"

"That's what I'm here for."

At the tiny shed being used as a construction office, Tony and Ryder studied the plans for the buildings. Ryder huffed out a breath. "I'd really like to start on the lodge and dining hall, but with just the two of us, that's impossible. We'll turn our efforts to cabin one. Exterior walls are up, so we can work on the interior."

"Great. Have you thought about bringing in a crew from outside Spencer? I'll need help with the treehouse, too."

Ryder nodded. "The owner of Dagleish Construction has contacts with other companies and will poach some of their workers when they're available. And we should be able to add some newly graduated kids once school lets out. I'm thinking they'd be good for painting and finishing work. Nothing too dangerous."

"Sounds like a plan. Think we can get walls up today?"

"Hope so. That's about all the two of us can do."

After a morning of work, he and Ryder had roughed in the interior walls of the cabin. Tony's muscles ached with the pleasant memory of hard work, but he knew he'd be stiff later. The simple, repetitive work had cleared his brain of mush and helped him focus on plans for his future. He had the nearly undeniable urge to discuss the possibilities with Cookie, knowing she'd have fantastic, creative ideas. But it was far too early in their relationship for that.

Relationship? He wasn't in a relationship. Okay, maybe he was. They were friends and enjoyed each other's company. And if being in any kind of a relationship with him helped her avoid Hartwood, all the better.

"What're you grinning at, fool?"

Ryder's question startled him from his thoughts, and he realized he was just standing there with a hammer in his hand, staring into the distance.

"Just thinking about how to get the better of Hartwood."

"That's worth contemplation." Ryder returned his hammer to a long wooden carrier and added the short saw they'd been using. "Let's call it a day. I haven't worked his hard in a while. I need a hot shower to loosen my muscles or I won't be back tomorrow."

Tony chuckled. "Or a massage from your lovely lady?"

"Hmm. Even better. Did this morning help?"

"Yeah, cleared my mind. I've got a mental list for this afternoon."

"Let's get back to town. Treat ya to Itza Burger."

※

Tony practically inhaled his double bacon and cheddar burger then groaned and patted his stomach. "Should of slowed down. Forgot how hungry construction makes me."

Ryder took a final, noisy sip of his shake then dumped his trash. "Nothing much better than a good fast food burger sometimes. Gotta run. Tomorrow?"

"I'll be there."

Needing to work off the greasy burger, Tony decided to walk around the town. If he was going to stay in Spencer much longer, he needed to find a place to live. Sure, his moms would love to have him stay with them, but their apartment was no longer comfortable for more than two. He needed his own space. Didn't need to be much. He'd check out the different options on his walk then make some calls.

He strolled by Cookie's apartment complex. One of the oldest in town, the recent remodels had vastly improved the property. Mom had mentioned that since the improvements, it was rare for one of the apartments to be vacant. There were other, newer complexes on the outskirts of town, but he figured he'd be competing with students from the community college. Possibly even some high schoolers aching to leave home, but not go too far.

He chuckled. He'd been one of those high schoolers who couldn't wait to leave home. Or Spencer. While he'd often thought himself an idiot for distancing himself by half the country, he'd been a successful idiot. Until recently. Some folks probably thought that even after all this time he'd come home with his tail between his legs to cry on his mommy's shoulder. Far from it.

The calm presence of his parents had helped him focus. And with support of family and friends he'd find his way. No problem. He was a survivor.

He wandered into Olde Town and sat on one of the benches. Living in a newer apartment held no appeal. He'd had enough of that back east. Some charm, character, all those things everyone seemed to be looking for on the home buying shows, now he understood. Charm and character could be added. A place just needed good bones. Like a strongly built treehouse.

Once one of the cabins was completed, maybe he could stay out at Stick Pony. Or in one of the bunk rooms on Jack's side of the property.

He rejected both ideas. He wanted to stay in town. Close to his folks. And Cookie.

He straightened with a jerk. Cookie had an empty apartment above her shop. She said it needed work, so maybe he could barter part of the rent for those repairs. The thought of being that close to Cookie made his heart pound. But could adding a landlord tenant component change their relationship in a way he wouldn't like? Change their friendship to business?

Only one way to find out. He stood and dusted off the seat of his jeans. There was probably sawdust embedded in his pores, but no helping that. He glanced at his watch. Her shift was nearly over so he didn't have time for a shower if he hoped to see her that afternoon. Maybe the evidence of his hard work that morning would help sway her to accept him as a tenant.

Ava, one of the college-age baristas, glanced up from the book she had open on the counter by the register and smiled. "Welcome to Cookie's. The regular?"

Had he been coming in here often enough that the staff knew his order? Probably. He returned her smile. "Yep. Not very busy this afternoon?"

She stuck a folded cupcake wrapper in the book to hold her place and moved to the coffee service area. "Not right now. We had a big rush right before lunch. And there's usually another one right before we close. Cookie's in the back with Darryl."

The staff suspected he didn't come just for the coffee. That was true. "Thanks, Ava. Okay if I go back? I've got business to discuss with your boss."

"Should be okay. I'll bring your coffee to you."

He caught Ava's eye and tossed a bill on the counter for his drink. "Tip's included," he said and made his way to where the baking magic happened.

He paused just past the swinging door and watched Cookie demonstrate her signature frosting swirl for an older gentleman who watched then repeated her motions on a sheet of parchment paper. Her economical movements and gentle teaching style captivated him. Maybe her offer to teach him to bake wasn't as silly an idea as his pot throwing had been.

With a jolt, he recognized the man. Darryl Thompson, creator of the local group Chickering Road. What was he doing here playing with icing? He thought the man had retired.

The opening metal door pressed against his back, forcing him a step further into the room. Ava grinned and handed him his latte. "Next time don't stop so close to the door," she admonished him.

"Sorry."

With coffee in hand, he crossed the small kitchen to the counter where the pair worked. Cookie glanced up and smiled. "Hey."

"Hey yourself. Darryl? How's it going?"

"Hey, Anthony. I heard you were back in town."

"And I thought I heard you were retired."

Darryl set his mostly empty, squished pastry bag to the side and wiped his fingers on a towel hanging from his apron strings. "From the band, yeah. Oh, I've got a few gigs here in town I'm still committed to, but for the most part I'm nothing but an advisor to the group now. My wife doesn't want me in the house all the time, so Cookie's teaching me to be a cupcake baker."

"And I can already see he's got some talent here, too," she said. "You've had a great few first days, Darryl. And your shift's up. Get going."

He touched a finger to his forehead. "Yes, ma'am. I'll clean up my practice area and be outa here in five."

Cookie moved toward her desk and sank onto the chair. She looked tired and a bit frazzled. When she hung her head and rubbed the back of her neck, Tony's fingers itched to take over and gently massage away the stress. The slight crackle in his hand made him loosen his grip on his cup. Then she looked up and smiled again.

"What can I do for you, Tony?"

"Are you done for the day?"

"There's always something that needs doing, but I could happily ignore all that right now."

"Can we go somewhere and talk?"

She was silent a moment before nodding. "As long as it's somewhere Cale Hartwood won't find us. That man has been dogging my steps all week. But I can't leave until my other employee gets here. I don't want to leave Ava alone."

From the front of the store came a disgruntled sound. "I'm fine here alone for a few minutes, Cookie. You get going. Besides, I see Ethan across the triangle. He'll be here in a couple anyway."

Tony bit back a laugh at Ava's comments and pitched his voice slightly louder than normal. "I'm not sure if your employees treat you with enough respect, Cookie."

"I heard that, Mr. Burnham. Just remember who makes your latte just the way you like it. Don't mess with the barista."

He cracked open the door and said, "Never, Ava. I value my life. And my coffee."

Cookie joined him at the door and Tony took her hand. "I have an idea where we can escape. How about we take a little trek out of town?"

"Sounds great. Then why don't I fix us some supper? Unless your folks are expecting you."

"I've been trying to stay out of their hair, so no, they don't expect me. That doesn't mean they won't cook for me, but sometimes I like the leftovers even better. My truck's over by Itza Burger. Do you mind the walk?"

"I really do have one more thing I need to do here today. Would it be possible to pick me up? It won't take me any more time than it should take you to get to your truck with those long legs."

So, she'd noticed his legs. His chest lifted with a rush of male satisfaction. But rather than strutting like a peacock, he nodded. "Works for me. Be at the back door in five."

＊

Cookie rushed to complete the final paperwork for depositing Darryl's first check. Her newest employee was a godsend. He'd taken to baking naturally and had a deft hand with flavors and decorating. Having a mature employee who was able to take the earliest shift meant that she didn't have to be in the store before the butt crack of dawn every day.

Not that she wouldn't be. She just didn't have to be, now that she'd discovered an interest outside of work. That subtle difference made a world of difference. She was pleased she'd taken the chance.

She had her tote over her shoulder and waited at the back door for only about thirty seconds before Tony's big truck rounded the corner and pulled into the loading zone. She rushed to the vehicle and after tossing in her tote, climbed into the tall cab. Dreading the discovery of a spying Hartwood, she glanced around the area. She hated she felt compelled to examine everywhere she was just to escape his advances.

He hadn't done anything improper. Except threaten her business. And made thinly veiled lewd suggestions that he must have considered flirting. She wrapped her arms over her stomach in a vain attempt to hold back a shudder.

"Cold?" Tony asked. "I'll close the window. I love the feeling of fresh air blowing over me when I drive. Sometimes I forget that others may not."

"No, I'm not cold. The window's fine. Just thinking about not such pleasant things."

"Hartwood?"

She wasn't surprised he guessed. This man seemed to be observant and notice everything around him. Nodding, she leaned her head back against the headrest. "He's wearing me out."

Tony was silent for a long moment. "I beg your pardon?"

She sat up and angled a bit in her shoulder restraint. "He won't leave me alone. Even when he's not physically present, there's an email. Or a call on the shop phone. Thank God he doesn't have my personal phone number. One small blessing. But it feels like every time I turn around, he's there, somehow. Like he's stalking me."

Tony's knuckles turned white around the steering wheel. His jaw tensed and she could practically hear his teeth grind together. "If you think he's stalking you, then you need to go to the police." At a stop sign he turned to look at her, fire brightening his light eyes. "Don't mess around with this, Cookie. Promise me. If you need someone to go to the station with you, I will. Or one of my moms would be more than happy to go. Promise me."

She lifted one hand to his shoulder, felt the rock hard, tight muscles and nodded. She'd been treating Hartwood's actions as a nuisance, like an irritating bug. She hadn't considered his actions could be more than that. She nodded again. "I never allowed myself to think about it in that way. I promise to be more careful. And I won't hesitate to report him if his actions escalate."

"They have already. Haven't they? Since I came to town. I'm afraid at first he was just pursuing you as a conquest, to have a beautiful woman on his arm."

Tony thought she was beautiful?

He continued without noticing her smile. "But once I got involved, he added a personal vendetta. Now he wants you and to use you to get to me." He pulled the truck into an empty parking lot and turned off the engine. "When I told you I stopped him from bothering my sister, that was only part of it. He'd been following her around, insisting she date him... the kind of stuff he's been doing to you. Fuck. I should have seen this coming. You need to talk to the police chief. The sheriff. Both if possible. They're both good men. Family, in fact."

"Tony, calm down. I'll talk to them if I need to. When I need to. But not yet. I..." She wasn't going to accuse a town trustee of stalking. Bringing this kind of notoriety down on her head or on the business she'd worked so hard to establish would be the death knell for her cupcake shop. She'd find another way around the problem.

"I recognize that look. Izzy had it, too. You can't handle this yourself."

"If I accuse a town trustee of any kind of misdeed, how will that affect my future in Olde Town? Even if he were found guilty, I'd always hear whispers behind my back about how 'she's the one who...'. I don't think I'm strong enough to face that. And then start over somewhere new."

"You won't be alone."

"I know you want to help. But just let this be for now. I do promise to be careful. And I do have your telephone number. Trust me on this, please."

He took a number of long slow breaths and gradually his grip on the steering wheel loosened. He ducked his head and peered at her sideways. "I don't have a choice, do I."

Cookie shook her head but offered him a soft smile. "Nope. I appreciate your concern and there may come a time when I'll need help. But I'm pretty self-sufficient."

"I don't like it, but I'll back off. You need to know one thing. One very important thing. My sister felt the same way you did. Actually, she was a lot like you in that self-sufficiency. Caring, strong, beautiful."

Had he noticed he'd called her beautiful again? In a roundabout way, but it still counted. Didn't it? Yes, it did. She appreciated his concern, but his powerful overreaction was unnecessary. Even though Hartwood made her angry, irritated her so much her skin crawled, and bothered her like a summer mosquito, he was still just a man and could be dealt with.

"But that didn't help Isabeau in the end." Tony fell silent and rested his forehead against the steering wheel.

A lump of uncertainty settled in her belly like an overly

sweet dessert. She reached toward him and stopped short of touching his arm.

He lifted his head and his frown morphed to a wicked grin. "I did beat him up, though. Had a little help from Ryder and a couple other cousins, but none of them know why I was so hot to beat on the bastard. We all thought he deserved a take down for one reason or another. I'm not proud of that moment. But I'll do it again in a heartbeat if he so much as touches you without your permission. And take the punishment like I did then."

Hoping to lighten the atmosphere in the truck cab, Cookie pressed her hands together between her breasts and sighed. "My knight in shining armor."

When Tony opened his mouth to speak, she shook her head. "I'm not making fun. There's no way I can understand how you must feel seeing him. Seeing him acting like he did back then. But I'll try. I promise I'll be even more careful. I won't let him do anything to me. And if I'm in trouble, I'll call you."

"Or Ryder, or Jack. Or the cops. Especially the cops. That bastard needs to be taken down legally." Tony rubbed his fists together like a prize fighter. "Although getting in a few punches would be worth the trouble."

She couldn't let him be charged with assault, even if that someone deserved it. Taking one of his hands, she stroked his fingers until his fist relaxed. "Now, you promise me you won't go looking for trouble. Don't give him any excuses to call the cops on you. He probably has them on speed dial so he feels in control. Because isn't that what all this is about? Control?"

"Yeah." He released a long breath. "And I've got enough control to keep my cool. Unless he touches you."

Trying again to lighten the mood, Cookie pressed her free hand to her chest and adopted a southern falsetto. "My hero."

Tony stared at her for a moment, then burst into laughter.

"I don't think you could ever be a helpless victim, sweetheart."

How wrong he was. But that was the past and would remain hidden in the past. There was no place for her father's domineering attitudes and influence in her life now. She grinned. "Or a very good actress."

CHAPTER EIGHT

"Can we put this conversation behind us for now?"

Cookie had no desire to continue this heavy conversation. Hartwood had ruined too many of her days already. She squeezed Tony's hand. He kept his fingers wrapped around his and rested their joined hands on his thigh. "I've got something else I need to talk about with you today. First, I want to show you what I was working on this morning."

"You do smell of sawdust and wood."

"I should have showered."

No, she liked the aroma on him. It spoke of hard work and determination. She'd found a few of his older shows on the internet and had watched them with a new eye, now that she knew something about the star. And she liked him even more. "Nope, it's fine. An occupational hazard. When I worked in a bakery right out of high school, I made a lot of cinnamon rolls."

"As good as I hear Vianna's are?"

"Different from hers but good in their own way. We used cinnamon from Ceylon that came in fifty-pound barrels. It was much finer than cinnamon you get at the store. Sometimes I felt like I'd absorbed the spice into my pores. Good thing I like cinnamon. And now I like the aroma of fresh cut wood."

A wide grin split his face and he sat straighter behind the wheel. She'd brought true happiness back to him after a painful discussion. She closed her eyes and took a deep breath.

Even though her ponytail would be a bitch to comb through, she enjoyed the drive with the open windows. The fresh air revived her. They headed west from town. She'd only driven this way once, just to be able to peer at the famous Aspen Gold Lodge from the road. The building and grounds had been impressive, even from a distance.

She leaned forward against her restraints when Tony eased the truck through a gap in a wire fence and followed a couple of tracks where the prairie grasses had been crushed by passing vehicles.

"Since the equine rehab part of this operation is next to the original homestead, it has a real road. Ryder decided to wait for paving the way into the therapy camp until the first cabins are completed. Then he'll decide exactly where the road needs to go." Tony slowed to steer into and out of a depression.

"How did you see that?"

"What? Oh, the dip. I've driven this a few times over the last couple of weeks. Guess I know my way."

"This land is amazingly beautiful. Surrounded by mountains and the wide-open sky. How could anyone not want to live here?"

"You sound like a native Coloradan."

"Far from it. I'm from Ohio. I'd never been further west than the Mississippi until I moved out here. I had no idea what I was missing."

"Why did you choose Spencer?"

"You know, I'm not exactly sure. When I'd finally saved

enough, I thought I could open my own storefront, I only knew I wanted to set up my shop in a town that wasn't too large. With too many people. I studied how often businesses like mine fail and took that into consideration. Colorado seemed like a good place. I discovered there's a great balance of tourists and customers here. Besides, Spencer didn't have a cupcake shop. So here I am."

"You certainly did your research."

A compliment from him, an accusation from her family. "I did. I wanted to succeed and figuring out all the pitfalls before starting was imperative. So far, it's worked out great. I was even able to purchase my building rather than rent space. I'd better not fail."

"Don't see that happening. You've got the right spirit for cupcakes."

He caught her off guard with that statement. She laughed. "The right spirit? Okay, I'll take that. What got you into treehouses?"

"You might have noticed my family enjoys movies."

"We've got that in common."

A plus on the positive side. "One of my favorites as a kid was *Swiss Family Robinson*. Now that was a treehouse. I was as passionate about it as the youngest kid in the movie was about animals." He chuckled. "Mom still has a box of my first drawings."

"That's sweet."

The note of sadness in her tone drew Tony's attention and he missed a second dip. They bounced across the landscape. He needed to pay attention so they didn't end up high centered. He glanced sideways as Cookie adjusted her shoulder strap. "Sorry."

"Watch the road, buster." She pointed toward the front of the truck.

"Sorry," he repeated. "We're here."

But until they stood on the slight ridge overlooking the

small clump of trees, he hadn't realized how important it was for her to approve of his plans for the treehouse. She'd made appropriate 'oohs' and 'ahhs' at the cabin work. And taken his hand as they hiked the short distance. He needed to encourage her to get some real boots. The clogs she wore in the bakery weren't the best for hiking.

He wanted to take her hiking high in the mountains. Along the winding streams. Across tiny valleys. Simply to enjoy being with her and watching her wide-eyed wonder at the nature around her. He gave himself a mental shake. He was getting way beyond himself here.

"I watched a few of your shows the other night."

Tony faced her. "And?"

"You've got some talent, Tony. Now you want to build here? And make it accessible to everyone. I'm impressed. No, that's not the right word. I'm, oh, I don't know, amazed. No, that's not right either."

He chuckled. She was so cute when flustered like this. He brushed a strand of her windblown hair from her cheek. "This is far different from what I've done in the past. But what I want, and what I need to do now. My agent still has a few things to iron out with the network, but it looks promising that they'll release me from the last years of my contract. Personally, I think they're relieved to get rid of me."

"I can't believe that."

"I've gotten to be a bit of a thorn in their sides. They don't realize I know the producer's been grooming one of my assistants to take over the show."

"Won't that bother you?"

He liked her honest, hard questions. "Maybe. Nah. It's time for me to move on. What we're negotiating now is how I'll be able to present myself and my knowledge in the near future. Like writing a book. Doing stuff on the internet. Networks can be stingy and unreasonable when they feel their rights are being stepped on."

"A book? That would be exciting. I've always wanted to write a cookbook."

"Let me guess. Cupcakes."

She slapped his chest and let her hand rest over his heart. "Of course, buster."

"What's with this buster business? I was hoping you'd call me Tone."

Her hand danced across his chest and she stared at the buttons at the base of his neck. "Oh, I don't know. Today you just seem like a buster." Then her fingers curled around the back of his neck. She rose to her toes.

She kissed him.

Too shocked to do anything but sink into the warmth and softness of her lips, Tony allowed her to direct the kiss. Her mouth moved over his and the tip of her tongue touched the center of his bottom lip. When she traced his lip with her tongue, he sighed and opened to her tentative exploration. Locking his knees to remain standing, he wrapped his arms loosely around her waist and encouraged her closer.

Then her lips were gone, leaving his cold and bereft.

She rested her cheek against his shoulder. "I probably shouldn't have done that."

He didn't regret a millisecond and tightened his hold. "I'm not complaining. I've imagined kissing you for... never mind. I'm not complaining."

"Me either. Next time will be better, though."

Next time? Hell, yeah. He wanted to pump his fists in the air and shout his agreement. How soon could he make next time happen? A sobering thought corralled his excitement. He hadn't asked her yet about the apartment. Her kiss might change their dynamics, so that renting from her might be impossible.

Reluctant, he released her and took a step back. She lifted her head, eyes filled with questions, and dare he hope, regret?

No way he had an ounce of regret about the kiss, nor would she, once they got to 'next time'.

"This treehouse isn't going to be a quick build. I don't have a crew I'm familiar with, and I'll be splitting my time to help with the cabins, too. I want to make a careful record of every aspect of this build, with notes, photos, video. That all takes time. When I'm done I hope to have everything I need for whatever venue I take to share with the world. Or at least whoever might be interested."

"That will be the world."

"You have that much faith in me?" Hearing her words of support gave him the push he needed to ask the difficult question.

At her nod, he took her hand and turned them back toward his truck. "This means I'm going to be sticking around Spencer for... I don't know how long."

"Good," she mumbled.

Next time. "Mom's apartment takes up the whole of her building, but there really isn't room for a third person there. Those ladies have a lot of stuff. No minimalist lifestyle by any stretch of the imagination." He chuckled. "It was always that way. At least when Izzy and I were kids, we had our own rooms. Those are now both crammed full of whatever my folks think is cool. I had to dig a path through the room to find the bed."

"You're kidding. Aren't you?"

He held his finger and thumb a short distance apart. "A little bit. But what I'm not kidding about is that I need to find a place of my own to live."

"There aren't a whole lot of options in Spencer. It took me a couple of months to find my place. I had to more or less camp out in the apartment above my store."

"And that's what I wanted to talk to you about. The empty apartment."

She stopped their forward progress and tilted her head to

one side to look at him. "That space is barely livable. And now it's stacked with overflow from the bakery. Coffee cups, cupcake boxes, that kind of stuff."

"I have no problem making the needed updates and thought maybe I could barter work for a part of the rent?"

She thought for a long moment and he watched and categorized the emotions playing across her face. At first, she rejected the idea, then wavered between agreeing and not. So much reflected in her eyes and the way her lips barely moved as she thought. He could watch her forever just to learn the tiniest bit of her mind. Except those lips, those soft, soft lips called to him.

He caught himself before he leaned in and initiated the first next time kiss. Muddying negotiations with a lip lock wasn't a good idea.

She curled one finger and caught the side between her lips, her gaze distant as she thought. She was killing him.

Then she blinked and drew a deep breath. "I don't have much to spend on repairs and improvements. I can only afford basic fixtures and simple patches."

"Supplies could be part of the bartering process if needed. And if I might brag?"

Waving one hand she cast her gaze to the sky. "Go ahead and brag."

"Despite what my past builds present, I can actually do a lot with a little. So, do we have a contract?"

"Hmm. I get final decision on the changes and improvements?"

"Of course. It's your property."

"Construction won't disrupt business in the shop?"

"I'll be out here most days, so work I do in the apartment would be evenings for the most part. If I need to bring in someone for an issue like an electrician, they'd probably have to be there during business hours."

"That's acceptable." She stared at her toes. "But, I will

require a signed lease. I've been on the wrong side of a hand-shake deal and won't do that again."

Pride at her business acumen and determination to take care of herself made him cup her chin with his fingers and lift her gaze to his. "I wouldn't want it any other way. Do we have a deal?"

"A deal? Yes. I'll take you on as a tenant with a bartering agreement for work and supplies to cover a portion of the rent. You haven't asked how much rent will be."

"I really don't care."

"You should."

A breathlessness entered her voice. Tony prayed it was because he had inched closer and rested his free hand at her waist.

"What if I insist on high dollars, or have unreasonable requests?"

He leaned to touch his forehead to hers. "You wouldn't believe some of the things I've been asked to do. There were plenty that couldn't be shown on television. What would be unreasonable to you?"

"Oh, I..."

Stroking his fingers over her soft skin from her chin to the back of her neck, Tony pressed his cheek against her sun-warmed hair. "Unreasonable to seal this deal with a kiss?"

"Do you have plans to take advantage of your new landlord?"

He jerked back then relaxed at her grin. "Would my new landlord approve of those plans?"

"You'd better believe it, buster. I'm done wheeling and dealing."

So was he, and brought their lips together for a light, teasing kiss. At her sigh, he deepened the kiss, drawing her closer until her body pressed fully against his. Heaven.

Then he tumbled to hell when he broke the kiss and stepped back. Now was not the time to pursue this. He needed to take his time, because even though she'd kissed him first, he sensed she wasn't sure how to proceed. Or if she really wanted to. Damn having that sensitive gene. He drew in a measured breath. Mom had taught him well.

The promise he'd made long ago to his sister still held true. He would never push too far. He'd be conscious of his partner's needs and wishes, and never allow fear into a physical relationship. With a series of short relationships that were built around little but sex, that hadn't been difficult.

Despite his body's interest, or maybe because of the instant attraction he'd experienced the first time he'd seen Cookie, now was the time to go slow.

Cookie matched his deep breath and grinned. "So, we've tentatively sealed our contract. Now, I'm hungry."

So was he. For her. "I could eat. What do you have in mind?"

"Spaghetti at my place. I know it's early for most people, but I'm up at four every morning, so supper and my bedtime are early, too."

"I understand early. I spent many a cold and dark morning trudging to a work site so we'd have the most daylight for filming. I can do early." He offered her his crooked elbow. "Shall we?"

❧

It had been late when they'd gotten back to town, so they settled for submarine sandwiches. With Tony settled next to her on the couch, her apartment seemed more welcoming, more like home. But when she'd started yawning, he'd kissed her and said good-bye. Despite the need thrumming at the edge of her consciousness, she'd fallen asleep easily and slept well.

Even though her four a.m. alarm was still just as early, she started the day with a smile.

That euphoria lasted until mid-morning when a high, lilting tenor voice asking to speak with her rose from the front counter. Wiping her hands on the towel she kept tucked through her apron strings, she peeked through the doorway. Ava turned and motioned to her. With a relaxed smile, Cookie shook hands with the dapperly dressed man and after learning he wished to make a large cupcake order, invited him to take a seat at one of the empty tables.

Once she'd gathered an order sheet and pen, she joined him.

"My name is Robert Weiss. I'm Cale Hartwood's personal assistant."

Cookie fought to keep her smile in place. Wasn't it bad enough Hartwood kept dogging her steps, now he'd sent his assistant? "How can I help you, Mr. Weiss?"

He gave her a limp-wristed wave. "Oh, do call me Bobby. Everyone does." Then he leaned his forearms on the table. "Mr. Hartwood is hosting an event in one month's time. He would like you to provide an assortment of cupcakes for the occasion."

The thought of baking for that man made her stomach turn in unpleasant flip-flops. But, the benefits of having her cupcakes featured at what she assumed would be a well-attended event could be a big boost for business. She'd hold off on her final decision until after she knew the specifics. "How many cupcakes would Mr. Hartwood require?"

Bobby threw out a number that made her widen her eyes. "That many?"

"Of course. He's expecting guests from out of town and is planning an event filled evening. Topped off by your deli-cious cupcakes."

Cookie made a note on the order form. "How many flavors? Any special requests for decorations or icings?"

"He will leave those details up to you, requesting only that you create your finest, most impressive cupcakes."

"I see." Carte blanche on flavors for such a huge order? Her mind whirled with possibilities. But first... "You said a month. When exactly are these cupcakes needed?"

Bobby gave her a date and time. She scanned the calendar she'd tucked under the order form. The date wouldn't be a problem.

"And will Mr. Hartwood be picking up his order?"

"He's requesting delivery, by you personally."

"I don't often make deliveries, but my staff will—"

Bobby slashed his hand through the air. "You will deliver the cupcakes or there will be no order."

Cookie stared at the flamboyant man. Although his suit was conservative, he'd paired it with a wildly patterned shirt and a striped bow tie. Given what she knew of Hartwood, she didn't see him having Bobby as his assistant. Perhaps the man was good enough at his job that the peculiarities were overlooked.

She couldn't pass up such an extravagant order. The extra income could be used for the improvements to the upstairs apartment. She nodded slowly. "Alright, Bobby. I'll deliver the cupcakes. I will need a deposit though for such a large order."

Smiling, he pulled a checkbook from an inner breast pocket of his jacket. "I have the authority to cut you a check."

She named an amount which would be approximately half of the order total. Bobby filled in the check without comment and after tearing it from the pad, handed the rectangle to her with a flourish. "Pleasure doing business with you."

With no further discussion he folded his copy of the order, tucked it in the checkbook, then rose and exited the shop. Cookie blinked and stared at the check that amounted to nearly a full day's till. Even though Cale Hartwood made her life difficult at times, this check bearing his signature would make a welcome difference in her bank account.

She tucked the order form and the check into her calendar and returned to the kitchen. Now she'd be able to step up from builder grade fixtures and finishes for the apartment.

Even though it involved Cale Hartwood, this had been a profitable day.

CHAPTER NINE

*B*efore Cookie left her apartment at five the next morning, her cell rang. Brow furrowed; she checked the number. Darryl?

"This is Cookie. What's up?"

"You on your way in?" Anger vibrated through the man's normally calm tone.

"Just going out the door. What's wrong?"

"There's been a break-in. I've called the police and they're on the way."

"Be there in under five."

Cookie kicked off her clogs and tossed them in her tote. Tying her athletic shoes tightly, she tried to contain her wildly escalating thoughts. A break in? How? Who? Why? Dear God, she so didn't need anything like this right now. Would she be able to open today? With her tote strap crossing her body, she rushed from her apartment.

Before leaving the safety of the building, she scanned the street and double-checked she had her phone. Phone in hand, and with the emergency call number queued up for an immediate dial if anything happened, she raced into the street. The speed of her thoughts kept pace with her feet. It was easier and quicker to jog to the store than to drive and park in a lot that actually wasn't much closer than home.

The cops arrived at the street side door to the bakery at the same time she did. Surprised to see her friend Ruby's husband there, she rested her hands on her knees for a moment drawing in harsh breaths before approaching where Hunter Lawe spoke with Darryl.

Despite her worry, she grinned solemnly at the older man's wild, angry gestures and indignation. He was such a good man.

Hunter turned to her. "Looks like a case of vandalism more than anything. We've had similar reports for the past couple of weeks. Unfortunately, your shop has gotten the worst of it so far. When my guys are done in there, I'd like you and Darryl to check and see if anything's been stolen."

Cookie blew out a long, slow breath. "The only thing worth stealing in there is equipment. And that's mostly too large and heavy unless the bad guys have a dolly and a truck."

"Money?"

"There's an overly large safe on the second floor. It came with the building. But it works great for a little cash and important paperwork. I'll check it first thing."

Hunter's radio squawked and he held up one hand. "Hang on. Go ahead."

The slightly mechanical, raspy voice was loud in the quiet early morning. "About done in here, Chief. It doesn't appear the vandals made it upstairs. There's, uh, flour everywhere and footprints, but none go toward the stairs. The owner can come in now."

"Okay, Ms. Lamont, let's go see if anything's missing."

Darryl took Cookie's arm. "It's bad in there. Steel yourself."

Straightening her shoulders, Cookie nodded. "I'm ready."

She froze a few paces inside the door, leaving just enough room for Darryl and Hunter to squeeze in behind her. Eyes wide, she covered her mouth with her hand. "Oh my God."

Flour and sugar covered every surface, and a white haze of dusty puffs lingered from the officer's footsteps as he crossed to meet them. The bright, shiny stainless steel of her tiny walk-in refrigerator was covered in swirls of ugly black graffiti, including words she would never use. Never. The thought that 'bitch' was the least offensive of the lot nearly made her laugh. She closed her eyes to block the sight and turned.

Hesitant to discover additional damage, she opened her eyes to squint. Flour footsteps led out into the storefront. She lifted her suddenly heavy arm and gestured with a shaky point. "Did they... out there, too?"

The officer glanced at his chief then shook his head. "No graffiti. But there is some damage to your display case."

"Cookie! What's going on?" Tony shouldered past the cop standing in the open doorway.

"Hold up, Tone." Hunter stopped Tony's advance by planting both hands against his chest. "Take it easy. Don't mess the scene up any more than it is."

Tony shook him off but remained where he stood.

Cookie was never so happy to see anyone in her life. When he opened his arms, she rushed into his embrace and hid her face against his shirt. She wouldn't cry. At least not yet. Not until they knew the extent of the damage. Then, then she made no promises.

Hunter cleared his throat. "What are you doing here, Tone?"

"The glare of your flashing lights hit my window just right and woke me. I came to make sure Cookie was all right."

"I'm fine." She eased back from the comfort he offered and gave an only slightly hysterical laugh. "But your shirt is buttoned wrong."

He glanced down, huffed and rebuttoned the plaid work shirt. "What happened here? A flour explosion?"

"Vandals," Darryl said. "Fucking, oh pardon me, Cookie, but fucking vandals."

Cookie bit back another inappropriate laugh. "I agree one hundred percent. I need to see what happened out front." She turned to Hunter. "Then I'll go upstairs and make sure everything is secure there. Darryl should be able to determine what's been damaged or what might be missing in here."

Tony spread his hands. "What can I do?"

The vandalism wasn't his concern, this was her shop after all. But, with him here, she wouldn't have to face the destruction alone. "Come with me?"

He glanced at Hunter and received a sharp nod. "Of course."

Feeling the tiniest bit stronger and able to face what she might find. Cookie took Tony's hand and together they entered the store front. First, she checked the expensive coffee service. A light coating of flour dulled the normal shine, but everything appeared in place, just as it was normally left at close down each day.

Flour footsteps covered the floor like a paper dance pattern. A good sweep would take care of that. Silent, she turned them toward the display case. "Oh no."

Cookie collapsed against Tony's side. He held her tightly then encouraged her to sit in the chair he grabbed from the closest table. She dropped her face to her hands and tried to take deep breaths. Too much. This was all too much. Her mind knew the damage was fixable, but her heart cried for what was lost. And for the rising feeling of invasion.

She'd been invaded. Her space had been violated. Her life had been intruded upon like never before. That made her mad.

Letting the anger roll over the despair and helplessness, she shook Tony's hand from her shoulder and moved to stand at her display case. Every colorful tray had been broken into small jagged pieces. A series of large cracks ran from front of the case to the back, marring the usually pristine, clear surface. She'd have to replace the entire unit. Her bank account might cover at least a basic unit. The replacement didn't need to be as fancy as this one.

She fisted her hands at her sides and screamed, "Damn it all to hell."

Footsteps rushed from the back, but Tony must have stopped the police from entering. He cautiously moved to stand next to her. "Cookie?"

She shook her head then her arms to diffuse the rage. "I'm okay. As much as I can be right now. I need to check upstairs, check the safe. Will you come with me there, too?"

"Anywhere you need, sweetheart."

"Easy for you to say, buster."

"I should have been here."

"What do you mean? This happened in the middle of the night. Hell, for a lot of people this is still the middle of the night."

"If I'd have moved in upstairs last night. After we made the agreement. Maybe the vandals would have been less likely to break in. I never expected anything like this could happen. I should have been here."

She rounded on him and poked his chest. "Don't you dare take any blame for this. Don't you dare give whoever did this less responsibility. No one could have guessed my shop would be a target. No one."

His expression said he didn't believe her, so she poked him again. "Don't. The only blame goes to the creeps who did this. Hunter said there've been other recent acts of vandalism. Tonight could simply have been my night. Maybe my door was the easiest to open. It could be we'll never know who or why. Or the cops could catch the culprits today." She dropped her hand and stepped back. "That would be a good thing."

"I'll move some stuff over today. I won't leave the building empty again after this happened."

It would be nice to know someone was watching over her space. But the apartment was barely livable. He'd planned to do a little work before moving in. She didn't want him to uncomfortable or inconvenienced. "You don't need to do that."

"I think I do. And once my moms find out, which will probably be in less than an hour, they'll insist. Shall we check the upstairs?"

The questions wouldn't go away if she ignored what happened. And the sooner she made sure her property was accounted for, the sooner she could get the store cleaned and start deciding how soon she could open for business. There was so much to do.

Tony cupped her cheek. "You're making lists of everything that needs to get done, aren't you?"

She nodded. "How do you know?"

"You've got that list-maker look in your eyes. We'll get everything taken care of and back to as normal as possible."

"You don't have to do anything. It's my shop—"

He silenced her with a tender kiss. "Yes, your shop, sweetheart. But Spencer is a community. We look out for each other. So, get accustomed to being looked out for."

That would be a new and welcome experience. She'd stood on her own feet, done everything for herself for so long, she wasn't sure how well she'd graciously accept help. She made a silent vow to be grateful for what she had, and that the damage to her shop was fixable. "I'll try. Upstairs?"

Nothing appeared disturbed on the second floor, and while she went down to report to the police chief, she left Tony examining the apartment. They'd made their agreement without him even seeing the place. Now she was worried he might consider the work too involved. Or the rooms weren't right for his needs.

If he decided not to rent the apartment, it wasn't a big deal. They hadn't yet signed the lease she'd printed off from a legal assistance site, so he had every right to walk away. As did she. But the more her thoughts circled around the vandalism, the more she believed someone being in the building at night could prevent a repeat. Tony's presence might not have stopped the break in, but perhaps the damage would have been less if the noise woke him. Her display case might still be whole and sparkling.

Once the police had the information and pictures they needed, Hunter left his card on her desk and promised to let her know as soon as they knew anything. Those famous words heard so often in movies and on television. She nearly laughed, but feared if she started, she'd become hysterical. And no one needed that right now.

Alone upstairs, Tony wandered the apartment for a good ten minutes, both to catalog the amount of work needed and to give Cookie time with the cops. Like the over-business apartment he'd grown up in, this place took up the whole second story. Even though this building was narrower, the main living area was spacious with tall windows facing the Olde Town triangle. A nook near the windows would make a great workspace, allowing him to take advantage of the natural light. The kitchen and bathroom were a mess. He'd bring in a plumber and an electrician to get everything up to code and working.

After the behind the wall details were taken care of, it wouldn't take him long to make needed minor repairs. He even had some decorating ideas to run by Cookie. Living here would be good. Both for him and for Cookie and the safety of her shop.

He glanced out the dirty front window and grinned. It wasn't even seven yet, and a cluster of shop owners armed with brooms, buckets, and mops crossed the triangle. Walking backward while leading the crew, his mom waved her arms, obviously enjoying directing the others like a drum major. He'd been right. It hadn't taken long for word of the break-in to spread and for the other owners to come together to help.

Leaping down the narrow stairs three at a time, he nearly barreled into Darryl who stood just inside the doorway, leaning on a broom.

"Hey, sorry man," Tony said.

"I don't know where to start," the older man said, then sighed. "It's too much."

"The cavalry is on the way."

Darryl brightened. "Many hands make light work."

"That they do. Where's Cookie?"

"Out front. She's really grieving over her display case."

With a nod, Tony drew in a measured breath. "Understandable. Can you get the incoming group started cleaning up back here?"

"You betcha. You go take care of our Cookie."

Our Cookie. Tony liked that thought. She'd handled so much on her own while getting a business running and successful. Probably much more than he suspected. She needed friends right now. Both to help with the clean-up, and for emotional support. He understood that need more than he cared to admit. Nothing he loved had ever been destroyed. Except his sister.

An insidious thought burned through his mind. Did Hartwood have something to do with the break-in? The man wouldn't be that stupid, would he? Tony cast his gaze to the ceiling. With Hartwood, anything was possible. After the mess was cleared away and Cookie was okay, Tony planned to talk with Hunter. He doubted Cookie had said anything about Hartwood's harassment.

Time to take a closer look at the motivations and dealings of the newest town trustee.

The sounds of shuffling feet alerted him to the arrival of the Olde Town shop owners. He followed the rise and fall of Cookie's voice and entered the store to stand beside her.

"Thank you, but I'm okay. You don't need to—"

"No, we don't *need* to, young lady." Tony grinned at his mother's determined tone. She used her 'mom' voice well. "But Olde Town is a family and family helps one another. I know you haven't taken part in the council—yet. Or attended more than one of our social gatherings—yet. But that doesn't mean we won't be here if you need us. And it looks to me like you need some help getting this mess cleaned up. Let us help with some of the dirty work. That will allow you to be able to assess what's what more easily."

"I appreciate it. I really do. But what about your own shops?"

"It's early, hon. Most of us don't open for another couple hours. With all of us working together, we'll have things set to rights here in plenty of time." Muffy chuckled. "As long as you don't stand in our way or slow us down."

Tony wrapped his arm around Cookie's waist. "You're not going to win this battle."

"It's not a battle. It's just that..." The tense lines at the corners of her mouth eased to a resigned half-smile. "Okay. Come on in, everyone. The coffee maker wasn't damaged. How about a hot cup before we get started?"

Tony leaned close to her ear and whispered, "That's the way to win everyone over."

A couple hours later and Cookie's Coffee and Cakes had been swept clean. The spray-painted words had, thankfully, been easy to remove from the stainless steel. Other than the loss of ingredients and a handful of dented pans, the only real casualty of the vandals was the display case.

While Cookie and Darryl took stock of what supplies

remained unpolluted, Tony leaned against the wall next to the latte machine, watching his folks whisper, pace the length of where the display case had stood, then whisper more. They had something up their sleeves.

He wandered closer. Janelle gestured again to the empty space. "It should be the perfect size."

His mom nodded. "Not as fancy, but it will do for the time being." She turned to Tony. "Can you get a couple of your strong cousins to meet us in our expansion store at nine?"

"Sure, I suppose. What are you two up to?"

"Up to? Why do we need to be up to anything? Just be there."

After a hug from each woman, he watched them stroll hand-in-hand across the triangle. Following orders, Tony pulled out his phone and glanced at the time. With luck, he'd catch Ryder and Jack before they left for a morning of construction at Stick Pony. He doubted they'd be upset with the delay, especially since it looked like a storm was moving in off the mountains.

He said a quick good-bye to a distracted Cookie and left the shop. He made the calls as he rushed home. He'd pack a few things and move into his new apartment that day. No way would he leave Cookie's store unprotected for even one night.

CHAPTER TEN

Once the impromptu help left the store, Cookie collapsed onto her desk chair. Darryl perched on the side of the desk while Ava, who had shown up for her shift in the middle of the cleanup, leaned against the freshly polished walk-in door. Cookie sighed. What next?

Ava straightened. "Do you have any thoughts on how long it will be before we can open?"

Cookie glanced around the kitchen. Everything had been set to rights, the only things missing were the ingredients needed to make batters and icings. The next scheduled delivery was scheduled in two days. She had time to add to her order. "If I can get everything we need on the next truck, we should be able to open the next day. So, in three days. I don't know how to keep the cupcakes displayed and covered though."

Darryl scratched his chin. "Let me check on something. The ladies at my church have what I've always thought was an over-supply of those covered plastic cake carriers. And I should be able to borrow a couple long tables and table-cloths. The display wouldn't be pretty, but we could line up the pans with a single sample in front. It's an idea anyway."

"And not a bad one," Cookie said. "Not bad at all. I wonder if I could find any covered cake plates at the antiques store. Like you said, Darryl, we can have a sample of each cupcake on display and keep the ones for sale properly covered."

Ava brightened. "I love antiquing. I could spend hours at Aunt Cora's place. If you'd like, I'll be in charge of finding the display items."

Her staff was amazing. Cookie counted herself lucky. "Sounds great. Turn in your receipts to me for repayment. Darryl, would you check with your church ladies?"

He gave a jaunty salute. "Aye aye, boss."

Relief soothed Cookie's frazzled nerves. Everything would be okay. She, and her shop, would survive. "Let's plan on everyone here the day after tomorrow for another cleaning and prep. Then we'll open as usual the next day. I'll call Ethan and the others to let them know what's going on. Having a couple of extra down days shouldn't hurt the shop."

"Want me to make a sign for the window?" Ava asked.

"That'd be great. There's some poster board and markers upstairs from the last time you made signs for me."

Ava started for the stairs but Cookie called her back.

"I forgot to tell you. I've leased out the apartment. We'll need to clear out the stuff stored up there today. Finding a place for everything could be interesting."

"I can do that before I leave," Darryl said. "You get on the phone and get us flour and sugar. Cupcakes won't bake themselves, you know."

While Darryl and Ava moved boxes of cups and lids from upstairs, Cookie called her salesman and placed a large order. Sticker shock would take her breath away when she got the invoice. Like it had when she first opened. But Darryl had said it well. Cupcakes didn't bake themselves.

Next she started a list of flavors for the reopening. Until they got into the swing of the new setup, she'd plan a limited menu. She rested her elbows on her desk and rested her forehead against her palms. She'd started from scratch before. And she needed to remind herself this wasn't exactly starting from the beginning. She had a building. She had staff that were willing to go the extra mile to help. They would all survive just fine.

A vandal's destruction wasn't her fault.

Ava paused by the desk and held up a large sigh. "How's this?"

Cookie's Coffee and Cakes is temporarily closed. Reopening on Wednesday. Watch for opening day specials! Thank you for your continued support!

"Perfect. I like the colors you chose."

"Guess my design classes come in handy at times. I'll put this out front then get shopping."

Cookie glanced at the clock and chuckled. "Does Aunt Cora's Attic open this early?"

Ava's shoulders drooped. "No. So much has happened already today. I can't believe it's not even nine yet." Then she straightened and grinned. "I'll be first in line though when she does. I'll check for cake plates at the thrift store, too. It's amazing what you can find there."

"I can't thank you enough for all your help."

"Don't mention it. I like working here. I'll get going."

Before Cookie started in on another list, Ava poked her head back through the doorway. "Uh, you might want to come out here."

Now what? Had they missed something during the clean up? Palms flat against the desk, she rose and rolled her shoulders. She had little energy or emotion left to deal with more crap today. The only tempting idea was to go home, curl up under a throw on her couch, and cry. Yes, she admitted to herself. She deserved a good cry over this. Not that it would solve any part of the problem

She steeled herself with a deep breath and with Darryl's

solid presence at her back, entered the front of the store. Ava grinned at a gathering of people on the sidewalk. "You're not going to believe this."

With heavy steps, Cookie moved forward. She didn't know if she could deal with people today. She couldn't sell cupcakes. And she certainly didn't want anyone to witness her imminent breakdown. The crowd needed to go away. "Believe what?"

Tony climbed the two steps to the door and waited until Ava flipped the lock and let him enter.

Cookie blinked back the sting in her eyes. She didn't cry. She couldn't cry. Not now. "What's going on?"

"Mom had an idea."

"What?" She was so weary and barely found any interest in her question.

"My folks own the store next to their pottery shop and are doing a remodel."

"So? What does that have to do with me? Tony, I can't... I just can't be around people right now." Admitting this was one of the most difficult things she'd done that day. "I'm barely holding it together right now."

His smile disappeared and concern tightened his lips. "I didn't think. I'm sorry. Just let us do this one thing, then we'll be gone. Okay?"

She dared not speak. It really didn't matter, so she nodded.

He returned to the group waiting on the sidewalk and spoke rapidly. The people parted and a trio of men pushed a large object forward.

Curious, Cookie moved to the doorway. Perched on a carpet covered, low cart sat a large display case. Polished dark wood made up the bottom half, while glass sparkling in the morning sunlight topped the piece of furniture. Silently, Tony assisted the men, who she now recognized as Ryder,

Jack and Joe, the county sheriff in lifting the obviously heavy piece. They carried it carefully to the steps.

"Please move," Tony said. "This thing is freakin' heavy."

When she didn't move, Ava and Darryl took her arms and eased her backwards to clear the doorway. With a fair amount of grunting and good-natured groaning, the men brought in the display case and, after a few minute adjustments, placed the piece where her old case had stood. It fit perfectly.

"What is this?" she finally managed to ask.

"A case for cupcakes. Remember, I told you mom was remodeling the store next door. They don't need this case. Ma thought it would fit. It does."

"I can't take this."

Janelle entered the store with a cloth and proceeded to wipe fingerprints from the glass. "I know it's not made for baked goods, but the glass panels in the back close securely to keep out dust and whatever else might bother your cupcakes. I also know how long it can take to have a case constructed to specifications. You won't want to be closed that long."

Tony's mother joined her partner. "Besides, it's too big for what we need. People like to touch the pottery, not just peer at it through glass, so not practical either."

"But even with my insurance, I don't know if I can afford—"

"Consider this a loan, young lady. And a favor. This way we don't have to pay to have this carted off and stored." Muffy grinned. "Not that we would. It's a glorious old piece, probably as old as the building. Not your modern sensibilities perhaps. But usable for the time being. Now, be a dear and say you'll accept our gift and we'll be out of your hair. Except for one thing."

Overwhelmed, Cookie didn't think she could deal with another 'thing'. She shook her head.

The older woman touched her arm. "I understand. This has been one hell of a day already. We only want to invite you to supper soon."

Cookie swung her arm back to indicate the display case. "This more generous than anything I can imagine. Thank you. Thank you so much. Give me a few days to get back into the swing of things and we'll have supper. Okay?"

"Of course. When you're ready just let our boy know."

Muffy and Janelle shooed the crowd from the store. Ava and Darryl slipped quietly out the back entrance leaving Cookie alone with Tony.

"Cookie, sweetheart, what can I do?"

She hated feeling so weak and helpless. Dealing with this in a calm, calculated manner to set everything to rights should be easy. The support of her neighboring business owners, especially Tony's folks, surprised her. With only Tony near, her strength left her mind and body. She lifted her hand and stared at her shaking fingers.

Tony took her hand. He stroked her fingers and a wave of calm realization washed over her. She didn't need to do everything alone. There were people in her circle of friends who she could call for help. She even had girlfriends now. She could talk with them about her troubles and concerns. And Tony. She had him, too. For now.

"Cookie?"

"Hold me?" She'd said the first thing that popped into her mind and although the request surprised her, she didn't want to take back the desperate request. She wanted, needed, his arms around her.

She stepped into his embrace. The strength of his arms supported her, the solid wall of his chest and the strong beat of his heart surrounded her with peace. This was where she wanted to be.

The knowledge should have surprised her. Instead she

welcomed the realization with a sigh and wrapped her arms around his waist.

"Everything's going to be okay," he soothed, rubbing his hand slowly up and down her back. "We'll get the store back to normal and you'll be fine."

She shook her head. If her life went back to normal, then this man wouldn't be a part of that life. A new normal. That's what she needed. One that included Tony.

"You'll be okay, sweetheart."

Despite the sting of impending tears, she grinned into his shirt front. He misunderstood. And that was okay. Yes, she'd come out of this setback just fine. Possibly even with an increase in business after the word spread of her misfortune. If other locals were as kind as those here in Olde Town, she'd have more orders as they supported her recovery.

She'd never expected such a thing, but every day she discovered how special Spencer was, filled with remarkable people.

Including the man who held her so gently, offering comfort and support. How did she get to be so lucky?

With a soft sniff to stem those tears she refused to shed, she rubbed her cheek against the soft cotton of his shirt. This was her comfort. Her belonging.

"You didn't just wipe your nose on me, did you?"

CHAPTER ELEVEN

*C*ookie stared at the contents of her closet. What did one wear to a wedding shower at a pole dancing studio? Not that she had many choices outside of her work outfits and a few pairs of jeans. She tugged dark blue dress slacks from their hanger and added a tailored shirt to wear over a sleeveless top. It would have to do.

She was more concerned with the appearance of the cake than her own. The cake had been scheduled to be delivered to Whimzy's the day of the party, so she'd contacted the owner Breezy, and told her she'd be bringing the cake. After a moment of Breezy's surprised silence, they'd made arrangements for the evening. Cookie would carry the cake in after everyone was there. If she was going to out herself as an erotic cake baker, she might as well do it in style.

She was particularly proud of this cake. Ethan had come up with a small platform run by a tiny motor hidden under the cake. The movement had operated fine in tests, but without the heavy fondant covering the crisp rice treats she'd used for the man's butt. She crossed her fingers and sent a silent plea. Her first special effects cake couldn't be a dud.

On the short drive the fresh air blowing through the open

window helped calm her nerves. In the parking lot, already half filled with vehicles, Ruby approached her. "Need any help?"

Cookie handed her the package containing her shower gift. "Carry this for me? I've got something else to bring in, too."

"Other than the guest of honor, you're about the last to arrive. But the cake's not here yet. Breezy says it'll be here on time, but I'm worried. It better be spectacular. And dirty." She waggled her eyebrows. "That I gotta see."

Before Cookie withdrew the large cake board from the back of her SUV, she adjusted the upside-down box covering the cake. It was heavy, and she lifted carefully. "Can you close the hatch for me? This is a bit awkward."

Ruby snorted. "Looks like it. What is that anyway? Some new shower game? I think those are silly."

"Nope. This is the cake you're so worried about. Help me get it inside."

"The cake? How'd you end up with—never mind. I've got the door." She juggled the present and stared at the covered cake.

Cookie grinned. "You'll get to see it when the bride-to-be and everyone else does. Thanks."

Ruby added their gifts to a large stack of wrapped boxes and tissue-filled gift bags and added Cookie's present then blocked any of the other women from wandering across Cookie's path. For that she was grateful. The cake was getting really heavy.

At the table, she lowered the board and took a deep breath. Wondering when Kate wanted to present the cake, Cookie took a peek under the cardboard cover. Everything looked fine. No travel damage she needed to touch up. Then Kate was at her side with a large wine glass with a selection of fresh fruits floating in pale golden wine.

Cookie took a sip. "Thanks. Just what I needed. Now, about the cake."

Kate propped one hand on her hip and caressed the swell of her belly with the other. "How did you end up with the cake? It was supposed to be delivered here."

"And it was. Just now. Uh, I'm the owner of Kinky Kakes. I made this cake."

Kate's mouth formed a silent 'o'. Then she grinned and pulled Cookie into a hug. "You should have told me," she whispered.

"I didn't know what kind of reception this kind of baking would get in Spencer. Cupcakes are one thing, but this?"

"Yes, this. Can I get a sneak peek? I want to wait until after the games to show off your work."

Games. Great. She agreed with Ruby. Nothing more fun than shower games. Cookie finally allowed herself a relaxed grin. "Nope. No peeks. Everyone gets to see the reveal at the same time. Baker's prerogative."

Kate pulled her lips to a pout.

"That might work with Jack, but not me." Cookie crossed her arms and adopted a fierce expression. Then the women laughed together and Kate steered Cookie toward a circle of chairs and the gathering of women. The doors opened and Vianna arrived, followed by Zoe Barlow and Willa Spencer.

Kate nudged her shoulder. "Don't worry. They'll appreciate your cake as much as anyone."

Cookie wasn't so sure, but she put on her brave face and actually enjoyed the silly shower games. She volunteered to gather the ribbons and bows as Vianna opened her gifts and created a bridal bouquet that didn't look half bad. By the end of the unwrapping, Vianna had broken five ribbons and was declared, much to her embarrassment, the future mother of five.

The wine supply was sorely depleted, as was the pitcher of mocktails. Kate called the group to attention. "Now, I'll bet you thought it was time for refreshments—beyond the stuff filling our glasses. But I've planned one more, umm, activity before we unveil the..." She opened her eyes wide and waggled her eyebrows. "...cake."

A chorus of groans met her declaration.

"It's not by chance that we're having this shower here at Whimsy Pole Dancing. Tonight, we're all getting pole dancing lessons."

A long moment of silence fell over the group. Then Zoe stood and squared her shoulders. "Sounds like fun. I'm ready. Where's my pole?"

Breezy moved from the back of the room and flipped a set of light switches. Soft spotlights highlighted six poles attached to the floor and ceiling. The other lights in the large space dimmed. "Ladies. Tonight you're just going to learn a few basic moves. Nothing too strenuous or...exotic. Pole dancing is actually a great exercise and I invite you to try out a class anytime.

"Okay, enough commercial. Let's have some fun. Who's going to join Zoe for the first set?"

Zoe marched to the center pole, grasped it and swung around to face the others. "Come on. You're not gonna let an old lady show you up, are you? Vianna, listen to your almost mother-in-law and get out here."

Cookie joined the others in a slow clap and stomp until the bride-to-be shuffled into a spotlight. She gestured to Kate, who laughed and, holding her belly, exaggerated her waddle to a pole. Three others joined them and Breezy began her lesson.

Even while watching the simple stretches and spins Cookie's mind was on the cake reveal. Had creating movement been the right thing to do? She was proud of the effort, but was making this cake for friends a mistake?

One of the shower attendees, some cousin of the groom— she couldn't keep the huge, extended family straight—

disrupted her musing by pulling her to a pole. "This is the last round and you're up."

Even knowing everyone in the room had experienced dancing around a pole what felt like an overly bright spotlight, Cookie's cheeks burned. Then once she relaxed and got the hang of how the pole eased and accented the simple moves, she had fun. Laughing with the others, she completed the routine. She might actually sign up for one of the classes. When she had time.

"Cookie," Kate said. "Will you do the honor and unveil the cake?"

All eyes had turned to her and an expectant silence filled the room. She blew out a long breath and moved toward the cake table.

Thankful Kate hadn't outed her as the baker, but knowing she'd still have to come clean, Cookie stood behind the table and the cardboard covered confection. "I assume you all know Kate ordered a special cake for tonight, from a specialty online baker. This is the cake. And I'm the baker. Kinky Kakes is a side business I started a number of years ago. Up until tonight, I was able to keep this a secret."

"Show us the cake!" came a call from the gathering.

"Cake. Cake. Cake."

The chant continued until Cookie lowered her hands to the cardboard cover. She shouldn't have been so worried. Although once the wine wore off, some of these women might react differently. It shouldn't matter to her, but it did. Besides, it wasn't like she was going to display her erotic cakes in her shop window.

Imaging the reactions of unsuspecting passers-by made her grin. "Okay. One. Two. Three."

She lifted off the cover and tossed the cardboard to one side. Despite the gasps and jostling women, Cookie studied Vianna's face. Her reaction was the most important.

A deep blush filled Vianna's cheeks and she ducked her

head. But when she looked at Cookie, she grinned and mouthed, "It's perfect."

Relief surged through Cookie and she released her held breath. Now for the big surprise. "Can everyone see the cake?"

After a moment of repositioning, the women fell silent.

"I attempted a special effect with this cake. Cross your fingers and let's hope this works."

Cookie pushed the small button on a wireless control. After a long, tense second, the mechanism jerked once before the man's hips moved forward and back in a slow, smooth motion. Tearing her gaze from the successful movement, she scanned the faces of the women.

Vianna had blushed an even deeper red. Kate's eyes were as wide as her smile. Other reactions were similar and no one turned away in disgust. Then as if on cue, everyone's phone was focused on the cake. A few flashes indicated still photographs, but Cookie was pretty sure most were taking a video.

Oh no. They couldn't post a video to the internet.

"Please, everyone. I don't mind you taking pictures, but please don't post them publicly. And please, don't post the video."

"The pictures—and video—would be great publicity for your business," Kate said.

"Yeah, they would. But I don't want the cake going viral or anything like that."

Cookie studied the cake in action. The man was positioned so his upper body was supported on muscular arms, allowing his lower half to move. She still didn't understand the meaning of the blue belt. She'd ask Vianna someday when she wasn't already completely embarrassed and flustered.

"Kate's right. Can someone send me their video and

pictures? I didn't take any. I'll use some on the Kinky Kakes website. With your permission, Vianna."

Vianna blinked. "What? Oh, sure. As long as you don't say who you made this for. This cake is amazing. Mesmerizing."

Kate elbowed Vianna. "Makes you want to leave the party early and rush home to Ryder, huh?"

"Well..."

"Shall I cut the cake?" Cookie asked.

"I don't want to ruin it," Vianna said.

"No worries. The couple was made to be removed before cutting the cake. You can take the topper home if you'd like."

Impossibly, Vianna's blush deepened. Cookie took that as an indication her cake was a success.

"Yeah, I think I'd like that."

❧

After their bi-weekly girls' night out the following weekend, Vianna and Kate sat with Cookie in her apartment. After a meal at Pearl's, the small group of women watched a chick flick and munched on popcorn. Now, with the others gone, the trio relaxed with their feet up on the old wooden coffee table, wine glasses in hand.

Kate sighed. "I'll be glad when I can have some real wine instead of sparkling cider." She took a sip. "This stuff really isn't that bad. It makes me feel like I'm being bad. And that's good."

Vianna swirled the liquid in her glass. "Alcohol and the spirit world aren't always compatible. This is my one drink for the month."

Chuckling, Cookie added another inch of a deep merlot to her glass then corked the bottle with a fancy stopper. "And I have no such restrictions. Other than how early I have to get up tomorrow. This will be it for me. I'm glad we could spend a little extra time together."

"And you haven't even mentioned Tony once," Kate said.

"There's nothing to mention."

"Of course, there is. You've been out with him a couple times, haven't you?"

Even though she knew she'd have to face it eventually, Cookie had been dreading this moment. Coming from a large city, she had no experience with a small town and how quickly news spread. Rumors spread even more quickly, gaining a life of their own. The internet had nothing on a small town. She lifted one shoulder. "Yes."

"That's it? A one-word answer?" Kate nudged Vianna's feet. "She's worse than you were."

Cookie relented. "Okay, we've gone out. The first time was when he saved me from Hartwood. Once to the ranch so he could show me where he wants to build a tree house. And once to the Olde Town potluck. Nothing more. Unless you want to count when I made dinner here. That was the same day we went to Stick Pony. I suppose it counts only once."

"Details?" Vianna leaned forward and set her glass on the coffee table.

"There isn't much to tell. We talked. Learned about each other's lives and interests."

Kate rubbed her stomach. "Oh, baby's awake. So, the big question is, are you interested?"

Heat filled Cookie's cheeks but she refused to look away from her friends' curious expressions. She nodded. "But it's complicated."

Kate lifted one finger like a teacher making a point to her class. "Anything between a man and a woman is bound to get complicated. But it's so much fun untangling the mess. And making up after an argument. Have you had to make up yet?"

Hiding a smile behind her wine glass, Cookie shook her head. Once she lowered her glass, she had control of her embarrassment. "Different kind of complicated. He's renting the apartment above the store and doing some work on the space as part of the rent."

"Any other kind of 'trade' in the works?"

Kate was incorrigible. This time Cookie shook *her* finger. "Not what you're insinuating. We have a written lease agreement, so everything is legal and above board. Enough about my boring life, Vianna, I want to hear what Ryder thought about the cake topper."

Kate sighed. "Great change of subject, Cookie. But I want to know, too."

Vianna curled her legs under her and grinned. Pink tinted her cheeks. An odd surge of relief passed through Cookie. It was nice to know someone who blushed more easily than she did. Good for her, not so much for Vianna.

After clearing her throat, Vianna spoke. "When I told him about the shower most of what I got was man agreement. You know, the 'I'm tired and don't really care, but I'm listening' grunts and 'go ons'. He was a little more interested when I told him about learning to pole dance. But he still didn't move out of his slouch on the couch."

Kate laughed. "Slouch on the couch. That's perfect. Jack does that, too. Have you had a slouch on the couch from Tony yet?"

Slouch on the couch? Cookie shook her head. Obviously, she had a lot to learn about guy stuff.

"But when I put the topper on the coffee table, he suddenly became interested. When I turned it on..." Vianna fanned herself with her hand. "I never got the chance to turn it off. He somehow found an overabundance of energy. I'll need to get a new battery."

"Oh, girl." Kate lightly poked Cookie's arm. "I'd say that topper was a success. You need to be proud of your business and your ability."

"I suppose I am. But I'm still leery about letting people know."

Vianna took a deep breath. "I wanted to ask you something."

The serious yet tentative expression on Vianna's face brought a flare of panic to Cookie's chest. Had her secret gotten out further than the women at the shower? "Uh, okay?"

"Don't look so worried. I was just wondering if you'd ever consider doing a wedding cake. Not out of cupcakes, but a regular cake?"

So not what Cookie was expecting. "I suppose. I made quite a few when I worked in a bakery in Ohio. Why?"

Vianna glanced at Kate, who nodded encouragement. "The bakery here in town does an okay job. I could have had the chef at the lodge make a cake, but the kitchen is doing so much already. And I've seen some of chef Young's cakes. Even the ones he says are plain are much too fancy for me. I know it's really short notice, but I only have a couple of days to cancel my bakery cake without a penalty. Can I talk you into making one for me? Please? Would you have time to make my wedding cake?"

A wedding cake. Simple yet elegant, like Vianna. Cookie even knew what flavor she'd suggest. "Of course. I would be honored. I am honored you thought of me."

"Oh, thank you. This makes me happy." Vianna clapped her hands. "This means so much to me. I'll cancel the bakery cake first thing tomorrow."

"Can you give me a couple days to create a few drawings? Then we'll need to schedule a tasting so you can pick your flavor. Or flavors."

Kate struggled to her feet. "I'd better be invited to the tasting. Be right back. Baby's kicking my bladder. Don't make any decisions without me."

Cookie rose to dig through her tote for her notebook then sat next to Vianna and began asking a series of cake related questions. Once Kate returned, she added her opinion. By the time her friends left, Cookie had a few solid ideas for Vianna's wedding cake.

She danced around her apartment. Creating this cake would be a great change of pace. And so much fun. Since she'd nearly perfected her cinnamon roll cupcake batter, she suspected that flavor would be a hit with the groom. She'd start on a variety of tasting cakes in the morning.

Life was spectacularly good.

CHAPTER TWELVE

A week later, Cookie attempted to stem her nervous fidgeting by double checking and adjusting the small cakes lining the counter. She'd pulled a table from the front of the shop so passers-by wouldn't think she was open because there were people in the store, after hiding in the kitchen when she'd seen Cale Hartwood striding through Olde Town. Today Vianna was taste testing wedding cakes. Cookie couldn't afford for anything to go wrong.

She glanced at the clock. Fifteen minutes until the wedding party was due to arrive. She ran through her mental list one more time. Everything was as perfect as she could make it. She sat on her hands to keep from twisting her apron strings into knots.

Footsteps sounded on the creaking stairs descending from the apartment, surprising her. Tony was leaving later than usual today. She half rose to go to the door to meet him, then sat back down. He was a distraction and although she could use a distraction for a few minutes, she didn't need to be distracted. She rolled her eyes at the twists and knots in her logic. She'd make herself crazy.

The footsteps stopped outside the interior kitchen door.

Soft knocking jerked her to her feet. To heck with finding a calm mind. She'd happily allow herself to be distracted. As long as he wasn't reporting problems with the apartment or his remodels.

When she opened the door, Tony leaned against the opposite wall, thumbs moving rapidly over his phone. He looked up, smiled, and the tension eased from her neck and shoulders. How did he do that with just one look?

Pocketing the phone, he straightened. "I didn't know if you'd be in today."

"I've been working on a special project."

"Figured. I just got a text from Ryder saying he and Jack wouldn't be out to the construction site until later this morning. Something about cakes."

Cookie stepped back and gestured for him to enter the kitchen. Maybe an opinion from someone not directly involved in the wedding would help calm the nerves. "Vianna asked me to make her wedding cake."

"I've heard cupcake cakes have been popular. You're the best cupcake baker around."

"Flatterer. She doesn't want cupcakes. She wants a real wedding cake. I've made a few, but it's been a couple of years. In about ten minutes, they're all coming over to taste sample cakes."

"Isn't a wedding cake just a wedding cake? White and sweet and, well, just cake?"

Just cake? Who was this man? Hadn't he been eating her cupcakes for six weeks now? "You need a cake lesson, Tony. Where are you off to now?"

He shrugged. "Nowhere in particular. I was hoping I could talk you into a trip to the mountains this afternoon."

"I'll make a deal with you."

Wariness filled his expression. "Okay?" he drawled.

"Help me with this cake testing. You'll experience what a wedding cake can be, how flavors are really important.

When we're done, I'll be delighted to take a day trip with you."

Eyes sparkling, he clapped his hands together. "Let's get to it then."

"We have to wait for Vianna and Ryder. And of course, Kate and Jack."

Tony stepped toward the counter. "Wow, these are beautiful."

Trying to see her sample cakes with fresh eyes, Cookie studied the smooth icing and flower decorations. Vianna had requested buttercream icing and no fondant. Suited Cookie just fine. She wasn't fond of the consistency or flat, overly sweet taste of fondant either.

A knock at the street-side door slammed Cookie's nerves back into full force worry. Tony patted her hand. "Calm down. This is gonna be okay."

What did he know? He didn't even understand the importance and variety of wedding cakes.

"I'll get the door, sweetheart. You take a deep breath and relax. Honestly woman, the nerves are rolling off you like tsunami waves."

Oh hell, she wasn't that wound up, was she? Cookie took the recommended deep breath and released it slowly. Yeah, she was. It wasn't just creating a wedding cake when she hadn't done such a large, fancy cake in years that made her nervous. This cake was for a friend. She couldn't fail. She wouldn't. Although her smile felt pasted on, she stood next to the small table crowding the center of the kitchen and waited.

Vianna entered first, followed by an exuberant Kate. Their men followed more slowly, wary expressions telling her they had no idea how important this experience was for a bride. Men.

"Come sit here, everyone. Tony, grab my desk chair and join them." Cookie clasped her hands tightly then forced herself to relax her fingers before she started wringing her hands. "Vianna, Ryder, welcome to your cake tasting. Hopefully by the time we're done today, you'll have decided on your flavor and the style of decorations. Then I'll have plenty of time to make you the best cake ever."

Vianna sat and tugged Ryder to the seat next to her. "I can't wait. And I already know it'll be the best cake ever."

Ryder chuckled. "It'll have to go a long way to beat the topper you made for that shower cake."

With a frown, Jack helped Kate to her chair then sat himself. "What topper?"

Ryder slapped Jack's shoulder. "Tell you later." Then he turned to Vianna and brushed the back of his finger over the blush filling her cheeks. "Only if it's okay with you, honey."

"I'm surprised you haven't already," she mumbled.

"Something like that, so... personal... I wouldn't without your say so."

When she lifted her gaze, Vianna's eyes twinkled. "Oh, go ahead." She turned to Kate. "You'll let me know what happens?"

Laughing, Kate nodded. "Of course."

The confusion filling Tony's expression as he sat at the small table brought Cookie a moment of debate. He'd ask later, but should she explain? Not something to think about now. She'd decide that when the moment arrived. Now, she had cakes to present.

"Okay, what you're going to do is sample four different flavors of cake and icing combinations. Any of these are interchangeable. Please look at the different ways I've created peonies—which will be the main decoration. You'll choose the one you like best for your cake. So... ready to get started?"

Tony surged to his feet. "Wait. We need pictures."

The others' startled expressions mirrored Cookie's confusion. "What are you talking about?"

He waved one hand toward the row of cakes. "I get the feeling that this is an important moment for the bride and groom."

Nodding, Vianna took Ryder's hand. "I hadn't really thought about it." Ryder shrugged.

Tony cast them a crooked grin. "You've got me all lined up to take video of your wedding day. And you have a still photographer, right? Are these going to be the only photographic memories of the occasion? How are you going to fill up an album to show folks that can't make it to the ceremony? Or your kids?"

Kate took up the cause. "He's got a point. Remember how one or both of his moms always had a camera pointed at us when we were young?"

"It got to be a joke," Ryder said. "Sorry, Tone, but they did go overboard sometimes."

"Yeah, I get it. But this is important. Humor me, okay? I'm gonna run up for a real camera."

"What about our phones?" Ryder called after Tony's retreating form.

He froze and turned back. "Phone cameras have come a long way. They take great pictures. But sometimes, you really need to have the ability to work with different lenses and apertures. Don't do anything important. I'll be right back."

While Tony returned upstairs, Cookie set a stack of small plates, along with forks and napkins on the table. She should have had this stuff set out before everyone got there but had been too busy worrying. Just proved what worrying got her.

Finally, after Tony was satisfied with photos of the cake line-up, she presented the first sample. "This cake is vanilla bean. Tony, this will be the closest to what you consider a wedding cake. There's a strawberry filling to go with the pink theme, and vanilla buttercream. The peonies on this sample are piped with buttercream."

After 'oohs' and 'ahhs' subsided, Cookie sliced the cake and put a narrow wedge on everyone's plate.

"Good, but boring," Ryder said.

Comments went around the table. The assessment of the cake was close to what Cookie had expected. Starting with the familiar was a good plan. Although she was delighted Vianna appreciated the hand-piped peonies. Not the easiest flower to produce accurately.

Holding her surprise flavor for last, Cookie presented a chocolate cake with cream cheese icing and gum paste peonies, then a lemon cake with lemon curd filling and buttercream with a hint of lavender. Edible paper peonies decorated that cake.

Both cakes received rave reviews. She hoped that boded well for her final offering.

She'd been working on this flavor for a long time, and even after Vianna had told her the secret ingredient, it had taken many trials to achieve the right balance of sweetness and cinnamon. With a flourish she set the final small cake on the table.

"I did some fancy piping on this cake. Piping like this can be combined with any of the peonies. We can be as creative as we like because I want this cake to be exactly what you want."

"Doing good so far. What flavor is this cake? I'm already having a hard time deciding what I like best. Did you have to make this so difficult?"

Cookie grinned. "This is a new flavor I have yet to introduce to the world. If you choose this one, I won't put it in my cupcake rotation until after your wedding. I've spent a lot of time on this one. I really hope I've done the flavors justice and that you like it."

She felt the weight of five pairs of eyes as she sliced into the cake and placed a bit on each plate. Then she stood back and held her breath.

Ryder took the first bite. His eyes widened, then closed as he sank back in his chair with a sigh.

So far, so good.

The others forked up their bites at the same time. Kate stared at Vianna and pointed at the cake with her fork. Vianna nodded. Jack rapidly shoveled a second bite into his mouth. "Oh, yeah," he moaned

After watching the others' reactions through his camera lens, Tony savored a bite. "It tastes like cinnamon rolls."

"Like Vianna's cinnamon rolls," Ryder corrected. "How did you do this, Cookie?"

"A lot of experimentation and ruined cupcakes. Even after Vianna confessed her secret ingredient, it took a lot of batter to make it right. I did okay?"

"Good lord, woman," Ryder stated. "Okay? I've never tasted a cake so delicious. It's like I'm eating one of Vianna's rolls." He speared another bite then spoke with his mouth full. "No question. This is the flavor. This is our wedding cake."

The love in Vianna's eyes while she watched Ryder chew made Cookie's chest ache, but she resisted the urge to press her palm against the heavy beating of her heart. So much feeling. So much love. She ached to experience that connection with someone.

When she looked at Tony, he watched her with nearly the same expression. There was a connection between them, and she longed to deepen their relationship. But how? When she initiated the intimacy of a kiss, he was always the one who ended the moment. Even with regret in his eyes, he stopped. She didn't understand. He didn't act as though she'd done something wrong. Perhaps today she'd dig deep and find the bravery to ask him why.

Breaking the contact, he blinked and glanced to the side before nodding. "It's a fantastic cake."

After Kate and Jack both agreed, all eyes turned to

Vianna. She hadn't said anything yet. Her's was the most important reaction and would tell Cookie whether she'd been really successful in duplicating the flavors.

Vianna took another tiny bite of the cake then set her fork on the table. "I can't believe you did this. Yes. Yes, this is what I want for my wedding."

Ryder took her hand and lifted it to his mouth for a kiss. "Honey, are you sure?"

"The surest." She laughed and held out her free hand with her pinky extended. "Pinky swear."

Cookie linked her little finger with Vianna's. The silly ritual was important to both Vianna and Kate, and who was Cookie to buck tradition. "Pinky swear."

Vianna pointed to the piped peony. "And I like this for the main flowers. I'll leave any other piping and decorations up to you. I know you'll make me a spectacular cake."

After they finished planning the cake and Cookie had packaged up the remaining sample cakes for her friends to take home, Cookie turned to Tony. He'd remained silent through the final discussion and had returned the table to the front of the store without her asking. A heavy lump of worry settled in Cookie's belly. Did he regret his earlier invitation?

Tony waited for Cookie to finish wiping down the counters before he moved behind her and wrapped his arms around her waist. She was remarkable. Her baking talent astounded him, and the ease and speed with which she'd sketched out a cake for approval made him proud. Waiting until the others had left the bakery had been hell. He wanted Cookie in his arms. Now.

Gentle, he pressed his mouth to the side of her neck. She angled her head allowing him greater access. He took advantage of her silent offering, skimming his lips over her warm skin before turning her in his arms for a proper kiss. As he sank into the pleasure of exploring her soft lips, he realized he'd never initiated their kiss. He'd been missing out on a world of sensual delight. Why had he been so...

Shit. He knew. He didn't want to push. Knowing how Hartwood's advances made Cookie uncomfortable, he hadn't wanted to do anything that could be misconstrued as an unwanted advance.

Her lips softened and her arms curled around him to caress his back. When he danced his tongue along her lower lip, her lips parted, inviting him to explore. Even though the soft and lingering kisses drove him wild, he held back.

Cookie moved her hands to his chest and shoved. Then she crossed her arms and he swore she looked ready to start tapping her foot. "Okay, buster, what is it with you? Do you want to kiss me, or not? Do you want to take this further, or not? You're driving me crazy. I don't know what to think. Is it you? Or is it me?"

The frightened, insecure rise of her final question broke through the haze. "Oh, no, Cookie. Not you. You're more perfect than I have a right to enjoy."

"I'm not sure how I should take that."

"Cookie, sweetheart, I..." Unsure what to say that wouldn't sound stupid, he stared at his toes.

"Out with it. Please. Don't leave me confused and needing you."

She needed him? He needed her. He didn't understand the need. Didn't want to take time to examine his feelings. He ached to act. To hold her, kiss her. And more. That more scared the heck out of him.

He opted for an easy, but true, cop-out. "I haven't had the best luck with relationships."

CHAPTER THIRTEEN

"Welcome to the club, Tone."

This wasn't a club membership he expected to share with her. Her foot tapped against the tile floor. She wasn't going to let him off with such a glib answer.

"Are you going to live in the past? Or would you like to move into the future?"

"No, I mean yes. I mean..." Shit, he was messing this up big time.

Cookie relaxed her stance and leaned back against the tall work counter. "This is what I want. I want to kiss you. Maybe more. But if you're going to pull back physically that's not going to happen."

His toes became interesting again. "When Izzy—"

"I can only imagine the pain you felt. But what does that have to do with us?"

"I don't want to push you."

"Push me into kissing you? Seems like I've been the one doing the pushing there."

He looked up and despite the flat tone of her words, she smiled at him. Unbelievably, the load he carried lightened.

Maybe he *was* being too careful. "I don't want you to feel pressured. Not you. Not any woman."

"The only pressure I feel right now is frustration."

"Cookie, I... Oh, hell. My whole body aches with the need to hold you, kiss you. It's difficult to rewrite old scripts and change old habits. Will you be patient with me? Help me?"

Her grin widened and her eyes sparkled. "I believe I have been patient. Now, I'm ready to move on to the helping. So, can we go upstairs for a while before our trip. To talk. Maybe."

Convinced his voice would crack like it had when he was a teenager, he gave a silent nod. Cookie checked the lock on the door then took his hand and tugged him toward the interior stairwell. "Come on, buster."

"I really don't know how I feel about this buster stuff."

She paused on the steps and turned to look down on him. "Come on, then, sugar honey lamb."

The overly sweet tone with just a hint of southern twang made Tony grimace and shake his head in mock dismay. "Stick with buster. Better yet, I'll always answer to Tone."

"So," she said as they reached the landing. "I haven't had a tour of the apartment since the electricity was completed and you had some furniture delivered. I'm looking forward to seeing what you've accomplished."

While the space had been improved by simply washing the walls, woodwork and windows, he'd added a few pieces of comfortable furniture. The apartment still needed a huge amount of work before he really wanted to show it off to Cookie. Or anyone else. He silently thanked whatever housekeeping gods that looked down on him since he'd actually straightened the bedding over the mattress on the floor.

Despite Cookie's words in the bakery, he didn't know if she was ready to take their relationship in this new direction. No, he amended. If she said she was, she was. He was the one with cold, dragging feet.

And what the hell was that all about?

He didn't have any misgivings about the few relationships in his past. Relationships that never lasted beyond the filming of a show or a short stay on a celebrity's property. He'd never had sex with a celebrity, but when he'd been inclined, their staff or associates had been willing partners. And that hadn't always been the best idea.

Why the fuck was he thinking about that now?

His focus should be on the woman who waited for him to unlock the door. He was a freakin' idiot. He liked Cookie. More than he would ever imagine. Liked her enough to not want to rush into a physical relationship.

Good God, she confused him. Sex was not what he wanted with Cookie. Despite how his body reacted, how he was drawn to her like a magnet, it wasn't for sex.

Not sex. Lovemaking. He didn't like Cookie. He loved her.

Tony followed Cookie with his gaze as she wandered the large room, dragging her fingertips over the back of the single overstuffed chair set before a small flat screen television. Memorizing her movements and expressions he faced a startling realization.

Dear God. He was *in* love with her.

The strength fled his legs forcing him to sag against the door frame. How was he supposed to handle this? Where was the playbook that told him what to do when he found 'the one' when he wasn't looking? Shit, and now she was staring at him as though he was deranged. Having no idea what his expression might be conveying, he managed a smile.

"As you see, the living room is set for optimal television viewing. Not that I've had much time for that. I'm hoping to create a dining area near the kitchen door. The light in here is wonderful in the mornings with those huge windows. The new plumbing is in. Of course, you already knew that. We need to decide on fixtures for the kitchen and bathroom. The small room where the safe is makes a great office, but it needs..."

He let his words trail off. Damn, he was rambling.

Cookie rolled her gaze to the ceiling, which needed scraping and a fresh coat of paint. Humor filled her expression as she crossed the room to him. "You sound just like your mother."

He blew out his frustration on a long exhale. "It happens sometimes."

"Like when you're nervous?"

She had the truth of that, but damned if he'd admit it. He remained silent.

"Me, too," Cookie said softly then rose to her toes to kiss him. "We got a late start on the day, I didn't eat breakfast, and I'm getting hungry. Can our outing include a picnic?"

It took a few moments for his brain to catch up with the change of subject. "I thought about showing off my progress on the treehouse, but the site's full of construction debris and tools."

He glanced down at her feet. She had on a pair of hiking boots. When she noticed his perusal, she lifted one foot. "I've been wearing these on my days off to break them in."

"Great. Are you up for a short hike?"

"That's why I got the boots."

Before they left the apartment, Tony called Pearl's and ordered a picnic lunch. But when they drove by the café, there were no available parking spaces.

"Let me jump out and get it, you circle the park," Cookie suggested.

"Deal."

As he drove around the park, Tony caught himself scanning the sidewalks for Hartwood. He wouldn't put it past the bastard to try and ruin the day. It was only a matter of time before Tony would have to confront the bastard. He still owed the creep a well-deserved beat-down.

First, he owed Cookie an apology. The two emotions—love and hate—were dangerously intertwined. If he wasn't careful in untangling his feelings, he'd make a mess of today. Even if he didn't mess up, Cookie could still walk away from him. She might not want to deal with his damaged soul. Or the simmering anger he'd become an expert at keeping hidden.

Forcing a smile to replace the tense anger that greeted him when he glanced in the mirror, he pulled up in front of Pearl's just as Cookie exited the restaurant. She gave him a bright wave then wove between the parked vehicles. She clamored into his truck, placed the bag between her feet and fastened her seatbelt. "Let's go. This food smells so good. I don't know if I can wait. So, where are we going?"

This grin was more successful. He'd asked his cousins a couple of not so subtle questions, so he knew no one else would be there. But he remained silent until they reached the edge of town before he answered her.

"The shack."

※

The small building was the same as the last time he'd been home, and his front porch addition had weathered to the point it now looked like part of the original structure. Cookie enjoyed the trek from the trail head and commented freely on the landscape and small wildlife. He wiggled his fingers. He hadn't thought through carrying their lunch and had given Cookie the small, soft-sided cooler. The handles of the plastic bag had cut into his fingers over the course of their one-mile hike.

Cookie's delight in the cabin eased his discomfort. When they stood at the cliff's edge, they'd taken a few selfies, then he'd pointed out landmarks he'd known all his life. Sharing those moments with her lightened his concern over the upcoming conversation. Once they'd eaten the excellent meal of cold fried chicken, slaw and fluffy dinner rolls with real butter, they sat on the porch.

He opened a bottle of wine from the cooler. She lifted her glass in a silent salute before taking a sip. Then she set her wine on the porch floor and leaned forward with her elbows on her knees. "Time for talking, buster."

Tony took a long, fortifying swallow and set his glass next to hers. "Don't you want to wait until after the pie?"

"You liked my little surprise?"

"I didn't even think about dessert. And you know I love pie."

She grinned. "I didn't really know how much until now. Maybe I'll have to come up with a pie cupcake."

"I volunteer to be a taste tester. If it turns out even half as good as your cinnamon roll cake, it'll be a hit."

"Hmm. Okay, Tony. No more stalling."

No more stalling. A frantic part of his mind searched for something else he could say, some other way to explain his actions. He cleared his throat. "I don't know if this will make sense to you."

"Try me."

Okay. He could do this.

Cookie stood and dragged her heavy log chair across the floorboards to sit directly in front of him. She took his hands. "Would it help if I asked questions?"

He shrugged. That might be easier, then again not. It depended on the questions. "No. I mean, yes. No, only partially. Hell, Cookie. Just listen first, then I'll try and answer your questions." He was sure she'd have many and dreaded the moment. And the answers. One long swallow of wine emptied his glass. Now or never.

"When we were in high school, Hartwood started following my sister around. She ignored him."

Questions waited in Cookie's expression, but she remained silent.

"She avoided him as much as possible. Spencer was even smaller back then, so doing that was difficult. One day..." Tony paused. "He attacked her. I was nearby and heard her scream. I pulled the jerk off her. Got in a couple of good punches before he ran off. Izzy made me promise not to tell anyone what happened. Not even our moms. I've kept that promise until now."

"Oh, my God, Tony. I thought his bothering her was just harmless teenager stuff. Was she okay?" Cookie took his hands and rubbed warmth into his skin. He hadn't realized how cold he felt.

"As much as she could be. Unfortunately, that incident escalated the animosity between us. Hartwood had a gang of wannabes. They beat me up. That one was hard to explain to Mom."

"How?"

"Since there'd been trouble before between Hartwood and anyone related to the Spencer family, I just said he picked a fight and I'd lost. When my cousins asked, I told them he was just being a typical bully. Lording his family name over everyone and expecting us all to kowtow to him. Couple weeks later Jack, Ryder and I cornered him for a change. He didn't get much more than a black eye. The guys and I were suspended for a week."

"I don't understand what this has to do with us."

"He hasn't changed, Cookie. He's still a bully. Still wants all the attention and glory on himself. I've heard rumors."

"About what?"

"Damn it, sweetheart. He's no good. He'll push, push hard to get his way."

Her eyes narrowed and she tilted her head to watch him silently for a long moment. "I know he will. He's tried a couple of underhanded maneuvers to get me to go on a date.

Like that day when you rescued me in the triangle. My knight in shining armor."

He didn't feel like a knight, shining or otherwise. But he'd do what he could to keep Cookie safe while keeping an eye on the bastard. "Don't trust Hartwood to be a good man, Cookie. I need you to promise me that you'll never be alone with him. Ever. Even if you're in the middle of Olde Town or in the park. He's bad news. Dangerous."

"I'll agree he's creepy and overly full of himself, but dangerous?"

Years ago, Tony had promised his sister to keep Hartwood's attack a secret. Now he'd broken that promise intending to keep another woman safe from the bastard's machinations. As much as he'd prefer it, he couldn't spend every hour of every day with Cookie to keep her safe. "Sweetheart, please. Promise me you'll be careful. Avoid him. Walk the other way if you see him. Please. I need you to do this for me. Damn it, Cookie, you have to promise me."

"I think you're overreacting, but okay. Yes, of course I'll make that promise. I'll avoid him—which is something I try to do anyway. I promise, Tony, to never be in a situation where I might be alone with him. Don't look so worried. I've been taking care of myself for a long time."

She took his hands. "Tony, I promise. Stop worrying so much. Now, I'm thinking that's not what we came up here to talk about, is it? What does the attack on your sister have to do with us, and…" Her face colored but she met his eyes and grinned. "And why we haven't started enjoying a physical relationship."

Tony pressed his lips together and closed his eyes on a deep sigh. He wasn't exactly sure how to make sense of it either. "Since high school, I've been ultra-aware of how saying certain things, or acting without consent, can turn a relationship sour in a single moment. I've been probably overly conscious of my actions around women."

"Not necessarily a bad thing, Tony."

"And that's worked for me. Until you."

Releasing his hands, she sat back and crossed her arms. Bereft without her touch, he waited as she visibly processed that much of his story.

"Until me. Why am I different?"

"Though it pains me to admit, my past relationships haven't been much of a relationship. More often just a fling while filming. That sounds terrible when I say it out loud." He stared to the side. This wasn't going well. He hadn't expected it to.

"So, you've had a series of non-committed, 'let's have some fun' relationships."

"Shit, when you say it that way..."

"No judgement. I'm not exactly proud of my past love life either. Good chance most of the population isn't. I'll ask again. Why am I different?"

Because I love you. "With you I feel more. Being with you is more important to me. Special. A need."

"And?"

Feeling as though he was baring his soul—and he was, partially—Tony held her gaze. "And I was afraid if I pushed."

A half-grin tilted her luscious lips. "For sex?"

"No. I mean, yes. I did talk to a shrink about it once, when I was building him a treehouse. He said that since I hadn't been able to protect my sister, I was behaving so that no other brother would need to be protective. I suppose that makes sense somewhere along the line."

"I think I understand. So, you didn't want me to be afraid. You didn't want to do anything that would force me—"

"I would never force—"

"Hush. Let me finish. You didn't want to do anything that would make me feel the need for a protector. You didn't want me to feel helpless. Or for you to feel helpless."

How was he so lucky to have found such a wise woman to love? Maybe she'd understand if he told her the whole story.

But he wasn't willing to risk that. "I guess I thought that if I didn't pursue a physical relationship as soon as I'd wanted..."

"How soon? Please tell me. I was attracted to you that first morning you came in for coffee. Wanted you not long after. Like that night we played in the clay."

She'd wanted him? He'd been too stupid, too wrapped up in his own insecurities to notice any signs of her deepening interest. He held out his hands and she rested her palms against his. A gentle tug brought her to his lap. "You wanted me?"

She nuzzled his neck. "I did. I do. You said that your cousins often brought their girlfriends out here. Did you?"

Oddly enough, he hadn't. "Not until today."

"So, I'm your girlfriend?" Her lips moved to his earlobe and his doubts snapped from existence. This was a chance that for once, he was willing to take.

"If you want to be."

"I'd like that very much. Now, about that bed..."

He rose with her in his arms and carried her through the open doorway. The bed springs squealed when he sat on the edge of the mattress. Taking her mouth with his, he poured his heart into his kiss. Then with his mouth still caressing hers, he said, "I think... I think I'm falling in love with you, Cookie."

She leaned back; eyes wide. Would his admission frighten her away? Despite his personal vow not to push, he thought his heartfelt words may have been too much. Too soon.

A tender smile softened her surprise and she captured his face between her soft palms and drew him close for a kiss that curled his toes.

This woman. Kissing him. He'd half planned for this moment but hadn't believed he'd actually use the condom in his wallet. She pressed forward until he collapsed to his back on the squeaky bed. Maybe they'd shake some of the rust off the springs. He grinned. "What's next, sweetheart?"

Tapping one finger against her cheek, Cookie glanced up as though there was anything to contemplate. Her eyes sparkled when she looked at him. But as she started to speak, his phone rang.

She laughed and stared at his pocket. "You gonna answer that?"

He wouldn't, not for anything in the world, except this was Ma's ring, and she seldom called. It had to be something important. He shrugged an apology.

"Oh, just answer the damn thing. We've waited this long. The length of a phone call won't make a difference. Just don't talk too long." She flowed to her feet and returned to the porch.

He stood to dig the phone from his tighter than normal jeans." What's up, Ma?"

"Sorry to bother you, Tone. But the furniture you ordered has arrived."

"Couple days early."

"The driver said they'd had cancellations. I'd let them in to the apartment, but no keys."

He imagined her spreading one arm to the side and lifting her shoulders. "There should be a set with both the outer and apartment keys in the key bowl."

"Sorry, Tone. We checked. Muffy also ran over to the shop, but since it's Monday—"

"No one was there. Ma, I'm not in town. The keys should be there." He remembered tossing the extra set into... "Shit. They're in my truck."

"Language, hon. Before you ask, I've already tried making other arrangements. But the driver is insistent that if the load isn't delivered—today—to the address on the invoice, he'll take it back to the store."

A delay would throw his remodel off schedule. "It'll take about an hour to get back. Can you delay the truck that long?"

"Your moms have it under control, dear. Just don't take your time. This guy's cranky."

Despite the sudden, unwelcome change of plans, he chuckled. Ma was a master of understatement. "As fast as I can, Ma. Love you."

After disconnecting, he hunched his shoulders and stared at the wide floor planks. The universe needed to cut him a break.

"Hey, Tone," Cookie said softly. "I'm guessing from your side of the call we need to head back to town. I've packed up the cooler and our trash." She bent to look up into his face. "It's okay. Really. We're okay. This just wasn't our time for this." She waved at the bed. "I'm not sorry. Don't you be."

"I'll make it up to you, sweetheart."

"Yes, you will, Tony. Yes, you will."

CHAPTER FOURTEEN

"We're so glad you could join us, Cookie," Muffy said.

Janelle set a bowl brimming with creamy mashed potatoes on the table. "It's about time we got together for a real visit."

Cookie spread a boldly tie-dyed napkin over her lap. "Well, I haven't been exactly the most social since I moved here. I didn't allow much of anything to take focus from building my business. I had the proverbial blinders on when it came to the world outside my little shop."

"Starting a business is time consuming, isn't it, dear," Muffy commented. "We've been here a long time—even before the trustees approved the development of Olde Town. And we'd be here even if there wasn't the tourist business. We love what we do and can't imagine doing anything different. Or doing it anywhere else."

Cookie understood the sentiment well. "I know what you mean. I love my little shop. It took me a few years to decide exactly what I wanted to do with my life. I knew I wanted to bake way back in middle school. But, my father didn't approve."

Muffy winked at Janelle. "Men."

The pair laughed until Tony entered the dining room carrying a platter of fried chicken. "Now what did the token man do?"

Muffy took the chicken then shooed him toward the chair across from Cookie. "Nothing, dear. Shall we eat?"

The conversation flowed around Cookie with well-worn familiarity. Tony's family was the kind she'd wished for when she was younger. No power struggles. No moments of one partner dominating the other. A picture of healthy relationships. She joined the conversation from time to time, but mostly enjoyed listening. The flow of words was calming. Comforting.

Lost in thought, she didn't notice when silence fell over the table. She lifted her eyes and the others were all looking at her. Smiling. What had she missed?

"Don't look so worried," Muffy said. "I was just apologizing for not having prepared a dessert. I got caught up in my work. I'm afraid that an air-drying pot isn't very tasty. But we could send Tony over to Pearl's for pie. Or just enjoy some coffee instead. I must show you the pots though, before you leave. The shape is new to me and while I like the flow, I'm not sure how the design will be received by the public. Of course, Janelle has exciting plans for the colors and glazes. She does most of the painting and glazing for our business."

"Mom," Tony interrupted with a grin. "Take a breath."

She laughed and pushed back from the table. "I do tend to ramble, don't I?"

Tony cleared his throat. "You know I'd never pass up a piece of pie from Pearl's, but Cookie and I have plans this evening."

"Do tell." Muffy shifted to sit on the edge of her chair and propped her elbows on the table.

Janelle shook her head and cast her gaze to the ceiling.

"Hon, we don't need to know their plans." Then she turned to Tony. "Unless you want to tell us nosey old ladies anyway."

"Old ladies? Since when, Ma?" He leaned back and folded his arms across his chest. "Shall we fill them in on all the intimate secret plans?"

Startled by his question, Cookie remained silent a moment then chuckled. "Well, since Tony tried to teach me to throw a pot, tonight I'm going to teach him how to make cupcakes."

Janelle hooted with laughter. "Our boy baking? I'd love to be a fly on the wall for that."

"Ma, I can cook. Sort of. I actually baked a cake before, too, if you remember."

Muffy stood and moved to a tall bookcase over-stuffed with books and photo albums. She studied the albums for a long moment before snatching one from the shelf and returning to the table. "Yes, dear, you baked a cake. A birthday cake for your sister."

She flipped through the pages. Cookie wanted to be looking over Muffy's shoulder to discover more about Tony. What he'd looked like as a boy. What he'd done that merited photographs. From the ramshackle appearance of the bookshelves, the family had a wealth of photos recording their history. No one in her family took many pictures, but she liked the idea. The only thing she really took pictures of were her cakes. And a few shots of the mountains on those rare occasions when she left town.

"Ah, here we are." Muffy held the open photo album against her chest and smiled.

With a sigh, Tony rose and cleared the dishes from his mother's side of the table. "You really don't have to show that off, you know."

"Yes, she does," Cookie and Janelle said in unison.

"So much for any privilege in being the token male," Tony

grumbled and took plates to the kitchen. "Go ahead. I don't need to see this. Not now, not ever."

Once he'd cleared the table, Muffy moved to Cookie's side, placed the album on the table, and pointed to a slightly faded instamatic photo. "He tried. He really did."

The small, faded square showed a grinning boy standing behind a cake plate, oblivious to the top layer of the three-layer cake before him. The camera caught the layer just at the moment it slipped from its perch. Candles tipped in every direction. The shaky lettering barely fit on the cake top.

"He was so proud of his effort. Until we cut the cake and it wasn't completely baked. I have no idea how he managed to stack the layers." Muffy shook her head sadly. "Didn't we end up going to Curley's for ice cream instead?"

Cookie chuckled. "I probably shouldn't admit this, but my first attempt at a cake didn't turn out well either. I used a box mix and for whatever reason, had only put half of the mix into the bowl. I ended up with a sagging, hollow cake."

Tony peeked his head through the kitchen doorway. "You're kidding, right?"

"Nope. It was a disaster. Luckily Mom threw it out before Dad got home. He wasn't understanding when it came to waste. Hopefully my skills have improved."

Muffy patted her shoulder. "I would certainly say so, dear. You two run along now. We'll clean up. All I ask is that if your cupcakes turn out, you bring us each a sample."

Easing next to his mom, Tony leaned to kiss her cheek. "I'll make you a whole damn cake."

"Language." Janelle shook her finger at him. "Get going. I know Cookie keeps early hours. Don't keep her up too late."

Pleasant warmth filled Cookie's cheeks. She really wouldn't mind being kept up late with Tony. They had unfinished business. But maybe their growing relationship really wasn't there yet. Did they even have a quote-unquote relationship? Friendship, yes, definitely. She was ready for more.

"I'll take care of her, Mom."

That brought barely repressed erotic images to Cookie's mind. Her cheeks heated further. Damn her fair skin and easy blushes. She cleared the thoughts from her mind. "Actually, tonight is good for teaching. Since the shop is closed on Mondays, I don't have to be in early."

Janelle's expression turned serious. "Do you feel you lose valuable business by not being open on Mondays? Weekend tourists are generally gone and the next week's haven't arrived yet. So, is Monday a good day to close? We've been considering closing one day a week, too."

The change of topic helped steady Cookie's wayward thoughts. "There's benefits and detriments either way. I realized before opening I needed to have a day to myself. Not that I've taken advantage of that. But now I've got a good crew. Darryl Townsend has turned out to be a skilled and competent baker. I probably could be open seven days a week. I'm just not ready for that yet."

"We're looking to take more time for ourselves as well," Muffy said. "We've been in business for a long time. Let's talk about this another time, shall we? You two get going. I'm excited to see how Tony does with baking."

"Gee, Mom, nothing like piling on the pressure." Tony shrugged then reached over Cookie's shoulder to close the photo album. "When my cupcakes turn out, we'll take a picture to replace this one."

After a lengthy good -bye and promises she'd return for a good visit, Cookie and Tony finally meandered through the Olde Town triangle to her shop. Hand in hand they strolled past the bright lights and juke box music coming from the soda shop. Lights hanging from posts set strategically around the triangle lit the sidewalk with a warm glow.

But not as warm as the glow filling her heart after spending time with Tony's loving family. She could easily fall in love with the women who so obviously adored and were proud of their son. She sighed. Years ago she would have done anything to have her parents be proud of her.

"Why the heavy sigh?" Tony asked.

"I adore your folks."

"That's something to sigh about?"

She remained silent until they circled the buildings and stood at the back door of her shop. Then she gave him a wry grin. "My parents... are not supportive. Never were. I get the feeling you could do just about anything with your life, and your moms would find a wealth of things to be proud about. My parents—not so much. The only time I received any encouragement was when I did exactly what my father wanted."

"That's hard to believe."

"I guess. For someone who never had to face constant criticism. Growing up I couldn't do much of anything right. And I heard about it, constantly."

"That's not..."

"Let me just say this and then we won't talk about it again, okay?"

Tony nodded slowly. He'd want to know more, have more details. Maybe some day, if their relationship progressed that far. Until then, she'd keep her insecurities well hidden.

"The only thing my father thought a woman should do, should be, was a housewife. Preferably one molded into the precise image of what he expected. A Stepford wife."

"Never saw that movie."

"I can believe that now that I've gotten to know your family a little."

"But I know what it means. And your mother? She conformed to that ideal?"

Memories of her mother's regrets filled Cookie. "She did. She was—is—a talented dress designer. But, that kind of a profession has no place in my father's world, so he brow-beat her into submission. He tried with me but I guess I must be flawed." She covered Tony's opening mouth with her fingers. "According to him. As soon as I was able to leave home, I did. Now I'm here. Successful. His attitudes hold no sway over me."

If she could believe her own words, she'd be in good shape. But the man's words and repeated demands continued to haunt her. Especially now when she was attracted to someone and considering her future as something more than a cupcake baker.

Tony's expression told her he only partially believed her insistence. Why would he, when she didn't believe her words herself? Enough. She wasn't going to let anything spoil this evening. She arched one eyebrow. "Ready to bake, buster?"

☙

Two hours later Tony grinned at the dozen cupcakes lined up on the shiny stainless-steel counter. Fluffy icing topped each tiny cake. He'd created a fancy swirl of red topped with a cherry made out of something Cookie called gum paste.

Cookie had been an excellent, and extremely patient teacher. Although it would take some time for him to call the cake a sponge and he really didn't understand what she meant by a tender crumb. None of that mattered. He'd done it. He'd baked cupcakes that actually looked good enough to eat. He pulled out his phone. "I have to send a picture of these to Mom."

Cookie took the phone and gestured for him to move to the other side of the counter. "Let's take one that's posed like the photo of you as a kid. How old were you then, anyway?"

"Ten. Eleven maybe. Old enough to think I knew what I was doing. Obviously, I didn't. How's this?" He posed with his hands spread to indicate the cupcakes. A wide smile brightened his face. He became little boy, all proud and full of accomplishment.

"Perfect. Let me take a couple so we're sure to get a good one."

After those pictures, he leaned on the counter and brought his face close to one of the cupcakes. "How about this?" He opened his mouth wide, threatening the cupcake.

Cookie laughed and took the picture. Then he proceeded to pose in increasingly odd positions with his cupcakes, keeping Cookie laughing at his antics. After the past couple of weeks, it did his heart good to hear her laugh.

"Stop," she said breathlessly. "I hope you've got that anti-shaking thing on your phone. I'm laughing too much to take a picture that's in focus otherwise."

"They'll be fine. One more, okay?"

"What pose?"

He knew exactly how he wanted this picture. He rounded the table and wrapped an arm around Cookie's waist. "A selfie."

She wiggled a bit then pointed to the cupcakes with the phone. "Better have one of those in the shot. You take the picture and I'll hold a cupcake."

Taking the phone from her, Tony angled them and, holding the phone at arm's length, took their photo. "I was wrong. We need one more picture."

"Okay?"

"This one is all you, sweetheart. I'd love it if you would at least pretend to take a bite. I want to prove to people that I made edible cupcakes."

"And you think this will help?" Cookie lifted a cupcake and grinned.

This was close to what he wanted. Her smile needed to be wider, her eyes more sparkling. He made a silly face and she laughed. He snapped a series of photos and luckily hadn't lowered the phone when she took a bite of the thickly frosted cake. A tiny smear of icing decorated the tip of her nose. God, she was adorable.

He wanted her as he had the first moment he'd seen her. This woman. Wearing frosting. And nothing else.

"Don't move," he said as he pocketed his phone.

"Why? What?"

He closed the tiny distance between them and swiped the icing from her skin. He'd really wanted to kiss the sweetness away but wasn't sure how she'd react. Leaning closer, he watched her dark eyes. Yes, the sparkle was there, and something else. Something deeper, more meaningful, something he ached to explore and understand.

He did understand the welcome invitation riding the surface of her expression. Determined to take advantage of the moment, he brought his lips closer to hers. The cupcake smashed icing first against his mouth.

Cookie laughed and stepped back. "I'm sorry. I couldn't resist. You looked far too serious. Besides, you haven't tasted your baking yet either."

With a low snarl, he snatched the ruined cupcake from her hand and ripped away the paper. He stuffed the entire thing into his mouth. Once the dark chocolate hit his tongue, he groaned in delight. His words were garbled when he said, "So good. I really made this?" He groaned again and tried to swallow the overly large bite.

"You idiot." Cookie pulled a bottle of water from an under-counter cooler and twisted off the top before handing it to him. "Drink carefully. Don't choke on me, Tony."

Sipping half the bottle finally cleared the cake from his mouth, although he mourned the loss of the flavors that burst through his senses. "I made that," he said. "You're the best baking teacher ever."

"Let's get these packaged up for you to take to your moms tomorrow. Before you mess them up." Cookie grinned as she placed the cupcakes in a square white box and closed the flap with a colorful sticker. "There."

Tony glanced at the clock over the desk. It wasn't as late as he'd thought. "Do you have time to come upstairs?"

She cocked her head and arched an eyebrow. "To see your etchings?"

What was she talking about? Oh. Duh. "No, I don't etch. But I did want to show you the progress I've made. After the guys from Dagleish Construction finished the plumbing and electrical on Thursday, I worked on repairing the plaster walls. I'd like your approval."

"I'm sure it's fine. As long as everything works properly, is safe, and you're comfortable, what more is needed?"

He had plans that he hadn't even completely admitted to himself. Those plans required her approval before he went further. Both with the remodel and with her. It was important to him to gauge her reactions. "You' re my landlord. And didn't our agreement include your final approval on the work? I'd sure like to not have to redo something if you don't like it."

Her grin softened. "I'm pretty sure I'll like whatever you do, but let's go. I'll admit I am curious. The construction noises when the crew was in were like a siren's call, but I resisted. And I'm curious how the furniture we had to rush back to town for looks in the place. But I don't want to be the kind of landlord that just shows up without warning."

She could bring her light and joy to his doorstep any hour of the day or night. He didn't need a warning. He did need her in his life. To that end, he'd made subtle changes in his original drawings for the apartment and in his furniture choices. Hope was a dangerous thing though, so he dared not hope too much.

"I don't see that as becoming a problem. Come on up for a bit. Please." He held out his hand and she rested her fingers against his palm.

"You'll have to go first." She stared up the long, narrow

staircase. "The steps aren't wide enough for us to go up side-by-side."

When they stood on the landing at the top of the stairs, Tony glanced back down the creaky steps. "I'll fix those squeaks."

Cookie shrugged. "If you want. I find the sound rather homey. Lived in. That's good isn't it? Unless you want to keep someone from sneaking up on you. In that case, you'd better fix the steps."

He filed her reaction away. Homey. Lived in. His initial reaction to this apartment had been similar. On shoots he'd been put up in hotels, sometimes fancy, other times not so much. Even the apartment he'd owned, but barely lived in was sterile and beige. He could have changed the decor but didn't bother. He wasn't there often enough for the sterile rooms to feel like home.

He opened the door and stepped to one side so she could enter before him. "It's not much. Yet. It's home."

※

An hour later, Tony walked Cookie to her apartment. The night had gotten cooler and he suspected a spring snow could be in the making. At least along the higher peaks. Hopefully there wouldn't be another late spring blizzard.

At her door, he took both of her hands in his and brought them up to his chest. "I had a great time tonight. I can't believe I baked edible cupcakes."

"And I enjoyed dinner." She glanced at him from under her dark lashes. "I'm hoping for a return invite and a chance to look through all those photo albums."

"No, you don't. Mom will be in heaven. Me, not so much. They took way too many pictures of Izzy and I."

Her expression dimmed. "It must be nice to have those memories."

The little bits of information she divulged about her past that evening made him sad. How she became such a vibrant, intelligent and successful woman with her background astounded him. Made him proud. And if he dared to admit it, protective of her. He never wanted her to feel unvalidated again.

He stroked a strand of her soft, dark hair behind her ear. "We made a good start on memories tonight. I'll send you the pictures."

"Thanks. I'd like to build more memories." She took a deep breath and stared into his eyes. He lost himself in the golden-brown depths. "With you."

She slipped her hands from his and wrapped them around his neck, spearing her fingers through his hair to tilt his face to hers. Soft and welcoming, her lips brushed against his. Tantalizing. Teasing in a way that brought him contentment more than lust.

Cookie ended the kiss but kept her palms against his scalp. The tips of her fingers danced against his skull and he fought to bring his breathing under control. What she did to him with such a simple touch filled his mind with hope, and more than a few erotic thoughts. Not. Going. There. Tonight.

To his relief—and dismay—she stepped back and reached behind her for the doorknob. "I'll see you tomorrow?"

Every day if he could. He nodded and leaned in for a quick kiss to seal his promise. "Until tomorrow."

CHAPTER FIFTEEN

The following Saturday was delivery day for Hartwood's huge cupcake order—unfortunately to the man's home. She squared her shoulders. She could deal with him for the amount of time it took for her to unload the cupcakes and get a check for the balance due. Then she and Tony had a date at Spampinato's, the fancy Italian restaurant she'd never tried.

After a good meal, she'd invite Tony back to her apartment. With luck, the day would speed by. She had plans for her man that evening.

Her man. A glorious thought. Hers. Still, that tiny voice in her head, the one that insisted on sounding like her father, made its presence known. Tony wouldn't stay with her. Her career made her unacceptable for a lasting relationship. Someone better, someone who would stay home and conform would take him from her. She wasn't good enough.

Stop. No more. She'd conquered that insidious voice. Over and over. When would it leave her alone?

When would she face the realities of her choices and her future?

Cookie sat at her desk and stared at the uncluttered

wooden surface. Sooner or later she'd have to face reality. Tony wasn't in Spencer permanently. Once he decided where his talent could take him, he'd leave for those greener pastures. She knew that. And she knew his decisions had nothing to do with whether she was good enough for him. Or had the proper, housewife sensibilities. She knew that. She did. But the promise of future pain still made her heart ache.

Straightening her back, she flattened her palms against the desktop. She was strong. Competent. Intelligent. And if she didn't quit mooning about what might happen in the future, she wouldn't be able to enjoy the present. She wanted to enjoy herself. Completely.

With her plans for the evening bringing back a smile, she turned to the task of packing up the last of the many boxes of cupcakes. When she'd come to the store that morning, she'd left her vehicle in one of the prime parking spots on the street behind the building, so she didn't have far to carry the heavy boxes. Since the order was more than her SUV could carry, she'd enlisted one of her staff to go with her with the rest of the load. Ethan had pulled up behind the building and left his hazard lights flashing.

Darryl helped her with the last few boxes. "Are you sure you don't need more help once you get there?" he asked as he carefully lowered the hatch of her SUV.

"We should be fine. But thanks. And thanks for taking over the baking tomorrow morning."

Darryl gave her a knowing wink. "It's about time you started taking some days off. Ava and I have tomorrow covered. Even with the weekend tourists, Sunday is usually pretty calm. Now, get going. You don't want to be late delivering cupcakes to our esteemed city trustee."

After a totally unladylike snort, Cookie chuckled. "If he has to wait a few minutes, he has to wait. Might be good for him. See you Tuesday."

"You got it, boss."

"Call if you need anything."

With a single sharp rap on the side of her vehicle, Darryl shook his head. "No worrying. Get going. Have fun tonight."

She answered him with a wave and a broad smile. He grinned in return.

Settled in the driver's seat, Cookie waved to Ethan then scanned for oncoming vehicles and backed carefully into the street. She'd memorized the directions to one of the swankier parts of town and Hartwood's home. Even expecting the large mansions on small lots, she stared open-mouthed at the homes she passed. She had no idea there was so much wealth in the small town—other than at the lodge. Of course, the owners of the huge homes could be mort-gaged to the hilt to keep up the pretenses.

She preferred the older parts of town, and how those homeowners had kept the historical accuracy and appeal. At least on the exteriors.

Enough gawking. She pulled into the driveway for her delivery and couldn't help but take time for more gawking. This house was more than huge, centered on what had to be at least two lots. A modern colonial painted in stark white with black accenting the peaks and trim, the house was surrounded by mature landscaping and a checkerboard patterned driveway.

This obvious display of wealth made Cookie shake her head. No wonder the man oozed privilege. As she opened her car door, she blew out a long breath. Despite the profits of this huge order, she dreaded the delivery and having to deal directly with Hartwood. The man gave her the creeps. At least Ethan would be with her, both for security and so she kept her promise to Tony. Shaking off the misgivings, she decided to take the first load of boxes to the door with her. With her hands full, she'd at least have that bit of protection for her personal space.

The heavy black door swung open as she stepped onto the porch area. Although her customer frowned when he spied Ethan pulling up behind her, Hartwood beamed and moved to one side so she could enter through the wide entrance. She struggled to keep her astonishment contained, but the tilt of the man's smile told her she hadn't been successful. But then, surely this grand foyer had been planned to illicit just such an effect on visitors.

The cupcakes were getting heavy. "Where would you like these, Mr. Hartwood."

"No formalities needed, Cookie. Here I am simply Cale." He made a grand sweeping gesture. "To the left. Tables are set up, but if we need more, I can pull out another."

Long portable tables formed a wide 'u' shape. Covered with pristine white cloths and skirted with black, the tables would show off her cupcakes well. Cookie bit back a grin. He must have had a professional caterer set this up. But what was with all the black and white? The only splotch of color she'd seen was a burgundy and blue cap tossed onto the seat of a white recliner. She wasn't curious enough to see the rest of the house to look for another splash of brightness.

The cupcakes would brighten this area at least.

"Ethan and I will bring in the entire delivery then set them out. Unless you have someone to do that." She could hope.

"Allow me to assist."

The minutes without the man's hovering would be nice, but since this was a big delivery any help would be welcomed and get her out of this cold mausoleum faster. She gave a single nod and kept her tone cool. "That would be nice."

Five minutes later the wealth of cupcakes boxes was spread across the tables. She removed the lids to check on the condition of the treats. A few had shifted, marring the perfect swirls of icing, but nothing drastic. She contained her sigh of relief and began transferring the small cakes to the display tables.

All the while she felt Hartwood's eyes on her. The heavy weight of his gaze gave her the willies, raising goosebumps on her arms. Where was Ethan? It wasn't like him to avoid work, especially since she'd told him he could leave early that day for a robot fighting event. Ignoring the sensation and her questions, she took a single step back to view the effect of the colorful display on the first table. Perfect.

Squaring her shoulders, she turned to Hartwood. Getting the man out of the room would make it easier to finish up quickly. So she could leave. "Final payment is due on delivery... Cale. If you'd like to take care of that while I finish setting up?"

He fixed her with a stare she didn't care to interpret, then shook his head. "Uh, about that..."

Great. Now what? "Is there a problem?"

The man had an expressive face. He knew and used that to his advantage. Now his expression of regret told her she wasn't going to like what next came out of his mouth.

"It appears we have an issue with the approval of the order."

"Approval? You did give Mr. Weiss authority to make the order, didn't you?" ·

"Oh, of course. Bobby has my okay to take care of things like that. It's just that, well, this time he didn't fulfill his duty properly."

Planting her fists at her hips, Cookie braced for his next words.

"Simply put, Bobby didn't sign the order. Therefore, I have no obligation to pay the remaining amount due."

"Mr. Hartwood...Cale... you've got to be kidding me. You're refusing to complete payment because of a missing signature? Just call Bobby in and—"

"Now, Cookie. Let's not worry Bobby about all this."

The glint in his eyes sent a shiver of misgiving down Cookie's spine. When Hartwood advanced, she struggled to maintain her position, hoping her glare burned him. "Well, then I guess I'll be taking half the order back with me. If you have a problem with that, I'll have my attorney contact you."

Once she had an attorney. She crossed her arms and waited for him to respond. He wasn't going to intimidate her. "Let me get Ethan and we'll start taking some of the boxes back to the cars."

Hartwood halted five feet from her and gave her statement a dismissive wave. "I gave the boy a generous tip and told him you didn't need him to stick around. He seemed anxious to be off."

A cold, heavy lump settled in Cookie's belly. She hadn't seen evidence of anyone else in the house. She should follow Ethan and leave. No. Hartwood wasn't going to chase her away without payment.

Hartwood gave her an easy, practiced smile. Probably the same one he gave voters before the election. He puffed out his chest and tugged on the cuffs of his white dress shirt. "The event I've planned is for a group of television executives visiting the area. As head of the newly formed Spencer Film Commission, it's my duty to encourage film and television companies to consider using the area for their productions."

Uh oh. What had he done?

"One of my first actions was to submit you and your business to one of the baking competition shows. Those are extremely popular and would bring recognition, tourists, and money to Spencer. And to your little shop as well. These cupcakes are our ticket in, Cookie. Yours and mine."

"You contacted a baking show about me? Without my permission? How. Dare. You?" It didn't matter she'd thought about applying to be a contestant a few years ago, he had no right to attempt to control her business or her life in that way. Her face heated, her breath came in harsh blast. "How dare you?" she repeated.

"Now, Cookie. Calm down. Everything I've done is for your benefit."

She doubted that. The man never did anything without a benefit to himself. A sinking feeling there was more nearly broke her determination to stay strong. "Bullshit."

He took a step closer. "It's gonna be okay, baby. You'll see."

Narrowing her eyes at his use of 'baby', she held her ground. She wouldn't be intimidated by the prick. Nor would he be able to sweet talk her into forgetting what he'd done.

As if he heard her thoughts, Hartwood cast her an easy smile and said, "Let's forget about the television deal. Probably a long shot anyway. I heard, though, that they want to talk to Burnham while they're here. Offer him a new deal. Some new show building his stupid treehouses. Looks like he won't be in town for long."

They wanted Tony back? But he'd told her that he and the production company were negotiating the termination of his remaining contract. Not adding to it. Now that she knew him, loved him, how could she let him go? No. Tony would have said something if he expected someone to show up in Spencer to talk to him. That meant one thing. Cale Hartwood was a conniving bastard. He probably said all that to confuse her, make her doubt.

Shit, it worked, too.

She lifted her gaze to discover the man had silently moved to stand directly in front of her. He smiled and rested his hands on her shoulders. "Now, babe. Forget about all that. And about Bobby's mistake. My guests won't be here for a couple hours yet. There's plenty of time for you to come upstairs. I can help with the tension I feel tightening your beautiful shoulders. Play nice and we'll work out a way to ensure you get paid."

Had he just said—? Propositioned her? She attempted to shrug away his heavy hands, but he jerked her closer and mashed his mouth over hers. His teeth scraped her lip. One of his hands tangled in her hair, holding her in place.

With a jerk, her moment of startled inactivity disappeared. She shoved at his chest. He tightened his grip on her hair and lifted his head. Staring into her eyes, he arched one brow and winked. "You're coming upstairs with me, babe. I'll make it worth your time. You'll enjoy it."

"No. I won't." Cookie tore herself from his grasp, covering the sting to her scalp with one hand. The other flew to his face, the slap loud in the cavernous room.

He pressed his palm to the red mark and grinned. "Ah, I like it a little rough, too, baby."

Reaching behind her, she wrapped her fingers around the nearest cupcake and smashed it into his leering face. Sliding on the highly polished marble floor, she ran from the room.

"You'll regret this, bitch. I'll close you down. You'll come begging to me. I'll enjoy it more when you're on your knees. Fucking bitch."

His shouted threats followed her from the house. Thankful she'd left her car unlocked. She slid behind the wheel and seconds later her tires squealed in her escape. Catching a glimpse of children in the development's playground, she slammed on her brakes then drove slowly toward town. She could do this. Hold everything together until she got home. She could do this.

No, she couldn't. She didn't want to accuse a town official, but she couldn't let this moment pass. Were those rumors Tony mentioned about him attacking women? Even though nothing had really happened, it was her responsibility, her duty toward other women to at least report the assault. Hunter might not be able to do anything, unless there were already other reports.

Her hands shook as she sat in her SUV at the police station still unsure if she was doing the right thing. Fighting tears, she rested her forehead against the steering wheel and took deep breaths.

A soft knock on the side window jerked her upright. A concerned face peered at her. Cookie nodded and the woman backed up and Cookie exited the vehicle.

"Are you okay?" the officer asked. "I'm Ivy. We've met before."

"I remember."

"I'm still on duty. Anything I can help you with officially?"

Cookie drew a long breath and straightened her shoulders. "I'd like to report an assault."

After an hour that felt at least a week long, Cookie had told her story both to Ivy and to the police chief. But once she'd made her statement, she hadn't wanted to press charges for an unwanted kiss. Hunter said regardless, her report would be added to a growing file. Sooner or later he'd have enough to put Hartwood's head on a pike. The image made her smile.

Drained she drove home, ran to her apartment and locked herself in, she collapsed with her back against the door. She slid to the floor and burst into tears.

Two hours and two showers later, Cookie sat on her couch, one foot tapping rapidly against the carpet. Her phone sat in the precise center of the coffee table. She'd debated calling off her date with Tony but didn't want to have to explain why.

She was strong. Nothing had really happened. He'd just frightened her. No need for her to make trouble for someone who could repay that action many times over. Or worse. She had no doubt he'd find a way to close down her shop. He'd threatened before. No, the best course of action would be to ignore the afternoon's events.

She tried a smile, but the movement felt forced. In the next half hour, she needed to get herself under control. By the time Tony arrived for their date, she had to be herself. She could do this.

Damn. Why did that rat bastard have to come on to her? Threaten her? He must have thought she'd been so impressed with his huge, cold house and the supposed power he wielded. She'd be honored he'd take her to bed.

And why not, her inner critic asked. Was she worth anything more than a short-term affair now? She wasn't wife material. God knew her father had told her as much so many times.

Waving her hands in front of her face to stem the rising sting of tears, she laughed.

The bitter sound centered her. She took a deep breath and rose. Although she was dressed for her date, she'd do a little extra primping. Make sure everything in her apartment was ready for them when they returned after supper. She glanced at the bed as she passed. Please. Don't let what that man tried spoil her time with Tony.

She touched where her bottom lip was still tender from the forced kiss and tried instead to imagine Tony's gentle kisses. How he cupped the back of her head as he teased her mouth. The glory of the passion a simple touch created between them. Her shoulders relaxed and under her fingers, she smiled.

She could deal with the aftermath of emotions by herself. Had handled much of it already. All she needed was to keep everything under control. No need to involve anyone else.

She could do this.

CHAPTER SIXTEEN

*T*ony stood outside Cookie's apartment door for a long moment. They'd had a couple of casual dates, they'd almost had sex, but this was their first official 'real' date, and he was unexpectedly nervous. The jittering in his belly and the constant flow of 'what if' scenarios through his brain surprised him. He'd never been so unsure before a date. But he'd never thought he might be in love before either.

He arranged the single fat pink rose in its nest of green fern-like leaves and sprigs of white baby's breath. Bringing her flowers again was taking a chance, but for him this cemented the idea of an official date. Then he smoothed his hand over the front of his button-down shirt and patted his back pocket for his wallet.

He wasn't that far gone, was he? Scowling at the door for a moment, along with a couple of deep breaths, calmed him enough to find a genuine smile and lift his hand to knock.

Cookie peeked her head around the edge of the door, before widening the opening to allow him to enter. She smiled in welcome, but there was something off. A tightness around her eyes. Maybe she was tired. She'd had that big order to deliver today. Had Hartwood been a dick? Concerned and a little puzzled, Tony held out the rose.

Her smile almost brightened her eyes. "Oh, it's lovely. Thank you. But you know, you don't have to bring me flowers, Tony."

He shrugged. "I wanted to."

After fussing with the bloom in a narrow vase and placing it on the bookshelf next to an old-school blown glass unicorn, she kissed his cheek. "Thank you. I love roses. And pink is one of my favorite colors."

Tony made a dramatic swipe of his hand across his forehead. "Whew. I'd hate to have brought you a flower you didn't like."

Although he'd hoped for a deeper thank you, he accepted the second press of her lips to his cheek. Maybe she was nervous, too. Wouldn't that be astounding? His Cookie was always so sure of herself, a self-reliant and powerful woman. Most of all, she put up with him. Hopefully she would—for the rest of their lives.

Shit. He was so far gone. Time to slow it down a little. She hadn't said the words, so he wasn't sure exactly what she felt for him. And now was not the time to delve into his own insecurities. "Are you ready? Our reservation is in fifteen minutes."

"You look mighty fine, Tone. I'm sure to be the envy of every woman there."

The compliment stoked his ego. He leisurely ran his gaze over her body. The deep purple dress caressed her curves and he curled his fingers against his palms to curb the desire to follow the flow of the soft-looking fabric. "I'll have the loveliest woman on my arm, so who cares what those other women think."

"If you don't stop looking at me like that..."

"Like what, sweetheart?"

"...we'll never get to the restaurant. And I'm hungry."

Hungry? So was he. For a taste of her. Giving himself a mental shake, he held out his hand. "Your wish is my pleasure to fulfill, Cookie."

Spamantino's was a delightful combination of modern and old-school Italian with muted lights brightening each table's white cloth and linen napkins, and wide clam-shell booths in the dimmer corners. The combined scents of garlic, basil and freshly baked bread made Tony's mouth water. While Cookie admired the décor and later praised the meal, Tony could tell something distracted her. Numerous times he'd begun to ask, but the shadows in her eyes kept him silent. Whatever the issue, he'd ask her in private. He just hoped to God it wasn't anything that he'd done—or not done.

Then he stood outside her door again, but this time, she held his hand as she turned the key in the lock. With a glance over her shoulder, she gave a gentle tug. He followed her into the dark interior. When she turned wrapped her arms around his waist, and pressed her cheek against his chest, he gathered her close.

"Cookie, what's the matter?"

She spoke to his shirtfront. "I planned to ask you to stay the night."

His heart leapt, and lower, his body reacted until her exact words registered. Planned.

"Have I done something?"

She patted his chest. "No. Not you. You're fine, doing fine. It's just..."

With gentle pressure, he rested his hands on her shoulders.

She jerked and stepped away from him. The streetlight glow filtering through her gauzy curtains gave enough light for him to see her wide eyes then the frightened way she covered her face as though attempting to hide.

Just like his sister had.

No.

Not that.

Ruthlessly Tony clamped down on the rising fear and anger. Her reaction could stem from something else, any number of possibilities. His anger wouldn't help. He put further distance between them and took a deep breath. "Cookie. Talk to me. Can you?"

After seconds that stretched to minutes, she lifted her face, tears glistening on her cheeks. She shook her head, then gave the barest nod. "No lights, though. Okay?"

"No lights. Whatever you need, sweetheart."

Using the faint light from the window, he followed her into the living room and waited until she sat, wondering if he should take the chair or sit beside her on the couch. She ended his dilemma with a watery chuckle and patted the cushion beside her. "Sit with me. Please?"

He sat and she curled her legs under her, turning so her knees touched the sides of his thighs. One of the damn hardest things he'd ever done, but he waited. Even with so many questions bouncing against the inside of his skull, he waited. Keeping his anger under control? Much more difficult. Possibilities ate at his patience until she drew a long, audible breath.

"Something happened today."

He nodded. "I thought as much."

"I didn't want—no, that's not right. I'd decided I didn't need to tell anyone. It's over. Done. But not forgotten. I thought I'd done okay, until I opened the door and saw your smile."

Angling a bit so he could see her face, he offered her an encouraging smile.

"Yeah, like that one. Then I knew, I couldn't. I can't let this stand between us."

"Is it about me then?"

"No. Oh no." She gave a bitter laugh. "Not everything is

about you. Just something you need to know. So we can move past this. Because I want us—to be us."

"I'm listening."

"Something happened today."

Nodding, Tony fought the urge to point out her repeated words. Thank God he hadn't had reason until now to practice the listening skills he'd perfected with his sister, but the hard-won sense of calm filled him without thought. He rested his hand on his thigh, palm up, inviting her to link her fingers with his if she wished. Sometimes a tiny bit of physical contact made speaking hard truths easier.

Prepared though he was, he dreaded what he might hear.

"It turns out Hartwood refused to pay the remainder of the balance on that huge order."

Not surprising, but not anything that should have produced Cookie's odd reticence. Silent, he waited.

"Yeah, he said since his assistant didn't sign... oh, Tony. It's not that."

"I know, sweetheart."

"I can deal with unpaid bills. I've been on both sides of them."

"Go on."

"Tony, I did like you asked and had Ethan go with me on the delivery. We needed two cars to get all the cupcakes there anyway. And everything was fine, until Hartwood told Ethan I didn't need him anymore, gave him a tip, and sent him away."

"Ethan should never—"

"It's not his fault. I'd already told him he could take the rest of the day off. But then Hartwood told me he'd talked to some television executives about me being a contestant or something on a baking show."

The prick overstepped propriety. Again. Cookie took his hand and stroked his tense fingers from the fist he'd made. "I was angry. He had no right."

"Agreed. He's always been like that, using another person to bring attention to himself. Even back in high school. I hope you told him off."

Finally, she gave him a ghost of a smile. "I did. Then he suggested a way to settle the bill before the TV people got there. He grabbed me."

His fingers convulsed around hers. "Cookie?"

"Kissed me," she whispered from behind her other hand.

The overwhelming urge to beat the bastard to a bloody pulp rose hot and demanding. Tony carefully eased her palm from her face and held both of her hands against his chest. "Can you tell me—did he do anything else?"

Fearing her answer, he held his breath.

She shook her head. "I slapped him." She glanced to the side then brought her gaze back to him. "He said he liked it rough. You're shaking."

"I'm angry. Furious. If he hurt you in any way, I'll kill him."

"No, you won't."

"Then I'll beat the shit out of that fucker."

"No, don't. Please. I couldn't bear if anything happened to you because of this. It's okay. Nothing really happened. He just frightened me. Now that I've said the words out loud, the experience doesn't seem so bad. Besides, I smashed a cupcake in his face."

Tony's rough chuckle startled him. His woman would be fine. If not, smashing the bastard's face was still an option. "Waste of a good cupcake."

"Well worth it, though."

Despite her assertions, he was concerned. Izzy had also claimed to be okay, and at first he'd believed her. Not long after her claims, she'd started acting out, had given up dancing and retreated into a silence he'd been unable to breach. Not that he'd tried that hard, he'd been a typical teenager. Then the failure had set in.

That failure mocked him now. The woman he loved had been attacked, violated, and he hadn't been there to protect her. His mind understood there was no way for him to always be there, but his heart felt strangled in his chest. What if Cookie hadn't been able to get away? What if history had repeated itself?

Cookie curled her fingers into his shirt sleeve. "In the future, I'll make doubly sure I'm never in a situation where I'm alone with... him. If there's any more interactions, they'll be in a public place. With others around. Yes, that will work. Tony? It's okay. I'm okay."

Repressed anger vibrated along every nerve ending, until his muscles were tight and aching for action. She wasn't okay. The impact of what happened would hit her again. Over and over. Staying in the public eye wouldn't help. Hartwood was a slimy, sneaking bastard. She needed to avoid him at all costs. Tony took a deep breath. His anger wouldn't help now, he'd save that for the next time he saw Hartwood. Another breath.

"You should report this to the cops. To Hunter. Or that new female cop."

"Her name is Ivy. I did. Right afterward. The police chief already has a file on him. But I didn't want to press charges. That would create more problems. He... he's a powerful man here in Spencer."

Tony snorted. "At least in his mind."

"Doesn't matter. If he thinks he's in the right, he'll convince everyone else. It will be my fault anything happened." She caught her lip between her teeth. "It wasn't, was it? My fault, I mean."

At the pleading hope in her tone his heart shattered. 'No, sweetheart. Definitely not. You were doing your job. He's the one who attacked you."

"Attacked is a strong word."

She was trying to justify what happened, to make the moments inconsequential. Just like his sister had.

Just like Izzy.

Cookie deserved to know. No, she *had* to know and understand what happened to Izzy. The knowledge might be the only thing to make her take care and protect herself. Because she was right. Hartwood wasn't going away. He hadn't even spent an hour in any form of punishment or reprimand in high school for any of his long list of misdeeds. Now as a trustee, he'd consider himself untouchable.

And the bastard was. Tony allowed his shoulders to slump. It was up to him to keep Cookie safe, to prevent a repeat. To do that, he had to come clean about the incident coloring his past. For all these years he'd held the secret he and his sister shared as a sacred trust. Now, breaking her trust could save another woman from the same possible fate. Izzy would be okay with his decision. He hoped.

Izzy had one hell of a temper, but he'd stand firm in the face of her anger to protect Cookie. He needed that same strength of will to speak the painful truth.

"Cookie, sweetheart? I need to tell you something. It's gonna be hard for me to say, even harder for you to hear."

She loosened her grip on his arm but took the hand he held out to her. "Uh, okay?"

"Remember I told you how my sister was assaulted?"

Her slow nod and curious expression encouraged him to continue.

"She wasn't just harassed." He lowered his voice to a mere whisper as though to say the words was to call the past into the present. "She was raped."

"Oh no. Oh, I'm so sorry. I know, that doesn't mean anything, doesn't help." Cookie clutched his hand. He accepted the squeezing pain as his due.

"She never told anyone. I only knew because I found her...

after. She made me promise to keep the secret. Even from our moms."

"Why?"

"Now I'm not sure. She's my sister, so I made that promise. I've kept it, too. Until now."

Cookie's eyes narrowed. "Why me? Why now?"

"I told you before. It was Hartwood."

The flat tone of his words made her arch her brows. "Hartwood?" The meaning of his words penetrated her understanding and she jerked her hands from his. "Hartwood...ra... did that to her?"

The burn of anger returned to his chest. Struggling to keep his voice calm, Tony stood and moved to the window. The night was still and dark, the street quiet and empty. Like his soul whenever this horrendous moment in his past intruded on his present. He pushed the curtain to the side and pressed his forehead against the cool glass. "Hartwood raped my sister. I told her to be careful. But I didn't protect her. Couldn't protect her."

He whirled to face Cookie. Her wide eyes exposed her growing understanding.

"Today, today I couldn't protect you either. From the same fucking bastard. I failed. Again."

Cookie rose and after a moment's hesitation, wrapped her arms around him. Tony closed his eyes and returned the embrace. Great. Now she comforted him when she'd been the one to fight off unwanted advances. Could he mess up any more?

She leaned back to look into his face. "We're a pair tonight, aren't we? Come back to the couch with me."

She waited until he nodded then kept his hands and backed toward the couch. Once sitting, she curled against his side and rested her head on his shoulder. "Thank you for wanting to protect me. I've spent too much of my life trying to prove I can handle everything by myself. It's nice to have someone care."

Care? Of course he cared. He loved her. But since she hadn't returned the sentiment, he kept silent.

"Can we talk more about this some other time? I mean, I feel okay now, but that won't last, will it? Once I start thinking about what happened?"

He shook his head. "Unfortunately, the repercussions can hit any time. Especially when you don't expect it. I'll be here whenever you need me. To talk. Or whatever." It was both the least he could do, and the most.

"I know it's avoidance, but would you like to watch a movie? Preferably something silly? I planned to ask you to stay tonight. But I don't--."

"I wouldn't expect... ask... want to..."

She covered his lips with her fingertips. "Be quiet, Tone. I know I'd still like you to stay. To hold me. Keep me safe. Be there if I have a nightmare. I want everything to be okay. But my heart aches like it's silently screaming with pain of what happened. I don't know how to contain it. But I know you'll guard my heart."

Forever. "You put too much trust in me."

"I don't think so. Will you stay with me tonight?"

The cautious, wistful look in her eyes offered him the hope she'd survive. He still owed Hartwood, but would forgo his retribution. For now. He'd figure out another way to let the bastard know his actions were being watched.

Tony gave Cookie his best smile, leaned back and kicked off his uncomfortable shoes. "Will there be popcorn with the movie?"

CHAPTER SEVENTEEN

*C*ookie slept fitfully, waking often, a couple times with her face damp from tears. Each time, Tony was there, somehow knowing when to allow her the space to grieve and come to terms with what happened, or to mold his body against hers, wrapping his love around her.

Not all of her night was spent reliving the previous afternoon, she also made a number of decisions. Now, when the sun finally cast bright streaks of light through cracks in the curtains, she needed to set her plans in motion. She eased from the warmth of the man she loved to sit on the edge of the bed.

This time he didn't wake when she moved. A soft smile relaxed her lips as she studied the planes of his face. Dark shadows under his eyes showed exhaustion and worry. A faint golden stubble covered his jaw and she wondered what he would look like with a beard. A mountain man perhaps. Her mountain man.

Soon. She'd tell him she loved him soon. Regretting not saying the words earlier, she stood. If she said anything now, he might think her declaration was in response to what had happened.

She'd be a mess for a while. Once she'd let her guard down and admitted she couldn't handle everything, issues she'd believed to be hidden away might rise to haunt her. Tony couldn't fix them—although he'd try. No, she had to handle these emotions herself. She'd accept his support, but she had to do the work.

Work. One of the first things she needed to handle. Hoping to have spent a luxurious night with Tony, she'd taken today off. She hadn't realized how difficult making the decision would be, even with her staff assuring her they could handle everything.

They could. During the night she'd accepted the fact and now she needed to let them know how much she appreciated and depended on them.

Tony stirred. He swiped his hand over the empty sheets, patted the pillow. His eyes burst open and he sat. "Cookie?"

"I'm right here."

His frantic gaze landed on her. "Are you okay? What—?"

She lifted one hand to stop his words. "I'm good. I need to go into work, though."

He rubbed his eyes and yawned. "I thought you took today off."

"I did. I need to talk to Darryl and Ava and I don't want to wait."

"Okay, give me a couple."

She pressed on his shoulder. He didn't resist and fell back against his pillow. "You're exhausted. I'll bet you barely slept last night."

"Doesn't matter."

"It does to me. I'll only be gone about an hour. If that long. You sleep." She took a deep breath and arched one eyebrow. "It might be interesting to find you still in my bed when I get back."

The bright blue of his eyes deepened to the shades of passion she'd discovered with his kisses. He twisted his fingers in the hem of the long tee shirt she'd worn to bed. His expression hardened. "No, I need to go with you."

"It's the middle of the morning. There's lots of people out and about."

"I don't care." He crawled from the bed and searched for his shirt.

Cookie wanted to be exasperated by the man's determination to watch over her, but she just couldn't. The honor and love in his actions tempered the horror of what happened to his sister and might have been repeated with her.

"Okay. But while I'm busy, I expect you to go up to your place and rest to build up your energy."

"I'll need energy?" The roughness of his voice sent trembling delight low in her body. Yeah, she'd be okay. They'd be okay.

"Count on it, Tone."

※

Less than ninety minutes later, Cookie tucked a file folder into the overstuffed drawer and smiled. With new morning and afternoon managers, she shouldn't feel the need to be at the store fourteen hours a day. Darryl and Ava had been surprised, and more than ready to accept their new positions. Together they'd spend the next week working on schedules and discussing the increase in their wages.

Cookie ran her own business, owned the building, and now had others to help shoulder the burdens of running a bakery. She was successful.

Take that, Dad.

She'd barely hidden her surprise when Hartwood's assistant, Bobby, had asked to speak with her. He'd offered a sincere apology for causing a problem by not signing the order form and presented her with a check for the full balance. Then he'd purchased a dozen cupcakes and with a flamboyant wave, exited the store.

Hartwood was obviously into games, underscoring the need to watch her back. She was fairly certain she'd seen the man skulking about the triangle shortly after Bobby's appearance. She didn't have the prickly feeling of being watched and he hadn't come to the store, but then she'd never had the need to be so specifically aware. She did live in her own head sometimes. Making a silent vow to improve on her awareness, she left the kitchen and, avoiding the squeaky stairs, grinned all the way to the upstairs apartment.

Tony better have gotten some rest.

❦

Tony slipped off his shiny wingtip shoe and grimaced. He'd wanted to look good for his date, but the fancy shoes pulled from the bottom of a box pinched his toes. They hadn't been the best to wear on the walk from Cookie's apartment this morning, either. With a sigh, he wiggled his toes and rested his feet on the coffee table.

Following Cookie's orders, he'd relax until she was done downstairs. Whatever she had planned at her place could be easily duplicated here. Or if she insisted, they could walk back to her place. At least he could put on his comfortable work boots.

His phone rang, startling him awake. He stared at the caller ID. Shit. Jack had crappy timing. He thought about ignoring the intrusion, but he'd never been comfortable not answering a call.

Ten minutes later, he'd agreed to head out to Stick Pony. Three horses for the riding camp were being delivered early. Tony froze with his second boot in his hand. What was with these early deliveries messing with his life? But with Ryder tied up with interviewing possible camp staff in Denver, Jack needed help getting the horses settled.

With the morning's possibilities ruined, Tony had tried to call Cookie, but her phone rang until the voice mail message started. He'd talk to her about that later. After Hartwood, she needed to keep her phone with her at all times.

The apartment door opened. Cookie wore a bright smile. A real smile. For him.

"I thought you'd be in bed." She dropped her ever-present tote bag on the counter. Her delectable mouth pulled into a pout, she wrapped her arms around his waist. "And you're dressed, too."

"I tried to call you."

She searched through her bag. "Oops. I must have left it at home." A faint pink tinted in her cheeks, tempting him to chase the color with kisses.

"You need to be more careful, sweetheart."

"I know." She lifted to her toes to kiss him. "Why are you dressed?"

He returned the kiss, resisting the urge to draw her into passion. It wouldn't take much—for either of them. Reluctantly, he eased back and touched the tip of her nose with his finger. "I need to leave for a while. The first of the horses for the camp are arriving early."

She frowned then nodded. "And Ryder's gone. So, you're helping Jack. But I didn't think the stables were done yet."

"Jack will keep the horses at his place. Ryder hasn't had a chance to hire anyone to run his stables yet, while Jack has a couple guys on staff. The horses would go there first anyway for medical checks." He glanced over her shoulder at the clock on the stove. "Supposed to be there in about forty minutes. So, I need to get going."

When she dipped her head, he caught her chin on a curled finger and lifted her gaze to his. "I'm not sure how long this will take, but if you want, I'll come back as soon as I can."

"Do you think I could go with you? I don't know anything about horses, but I think I'd like to learn. I'll stay out of the way. It would be nice to visit with Kate, too."

So much hope filled her expression he couldn't deny her, even if he'd wanted to. "You'll do whatever Jack or I say? I won't put you in harm's way, sweetheart."

"I will. Oh, this will be fun." She glanced down at the working clothes she'd put on automatically. "I'd better change, too. Is there time to stop at my place?"

Once there, Cookie disappeared into the bedroom. She'd been talkative on the short drive over. Tony tilted his head and considered her actions. Her tone. A little forced, a little too bright. But not enough to seriously concern him. Much. His Cookie was resilient. More so than his sister had been. He turned to the window. He needed to call Izzy. See how she was doing. Talk her into a visit at least. Their moms missed her.

He did, too.

"Will this do?"

He turned at Cookie's question and after a breath, chuckled. She'd put on jeans and a sleeveless knit top. With a long-sleeved blouse tied at her waist, she was the picture of a stereotypical farm girl. All she needed was a straw hat. He dropped his gaze to her feet. Good. Her hiking boots were the best choice to protect her toes. He spread his arms. "Come here."

She rushed into his embrace and met his kiss with fire and passion, startling him. Stepping back, she patted his chest. "This is going to be fun."

❧

While not exactly fun in the purest sense, Tony did enjoy working with the horses. The lessons he'd learned as a boy came back easily. These horses were calm and well-behaved, a requirement he supposed for animals used in riding therapy. So other than one being skittish in the new environment, the trio had been stabled, brushed and fed.

After an initial hesitancy, Cookie helped Kate stroke and talk to the smallest horse. Cookie beamed over the animal's back at him. He pulled out his phone and took a few photos when she wasn't paying attention. Then when she praised and hugged Madison's colt, Zombie, Tony knew he had a horse-lover in the making and wondered when he'd be able to talk her into a ride. He'd ask Matt at Timberline Outfitters if they could take out a couple of his mounts.

Kate had insisted they stay for a meal and even though they'd had Italian the night before—had it only been last night—there was no way he'd pass up Kate's three-inch-thick lasagna. Or the dark chocolate lava cupcakes Cookie baked while he and Jack finished up with the horses. Ryder had called with the news he'd hired three of the applicants he'd interviewed, with two of them able to move to Spencer to start work within a month.

Tony glanced around the table at Jack's growing family then let his gaze rest on Cookie while she told Madison a story about a cake disaster. Cookie's animated expression and wild hand movements made the girl giggle. He'd spent years chasing his dream, caught it, too. But he hadn't realized how much he missed being a part of a family. A real, loving caring family.

Even if Cookie never loved him or wanted to become a part of his family, he'd never leave Spencer again. This was where he belonged. These mountains, the high meadows, the trees, the town, were home.

Jack slapped his shoulder. "Head out of the clouds, dude."

Tony brought himself back to the present. "What?"

Jack jerked a thumb across the table at Cookie. "She can't stop yawning. Take her home, man."

Cookie waved one hand. "Oh, don't worry..." Another yawn interrupted her denial. She shrugged.

Kate struggled to her feet and made shooing motions at Cookie. "You two get going. Even if you *claim* not to be tired, I'm beat. Baby boy here takes up a lot of energy. Get going. See you later."

The radio played soft classic rock on the way back to town. Cookie leaned her head against the headrest and closed her eyes. Tony berated himself for allowing her to become overly tired. The emotional rollercoaster of the previous day had surely drained her, then the unaccustomed work with the horses, and baking, must have taken the last of her reserves. He'd get her home, apologize then find his way to his lonely bed.

This two apartment thing was going to get old really fast.

CHAPTER EIGHTEEN

*T*hree days later, Tony toted a large box of cupcakes toward the first completed Stick Pony cabin. The construction crew had worked their asses off to get this one finished as well as continuing to work on other cabins and the main lodge. He'd put in long hours, too. Today, they'd celebrate with a late start, some treats, then hit it hard for the rest of the day.

Next to him Cookie pulled a rolling-cooler filled with ice cold water, tea and soft drinks. This was her surprise for the hard-working crew. And, he supposed, a way to distance herself further from the incident with Hartwood.

Struggling to relax his jaw, Tony led her up the short ramp to the wide porch at the front of the cabin. "Most of the cabins will have four to six bedrooms with a huge shared bathroom. Everything's compliant and should be easy for our campers. Some cabins will have increased accessibility options as well as space for personal aides."

"Ryder's done a great job. It's beautiful from the outside. I like how the cabins are set far enough apart to feel private, yet they all face a central area."

"Once the camp is up and running, Ryder plans to duplicate this basic plan around the area. He's working on balancing being able to offer services to as many as possible with having a manageable number of horses and staff. Tons of rules and regs for that, too. Better him than me."

He set the cupcakes on a card table he'd set up earlier. "Wheel those drinks under the table and I'll give you the quick tour before everyone else gets here."

Cookie pushed the cooler with her foot. "What about the treehouse?"

He hadn't spent as much time working on his project as he wanted, for a number of good reasons. Including the time he spent with her. He shrugged. "Okay. I've been helping out here, so I'm not as far along as I'd like. Now that there's a full crew from Dagleish, construction should shift into high gear. I can focus on the trees then."

She looked at him from under her eyelashes. "Have you been spending too much time with me?"

"Much as I'd like it otherwise, we only see each other in the evenings. Gets kinda dark out here. Hard to build in the dark."

"Yeah, right. Daylight's lasting longer. But I'm not going to argue with you. I like those evenings, too."

She'd left the lease for her apartment on the kitchen counter the day before and he'd snooped. There were only a couple months left on that agreement. One of these evenings he'd ask her to consider moving into the apartment above the bakery. With him. Fast tracking the remodel would cut further into his time working on the treehouse. He'd take that delay, as long as it meant she'd move in with him.

He just wasn't sure how to approach the topic.

"Hey, Tony. About that tour?" She tugged on the front of his shirt until he leaned toward her, allowing her to initiate a sweet kiss.

"Uh. Yeah. Sure." He cleared his throat and grinned. She was a master at keeping him off balance. He could do that too. He angled close to her body, but instead of accepting the invitation of her full lips, pressed on the lever style handle, shoved open the door, and backed her into the cabin's main living area.

He froze. "What the fuck?"

A frown wrinkled Cookie's forehead before she whirled to face the room. "Oh, my God."

Thick black graffiti covered the interior log walls and the freshly painted drywalled. Ripped from the ceiling, light fixtures hung by the wiring.

With another muttered curse, Tony stepped around her and tripped, catching himself against a window frame. He glared at the nail gun left on the floor then slumped against the wall. "Fuck."

Walls could be washed. Lights repaired. But the vandals must have broken into the locked tool shed and used a nail gun to desecrate the engineered hardwood flooring. He scanned the room. Some nails were imbedded deeply, others appeared as though the asshole stood in one place and shot nails through the air.

Cookie bent toward the nail gun.

"Don't touch it. Leave everything like it is. Let's get out of here. I'm calling Joe."

"Joe?"

"The sheriff. Then I've got to break this news to Ryder. And Jack."

"That writing... on the walls. The shape of the letters, the bad spelling looks a lot like what was left in the bakery."

He took her hand. Her calm, tamed the anger rising in his chest.

She continued, "It could be the same vandals. Should I call Hunter?"

"Not his jurisdiction, but if the damage is similar, he may have leads. I'll mention it to Joe, but I'm sure they keep each other informed about what's happening in the area. I don't know how I'm going to tell—"

"Just show them. Isn't that Jack's SUV?"

It was. The prospect of opening the door to the destruction was far less appealing than making a call. Before Ryder exited the passenger seat, Tony crossed the parking area, waiting until both men faced him.

Cookie hovered on the porch, gnawing on her thumbnail. She needed to get her emotions under control to support Tony and his cousins. This destruction brought back the anger, helplessness, and godawful feelings of violation. He'd been at her side when the vandals made a mess of her bakery, and after... Hartwood. Now she could be here for him.

For the most part, the vandalism at the bakery had been easily fixable with a rag and broom. Here, there was so much damage. Especially to the floor that might need to be completely replaced.

At a loud expletive, she looked up then moved to the side as the three men jogged toward the building. Tony held back while Ryder and Jack crowded through the doorway. An explosion of language worthy of a crew of sailors rolled over her. Then heavy silence preceded the men from the cabin. Ryder sat on the single step next to the ramp and dropped his head into his hands. Jack joined Tony who moved away to call the sheriff.

A deep sigh drew her to Ryder. She hesitated then rested her hand on his shoulder.

Bright red infused his face, and his green eyes sparked with anger. He took another deep breath and shook his head. "Always something. Sorry about this, Cookie. You're not seeing my best side. But, shit... why now?"

"No, I'm sorry. This is senseless. Why do people feel the need to destroy things? Especially something beautiful. I never expected this kind of vandalism in Spencer."

Shrugging, Ryder stood. "Guess it's a way to holler for

attention or to vent anger or something. Don't know why anyone would be angry about Stick Pony." He paused and rubbed his hand down his face. "Or a cupcake shop."

Before she could comment, the other men joined them. Tony pocketed his phone. "Joe's on the way. About five minutes. He said not to touch anything."

"No duh," Ryder commented dryly.

Jack checked his watch. "Crew's scheduled to show in about fifteen." He turned to Cookie. "We should probably move the cupcakes from the crime scene and keep everyone out of the way."

While he and Tony moved the table and goodies to one of the half-finished cabins a short distance away, Cookie left Ryder to wait for the sheriff and wandered around the cabin. Near the back corner of the building, she discovered a couple spray paint cans. Empty fast food bags and crumpled take out cups littered the area. Of course vandals wouldn't clean up after themselves.

There might be fingerprints or some other clue the cops could get off the paint cans. Searching for anything that looked out of place, she scanned the area behind the cabin. Sunlight highlighted a splotch of color peeking out from under a toppled sawhorse. Cookie approached warily and bent low to study the burgundy, blue, and silver ball cap. Unless a worker had left this here, she'd discovered something important.

She completed her circle of the cabin just as the sheriff's vehicle pulled up next to the men. She waited while Tony explained what happened and four tall men crowded into the doorway. Even with the serious situation, she couldn't help her grin when the sheriff's expletives burst through the silent air. When they returned to the gravel path, she joined them.

Tony nodded toward the sheriff. "Cookie, Joe Cavanaugh."

He offered his hand. She shook it and his serious expression softened. "You're the cupcake lady? Instead of donuts, some of my guys have been bringing in cupcakes. I haven't made it over to your shop. I'm gonna have to rectify that. I really like your chocolate cherry ones."

"Thanks. Stop by and I'll treat you. And coffee to go with it."

"Deal." He turned his attention to Ryder. "So, coz, made any enemies lately? Could this be an act of revenge from someone associated with that bastard, uh, guy who kidnapped Vianna and Kate?"

Wait? What? Her friends had been kidnapped? How could she not know about that? Then again, she doubted she'd broadcast the news either. And had Joe called Ryder 'coz'? Another cousin? Feeling as though somehow she'd known that, she studied the four extremely attractive men. They grew 'em good here in Colorado.

Passing over the three dark-haired men, her gaze lingered on her favorite of the group. Favorite? More than that, she loved him. He'd said the words to her, now he needed to hear them from her. Soon.

"Notice anything else? Anything missing?" Joe asked.

Jack slapped his forehead. "Hadn't thought to look. I'll check the equipment shed." He loped toward the small building.

Time to add her bit of knowledge to the mix. "I might have something."

When three pairs of eyes turned to her, she lifted her chin. Tony gave her an encouraging grin.

"I walked around the cabin. Near the far corner are some paint cans. And a lot of trash. Looks like whoever did this must have had a party, too. Further on there's a baseball cap stuck under a sawhorse. It could belong to a worker, but I really don't think so."

"Show us." Joe stuffed his note pad and pen in a pocket and gestured for her to lead the way.

Jack re-joined them at the party site and bent to retrieve a crumpled can. He held it aloft for examination. "Beer. From this, I'd guess teenagers. No self-respecting adult would drink this brand."

A second official vehicle arrived and Joe waved over his deputy. "Search this area, Mason. Bag anything that might have a print or other ID. You know the drill. Cookie? Show us the hat."

Conscious of her followers, she stopped a few feet from the sawhorse and pointed. "There."

Joe knelt and while Tony carefully lifted the wooden sawhorse, pulled the cap free. "Looks like Avalanche colors."

"Avalanche colors?" Cookie asked.

"Denver's ice hockey team. But there's no logo."

When he shifted the cap in the light a memory overwhelmed Cookie. She gasped and took a stumbling step backwards. Tony was at her side in a flash, his arm a solid support around her shoulders.

"What's wrong?"

She pointed. "I've seen that before."

The others crowded closer. Tony actually growled and they backed off. Jack poked his elbow into Ryder's side, but Joe just sighed and lifted both hands.

"We're not gonna do anything to hurt her, Tone. Lighten up." But he gave her a long look, as if he'd figured out why she'd had such an odd reaction. "Cookie, where and when do you think you saw this cap?"

She took a deep breath. Speak the facts and avoid the most painful parts of the memory. She could do this. "Last Saturday I made a cupcake delivery to Cale Hartwood's house."

Glancing from one man to the other, she leaned into Tony's solid comfort. Three sets of narrowed gazes studied her. If she turned her head, Tony's expression would prob-

ably be exactly the same. This family really stuck together—
at least in their dislike of the bastard.

She had to call him that to herself a few times before she
continued. "His house is... well, everything is black or white. I
mean, everything. I noticed a spot of color on a white leather
chair. It caught my eye because it was so unexpected. It
looked like this cap, just tossed onto the cushion. If it wasn't
this cap, it was one just like it."

"You're sure?"

"Yes, sheriff. As sure as I can be. But creepy as Hartwood
is, I can't see him doing something like this. It's too... messy."

Joe gave her a tight smile. "You've got him pegged.
However, there is a Cale Hartwood who fits the profile.
Junior's been causing trouble in town. He may be spreading
his wings. I need to talk to Hunter."

Ryder leaned against the cabin and crossed his arms.
"How long until we can repair the damage?"

"We'll get photos for documentation. I'd like you to give it
couple days, though. Maybe I'll bring Junior out here for a
few questions."

After Ryder agreed the group completed their circle of
the cabin. When they returned to the front, Vianna and Kate
waited by Kate's car. The women rushed into their men's
arms.

Jack leaned back and held Kate at arm's length. "How did
you know?"

"Chet told Zoe, who told Vianna, who called me. If it's on
the police scanner..."

"Crew's here," Ryder said. "Let's give them the news along
with their cupcakes. Maybe someone will have some ideas on
getting past this setback."

As the men walked away Cookie moved to Kate and
Vianna, wrapping her arms around her friends' waists. Kate's
baby pushed against Cookie's hand and she jerked.

Kate chuckled, took Cookie's hand and returned it to her

side. "He's been really active lately. I hope it means he'll be ready to be born soon. Doctor says almost a month yet, but I'm not so sure."

Experiencing the tiny taps against her palm, Cockie sighed and nearly forgot the mystery dancing through her brain. She cleared her throat. "Okay, so, why didn't I know my best friends were kidnapped?"

CHAPTER NINETEEN

*T*ony plopped his sleeping bag behind a half-constructed wall of the building nearest the vandalized cabin. This was his third night of playing security guard and while making sure no other destruction occurred at the camp, he missed the warmth and comfort of his bed. And the possibility of a warm, loving body next to him. But with Ryder's wedding a couple weeks away, Cookie was already busy with the cake, and assured him she wouldn't be good company anyway.

He needed her. It wasn't about the possibility of sex. He needed her more than the physical. That amazed and more than frightened him. It had been easy enough to fall in love with her. Easy to say the words that one time. The realities, the possibilities, were overwhelming.

She hadn't returned the words to him. The fact ate at his confidence. Now he didn't know where he really stood.

He settled in for the night and the never-ending circle of his thoughts. The previous nights' weather had been mild. Tonight an air of anticipation and expectant waiting surrounded him. Probably just him projecting his thoughts and feelings on the night. He sat in the shadows, alert and aware of the soft night noises and rustle of nearby animals and birds.

This ranch land was a great spot for Ryder's camp. And for Tony's latest tree house. His fingers flexed with the need to be working on his project. After these night shifts, he'd stuck around and helped the construction guys. By mid-afternoon, he was exhausted and had no energy left for his own work. Although he'd forced himself to work on his apartment before collapsing into heavy, dreamless sleep. He yawned.

Probably a good thing he hadn't spent much time with Cookie. He'd be a zombie. The time would come for him to return to the trees. He smiled to himself. And to her.

A soft crunch along the white stone path drew his attention. Easing to his feet, he peered through the night toward the sound. A tiny spot of light bounced along the trail, paused a moment before the vandalized cabin, then disappeared inside.

Ah-ha. Checking his pocket for his phone, Tony used the pale light of the half-moon to guide his way to the cabin. He paused at the door to listen. Soft grunts followed by the clink of metal against wood deepened his frown. What was going on in there?

He moved into the open doorway and, shading his eyes, flipped a switch to activate the spotlight Ryder had installed in one corner.

A shout of surprise. The thud of a body hitting the floor. Prepared to physically contain the intruder, Tony took a step forward.

"Shit, dude. What'd you do that for?"

He froze at the young voice and stared at the teenager sprawled on the floor. The boy gripped a claw hammer against his chest and struggled to sit.

Hands fisted at his waist, Tony narrowed his eyes to glower at the intruder. "What are you doing here?"

Bright red infused the boy's face before he ducked his head. "Trying to fix this."

Then Tony noticed the pile of bent nails next to a cleared spot on the floor. He arched a brow.

"I... I was stupid. Thought if I went along with this, I'd be his friend."

"Whose friend?"

The boy shook his head. "Stupid. He ignored me. Laughed at me. I'm so dumb."

Although Tony never had to prove himself to belong in a group, his sister had felt the need. He closed his eyes for a moment. He'd been too late to help her. Maybe he could make up for that failing and help this kid. He crouched at the boy's side. "You're not stupid."

"Huh. Dumb though. I helped write on the walls. But I didn't do this." He pointed at the nail studded floor. "Then I thought if maybe I fixed the floor, I wouldn't feel so... guilty. I suppose that's kinda dumb, too."

The kid needed something positive, a nudge in the right direction and he'd be fine. That much Tony could do.

"Yeah. It's dumb to come out here in the middle of the night. What's your name?" Knowing the importance of how the kid responded, Tony held tight reins on his impatience.

"Braydon."

Tony held out his hand. "Good to meet you, Braydon. I'm Tony."

After a long moment, Braydon shook Tony's hand. "You gonna call the sheriff?"

"Do you think I should?"

A deep, resigned breath. "Probably."

Tony rose and glanced around the room. "It's gonna take a while to pull all these nails."

"Yes, sir. And I'm ready to pull every one of them."

Cupping his hand over his mouth and chin in a contemplative gesture, Tony hid his grin. The determination in the young voice proved this was a good kid who only needed some guidance and advice. "How did you get here tonight?"

The question surprised Braydon and he gave Tony an assessing look. "I drove. Left the car across the road about half a mile past the gate. Walked across the pasture. Why?"

"Got a deal for you, kid."

"I ain't a kid." Braydon squared his shoulders.

"I still have a deal. Leave now and come back early Saturday morning ready to work and I'll tell Mr. Barlow and Mr. Spencer you're volunteering to help clean up the mess. I'll need to tell them you were also here when the vandalism occurred, but you want to make restitution for your part."

"And I won't get in trouble with the cops?"

"I think we can keep your name out of this if you do a good job. What about the others? Who are they?"

Tony watched emotions cross Braydon's face and knew when he'd made the decision Tony unfortunately expected.

"No, sir. I can't say."

"I understand. Think about it, and if you change your mind, you can always talk to me first. I can help."

The boy ducked his head again. "Thanks for giving me a chance."

"Don't disappoint me. Now, get going. I'll see you Saturday morning."

"Yeah, I'll be here. Thanks." As though fearing he'd stop the progress, Braydon eased around Tony and shot out the door. He jogged across the pasture, his tiny flashlight beam bouncing across the undulating hill.

With a sigh, Tony returned to sit on his cold sleeping bag. He leaned against the wall and closed his eyes. The kid had a good heart. With the right guidance, Braydon would do fine.

A muffled curse woke Tony. He cracked the kink from his neck then angled his head toward the sound. Busy night at camp. Fairly certain this encounter wouldn't be as easy or successful as the first, he eased to his feet and strained to determine the location of the rustling footsteps.

Muted light, probably from a phone, danced across the area behind the vandalized cabin. This could be what they'd been hoping for. With the construction crew as witnesses, they hadn't attempted to hide the vandalism. But no mention of the cap had been made. Ryder hoped whoever lost it would be dumb enough to return. Joe had agreed and given them four days for the experiment.

Containing his satisfaction, Tony slipped through the darkness. He leaned against the corner of the cabin to watch a dark figure searching the ground and around piles of logs and lumber. Occasional frustrated muttering made him grin. If this wasn't so serious, confronting this interloper would be fun.

Apparently giving up, the tall figure turned toward the cabin and Tony stepped from the shadows. "Looking for your cap?"

The figure feinted to the left then ran to the right. Tony mirrored his actions, snagging a handful of the kid's tee shirt. With his fingers tight in the soft fabric, Tony yanked backwards. Falling with an oomph, the trespasser sprawled on his back. Tony knelt and pressed his palm against the kid's shoulder with just enough pressure to keep him on the ground. With his other hand, he pulled out and dialed his phone.

"Trespasser at the pony. Five minutes? Great. Doesn't act like he wants to stick around."

After disconnecting, Tony pressed the flashlight icon and brought the phone close to the boy's face. "And who do we have here?"

"Let me up."

Tony shook his head. "Nope. Not until the sheriff gets here."

"You got no right to keep me here. No right to hold me down."

"Yeah, you forgot I'll pay for it someday."

The boy laughed. "Once my dad—"

"Don't even go there. I'll let you up, but don't run. Don't even think about it. Got it?"

"Fuck you."

"Listen, kid. You're staying on the ground. I'm moving away, but if you make one move, we're right back to where we are now. Understand."

"You're just a wanna be Spencer. You ain't nothin'. Not a real part of that fucked up family. Not like me. My dad owns this town. He'll deal with you. I can do what I want. You'll see."

The rant confirmed Tony's suspicions to the teen's identity. Hartwood's kid.

Continued muttered taunts bounced off Tony. He'd heard them many times as a teenager. Standing, he kept his foot next to the kid's side and his muscles tensed. If Joe didn't get here soon, the kid would try something and Tony would have to let him go. He had no clue how many attorneys Hartwood might have in his pocket, so he needed to keep his actions clean and without reproach.

The crunch of tires over rock and the swing of a spotlight over the area relaxed his shoulders. The bright light illuminated on the boy's defiant expression and clenched fists. This encounter was a polar opposite of the one with Braydon. Wasn't going to be easy this time.

Joe clasped Tony's shoulder. "So, who do we have here?"

Glaring, the boy sat, his fists lifted slightly from his thighs. "You know who I am. Let me go."

"What are you doing here in the middle of the night?"

"Ain't your business."

Joe crouched to be closer to eye level with the boy. "It is

my business. You're trespassing. And I think not for the first time."

"I don't give a fuck what you think."

Joe glanced up at Tony who shrugged. Let the brat dig himself a deeper hole.

"I think you and some—friends—were out here a few nights ago. Had a little destructive fun. A couple of beers. Lost an Avalanche cap. What are you doing here tonight?"

"I ain't sayin' nothin'. My dad will have you fired."

Standing, Joe pulled his notebook from a pocket. "What's your name, kid?"

"You shittin' well know who I am...*sheriff.*"

Joe's eyebrows arched. "Just tell me your name."

Catching both men in his angry glare, he planted his fists at his hips. "CJ Hartwood. Got that? I'm a Hartwood. You're nothing."

Joe glanced at Tony. "Give me a few minutes with our young friend?"

"I ain't your friend."

Tony nodded and strolled toward the sheriff's vehicle. Joe was good at his job. CJ might not come clean here and now, but Tony was pretty sure Joe had an ace up his sleeve. Something the kid couldn't deny or bluff his way through. Hopefully after tonight the vandalism would cease and he could go back to his warm bed.

The sound of a short scuffle made him turn around. Joe had CJ's shoulder in a firm grip as he steered him toward the vehicle. The boy complained, cussed and promised retribution the entire time Joe loaded him into the back seat. Before he shut the door, Tony leaned into the vehicle. "Have a nice ride back into town, kid."

"I'm not some kid. I'm the son of the founder of this town. I'm a Hartwood."

"Give it a rest, CJ," Joe said wearily.

Tony adopted an innocent expression. "What does CJ stand for?"

"You know damn well, you fucker. I'm named after a great man. My dad. Don't ever call me kid again. Call me Cale Hartwood Junior."

Giving up on holding back, Tony chuckled.

Junior gave him the finger.

Tony shook his head with mock sadness but before closing the door on the sputtering youth, said, "You realize you're named after a leafy green vegetable, don't you?"

CHAPTER TWENTY

*R*yder and Vianna's wedding day dawned with a spectacular colorful display over the mountains. But Cookie was too tired to appreciate the majestic pink and orange spectacle. She'd been up most of the night perfecting the finishing touches on the cake. Thank goodness the staff at the lodge had allowed her early access to the ballroom so she didn't have to stack the layers and finish piping mere hours before the event.

The lodge staff had pretty much left her alone. Other than a couple of visits from Steph Cavanaugh, the lodge's event planner, the crews had avoided her corner of the room as much as possible. When she'd placed the final piped peony on the top of the cake and stood back, she'd been surprised at how beautiful the decorated ballroom had become. The area was a far cry from the sparsely furnished, open room where she'd set up her cake components.

She had few hours to run home, take a power nap, and clean up before she needed to be back to check on the cake prior to the ceremony. Pressing her fists against the small of her back, she arched and eased the pressure along her spine. What she wouldn't give for a massage.

After double checking the cake would remain undis-
turbed and hidden behind a tall, portable screen, she drove
home. Tempted to swing by the shop, she drove toward Olde
Town. Tourists were out early exploring, but she drove past
her corner and around the park to her apartment. Her staff
could handle any crowds needing coffee and cupcakes she
reminded herself for the millionth time.

A short break and she'd be fine.

The cake had turned out spectacularly and she couldn't
wait for the reveal to the bride and groom. Then the guests.
If today was a success, her business might expand to include
special event cakes. The critical voice sounding like her
father intruded to demand she keep things just as they were.
Maintain the status quo. Don't try to be more than she was
or do more than she could.

Shoving the critic into a mental box, Cookie climbed the
steps to her apartment. She was dragging and needed to dig
deep to find some energy for the rest of the day.

Two small packages leaned against her door. Cookie
eyed them for a moment. She didn't remember ordering
anything. Retrieving the boxes, she discovered neither had
any labels indicating they'd been mailed or sent through a
delivery service. She recognized the messy handwriting.
Tony's.

What had the man done now? After dropping her tote on
the kitchen island, she took the packages into the living
room and after placing them on the coffee table, sat staring
at the brown boxes.

With a sigh, she reached for the smaller. She wouldn't
know what Tony left for her if she didn't open the boxes. She
had to search her kitchen junk drawer for a pair of scissors
to cut through the heavy packing tape. He certainly hadn't
wanted the box to come open unexpectantly. What was it
with guys and over-using tape?

Finally, the top of the box was free and opened to reveal a

small, ceramic pot. Cookie lifted the pot from a bed of packing material and held it to the light and laughed.

Was this her pot? The one she hadn't finished 'throwing' when Tony tried to teach her how. Bright colors swirled over the surface following the slight indentations that perfectly matched her fingers. The glaze sparkled in the sunlight coming through her window. Janelle and Muffy must have finished the pot for her. To her surprise, it really didn't look half bad.

She glanced at her bookshelf. This pot deserved a place of honor there so she'd have to clear off a spot later.

Why had Tony chosen today to leave her presents? After cutting through the tape on the second box, she discovered a note.

Today is a special day for our friends and family, and I won't get to see you until later. I can't stop thinking about you.

He'd drawn a heart and signed his name.

Cookie dropped the note on the coffee table. A heart? What did that mean? A rise of hope filled her chest, but she shoved away the emotion. They had a relationship. But exactly how far beyond friendship and kisses and where it was going still eluded her. Pinning him down for an answer could be a recipe for disaster.

A wad of tissue paper filled the box. More evidence of a man's 'skilled' wrapping ability. She plucked the paper from the box and frowned at the long rectangular jewelry box cushioned by another wad of colorful tissue paper.

Slow and hesitant, she lifted out the black suede box and cradled it in her palm. Were they to a jewelry point in their relationship? Did giving jewelry mean the same to him as it did to her? Maybe there wasn't even jewelry in the box. Maybe it was something else.

But what else might fit into this box?

The only way she'd know would be to open the box and look inside.

She caught her lower lip between her teeth and opened the box. "Oh," she whispered.

A small ceramic heart attached to a short silver chain lay on the soft cream-colored lining. Cookie touched the heart with her finger then slipped the chain over her hand and lifted the bracelet to the light. "It's beautiful."

Another slip of paper peeked from the edge of the jewelry box. She wrapped the bracelet around her wrist and easily fastened the clasp. It fit perfectly. Then she drew the paper from the box.

Cookie, Mom made this after you came to dinner the first time. I hope it fits. She said it would. Thank you for being you.

The swirl of colors across the surface matched those of the pot. And matched the dress she planned to wear. She'd wear the bracelet to the wedding. Just for him. Amazed at the coincidence, she removed the bracelet and returned it to the box to stroke the cool chain and the smooth surface of the heart.

A nap now would be impossible. Her mind was filled with Tony, his thoughtful gifts, and what he might be trying to convey to her.

Even though he'd said it once, she dared not think about the 'L' word. His declaration could have been spurred by nothing more than the heat of the moment.

Maybe this bracelet meant he would no longer hold back, and they could experience more than shared kisses.

She was so ready. Hopefully tonight. Didn't weddings bring out the love in people? She'd change the sheets on her bed. Just in case.

Smiling at her plan, and finding renewed energy, she danced around her apartment. One way or another, tonight would be a good night.

✢

Tony couldn't believe how early the wedding party began getting ready, but he'd still arrived a few minutes later than his assigned time. He'd been enlisted to help with a prank Kate and Jack planned to pull on Ryder.

And the prank had been spectacular. The look on Ryder's face when he'd turned and discovered Jack in a wedding dress instead of Vianna had been worth the effort.

Now after what already felt like hours of filming, it was time for the ceremony. He'd take a video of the moments while the local photographer, Linc Simmons, shot still photos.

Tony had filmed a handful of marriage ceremonies when he'd started out working behind the camera, but with the passage of time since then, he hardly felt like a professional. But was confident his shots were good and captured the expressions and emotions during the ceremony and vows without getting in the way of those gathered for the celebration. He hated when the photographer was right in the couples' faces and blocking everyone's view. Thankfully, Linc had the same aesthetic and they moved through the ceremony in an easy photographer's dance.

One issue haunted Tony during his assigned job. He kept looking for Cookie every time he scanned the crowd with his camera. As much as he ached to watch her watching the ceremony, it wouldn't do for one person who wasn't in the wedding party to have the most time on film. Besides, she'd taken a seat at the rear of the room about as far from him as she could. The seating choice wasn't about him, but about being able to get to the reception ballroom to check on her cake.

She'd already been at the lodge when he arrived, but because he was running late for the prank, he hadn't had time to seek her out and talk to her before the ceremony.

Still filming, he backed toward the door as Ryder and Vianna turned toward the applause after their first kiss. He'd get the wedding party moving back down the aisle then crossing the lobby to the reception area. Linc could handle any pictures needed of the hugs and handshakes as they greeted guests. Old man Spencer loved his family reception lines.

And Cookie would be in the ballroom, guarding her cake. They'd have a few moments alone.

He paused in the doorway, sighed and lifted his camera to take a long shot of the highly decorated, still empty ballroom. Even more lavishly decorated than the ceremony space, vases dripped the fat-blossomed peonies. Candles flickered, making bright spots on the tables and along the wall. Tables set for a multi-coursed meal filled one end of the room, the dance floor and band riser the other. Slightly off center from the doorway was the cake. And Cookie.

Busy brushing wrinkles from the tablecloth, she had her back to the door. Tony took a moment to study her in the soft spotlight focused on the cake table. She wore a dress that flowed over her figure and exposed her legs to just below her mid-thigh in a way that literally made his mouth water. He swallowed heavily and must have made some noise because she froze, straightened and turned.

"It's you," she said. "Wait, you're not filming me, are you?"

He was. He switched off the recording and crossed the room. "No."

"Good. Do you have good shots of the cake? Linc took a bunch of photos earlier and I'm hoping to use one or two in case I decide to add special event cakes."

Although her hands fluttered around the table, then disappeared into the folds of her skirt, her breathless, rushed words were a contrast to her calm appearance.

"We have a few minutes before guests start trickling in. Let me take some shots."

"Wait, I'll get out of the way."

"No, please stay there for a moment. I wouldn't be a photographer worth my salt if I didn't show both the cake and the baker in at least one shot."

"Worth my salt?"

"Something Mom says quite often. It means—"

"I know what it means I'm just not accustomed to hearing the phrase. Okay, I'll stand here, but not long. Did you want me to do anything?"

"When I came in you were fussing with the details. Just do a little of that, then look at me and smile."

She did as asked. Her smile shot straight to his heart, and lower. That smile wasn't for the cake, or for the wedded couple. That smile was for him. He didn't want to share this moment with anyone. He lowered the camera. "Cookie, I..."

She circled the cake table and pushed on the camera until he held it at his side. "I'm glad we have a couple minutes of quiet. I want to thank you for the surprises you left at my door this morning. I spent most of the night here with the cake, and was so tired when I went home to change. It was a pleasant surprise to find packages on my doorstep."

"I can't believe you'd trust anyone else to guard this cake."

She ducked her head. "You're right. Seriously, Tony, thank you for the gifts. My poor little pot looks better than I thought possible. Did your mom finish for me?"

The tips of his ears heated. "No. I did."

"Oh. It's beautiful. It's going to be perfect on my bookshelf." She held up her wrist. "What about this?"

"A joint effort. I made the dangle. Mom and Janelle put it on the chain. Do you, uh, like it?"

She lifted to her toes, kissed his cheek then whispered, "I love it. Even more now that I know you made it."

If he'd known being creative would make her so happy and breathless, he'd have done more. No, probably not. The romantic creativity had only appeared once he recognized what his heart had known long before his brain. "You are my inspiration, sweetheart. How could anything that comes from you be anything but beautiful.?"

She gave him an odd look—like he had grown more heads or something. "Yeah, right."

He took her hand and slid the bracelet around to peer at the ceramic heart. "It matches your dress."

"Don't sound so surprised. With that swirl of colors it matches a lot of dresses." She kissed his cheek again. "Yes, it does. Perfectly. And I love it. Thank you."

Aching to kiss her properly, Tony said instead, "You're welcome. I'd better get the rest of the video I need. The crowd's getting restless out there."

Cookie nodded and stood back. He did a full three-sixty shot of the cake then zoomed in for close ups of the flowers and swirls of icing. "These decorations are spectacular. Beautiful."

"Like the bride. She was my inspiration. And the love that's so evident between her and Ryder."

Did he hear wistfulness in her tone? He was more than ready to put his camera away to explore the possibilities. But he'd volunteered to be the videographer and there was still the reception to document. At this moment he hated, absolutely hated that he knew his way around a camera. Being unable to deny Vianna's hopeful request had sealed the deal.

There might be a way to salvage the evening. "Will you sit with me for dinner?"

Cookie chuckled. "I'm pretty sure when Kate helped with the table assignments, she put us together."

"Table assignments?"

"Haven't been to that many fancy wedding receptions, have you, Tony? Everyone gets assigned a table for dinner."

"That's, uh..." He didn't mind, as long as he was at her table. "Whatever. I'll need to be wandering the room off and on all evening but I promise to give you as much of my time as I can."

"Good. I'm looking forward to that. As long as you don't get that camera in my face again. Okay, looks like it show-time. Here comes the wedding party."

Cookie's feet ached. More accustomed to the roomy clogs she wore at the bakery, this foray into a fancy pair of strappy sandals had become torture. But she couldn't have presented the beautiful cake with clunky feet. She stretched her legs under the table as far as she could and scanned the room.

The lodge's chef had outdone himself with the wedding supper. After the official cake cutting, she'd finally relaxed. While there had been some good-natured, disappointed comments when neither Vianna or Ryder had shoved cake into their partner's face, Cookie had actually been glad. One of those silly traditions.

The comments she'd overheard and those directed to her once it became common knowledge she'd baked the confec-tion, eased her concerns. Both the decorations and the flavor of the cake were well-received and more than a handful of people had mentioned they'd contact her for future cakes. Now she only needed to make sure that she was ready to expand her business. She wouldn't set herself up for failure by jumping into anything without knowing what was what.

Ryder and Vianna had danced their first dance. But Tony hadn't been able to get out from behind his camera much and they'd only had one slow, swaying dance. Her sore feet hadn't minded but her nerve endings continued to tingle from his touch and the heat of his body.

To distract herself from her thoughts, Cookie scanned the room. Tony was nowhere to be seen and she frowned at the longing in her heart. He wouldn't have left already. Not without saying something to her. Pure, sensual invitation had shone in his light eyes. Then there he was, across the room, but with a smile and wave for her.

Relieved, she continued to look around. Tired children had curled up on sets of chairs pushed together. A couple had even stretched out under the tables. It wouldn't be long until the party started to wind down. Ryder leaned against the far wall talking to the event planner. But his gaze never strayed from where Vianna sat talking with her new mother-in -law. He looked ready to grab his bride and bolt from the room.

The idea had merit.

She glanced at her watch and widened her eyes. That late? Her gaze shifted to the band. This was Darryl's farewell performance with Chickering Road. She suspected the group would continue playing as long as one person remained to listen. Glad she insisted he take the next day off—and he'd insisted on the same from her—she spent a few moments worrying about how her store would fare with them both gone.

Ava could handle a Sunday just fine. There were plenty of cupcakes available, and even more in the freezer if needed. The niggling concern she should have checked in before the wedding made her rub softly at her temples.

Kate eased into an empty chair. "Stop worrying about work."

"How did you know?"

She patted her chest. "Small business owner. I know the look."

Cookie nodded. "I've got great staff. They can handle everything. They know to call if an emergency comes up."

"I'm gonna have an emergency if the bride and groom don't leave soon. I can't relax until they do. And I'm exhausted for two." She patted her distended belly. "Baby boy is cranky. I can't wait until this kid pops out."

"Still think the doctor's wrong?"

"If you go by the fact Madison was early, it could be any day. I hope to high heaven I don't have to carry this kid around like this for the couple of weeks the doctor predicted. Once my boy's swaddled in a blanket and in my arms, everything will be so much better."

An odd sensation settled in Cookie's chest. She'd never thought about children, and had never been in a relationship where she thought kids were a possibility. Catching Tony's movements as he recorded couples on the dance floor, she revised her thought.

Until now.

Hoping to take their relationship into the sexual realm—tonight—made her consider the idea. Tony and children. He'd be a great father. His kids would have the best grandmothers. There was so much love in Tony's family, it would make up for the lack in hers. She had no delusions that a grandchild would be approved of by her father.

Damn the man for still making her question her life and decisions.

Kate poked her shoulder then pointed across the dance floor. "You need to get over there."

"Huh? Where?"

"By the doorway. All the single ladies..." She waggled her hand in a well-known movement from an old music video. "...are gathering for the bouquet toss."

Cookie shook her head. "No. I don't need—"

"Yes, you do. You're not married. It's tradition. Now scoot. Don't make me go all crazy pregnant lady on you."

Chuckling, Cookie relented. "Okay. I'll stand at the back. Just for you."

"Go. And good luck."

Cookie slipped her shoes on and rose. She looked around for Tony. She didn't see him so there would be no rescue from him. She straightened her shoulders and went to join the hopeful women. She wasn't competition for any of them, she was just here to please her friend.

The crowd silenced, then a single voice shouted, "One. Two. Three."

The women to either side of her scrambled forward, arms lifted to catch the small, tossing bouquet. Grinning, she watched the small bundle of pink and white flowers sail high over the heads of the crowd. Straight. Toward. Her.

She lifted her hands both to deny the bouquet and to protect her face from the flying flowers. Her fingers closed around the soft blossoms. Oh no.

Groans of half-serious disappointment surrounded her. Then the women started to clap. When the band joined in, and her name became a chant, Cookie accepted the inevitable. She lifted the flowers in a stance that made her feel like an athlete on the gold medal podium. Her heart was certainly racing enough.

Vianna appeared before her and leaned close to press her cheek against Cookie's. "I'm glad you caught that, Cookie. Tradition says you'll be the next bride."

"Great."

Vianna laughed at her dry, sarcastic response. "Just keep an open mind. Gotta go. We're going to sneak away."

"Then you shouldn't be telling me."

"You won't say anything, will you?"

Cookie shook her head.

"Thanks again for the gorgeous, spectacular cake." With that Vianna was gone.

Cookie stared down at the fat peonies then lifted the bouquet to her nose. The sweet scent surrounded her. Amazing how even with the whole room filled with peonies, practically the entire lodge, she could still distinguish the scent from these.

"Good catch."

She jerked at the words Tony spoke close to her ear. "Uh, thanks?"

"No really, it was spectacular. Worthy of the Heisman Trophy."

"That sounds so romantic. I suppose you recorded the moment."

"Saved for all eternity." He patted the camera. "I'm ready to call it a night. I'm done with being a walking camera and getting into everyone's business."

"Don't tell anyone, but there is at least one more thing you should record."

He wrinkled his forehead. "And that would be?"

"Vianna and Ryder are trying to slip away without anyone noticing. If we wander toward the door, we might catch them. If not, at least we can be on our way. I'm tired and sore."

"Sore?"

"My back's stiff from bending to finish the cake. And my feet hurt. Professional hazards. I just need to relax somewhere peaceful and quiet."

The clear, light blue of Tony's eyes darkened. His nostrils flared. His reaction to her words made pleasant jitters dance along her spine. "I imagine you're feeling the strain of being behind the camera all day. Would you... do you want to..."

"Yes."

"You don't know what I was going to say."

"Doesn't matter. The answer is yes. Here comes the bride and groom. Let's slip behind these plants and I'll get this last shot. And then, yes, I'm all yours."

All hers. Just what she'd wanted for weeks now.

CHAPTER TWENTY-ONE

*T*ony had been planning this night since their visit to the shack. Now was the time to take their relationship further. In the short hours he'd carved out he'd finished the tile in the expanded bathroom. While boxes containing tiles for the kitchen backsplash remained stacked in a corner, the rest of that space looked okay.

Even though Cookie had seen his progress a couple weeks ago, she hadn't been back since then. This reveal would be spectacular. At least for the one area he'd completed.

The master bedroom suite.

He probably should have spent more time on the kitchen and living room, but passion had taken over and directed his work. Yes, he was passionate about his work, but not with this overpowering need to make it perfect for Cookie. Love made a man crazy. Yep, he believed that now.

Because she wouldn't leave her car at the lodge they left in separate vehicles. He followed her to the parking space provided for her apartment. He was prepared with a list of reasons why they should go to his place, but she didn't ask, simply climbed into his truck and smiled at him. The parking area for those who lived in Olde Town was nearly as far from the cupcake shop as her apartment was. He could have left his truck parked on the street there.

The walk through the quiet of the late night amped his nerves. Shit, he'd never been so unsure before with a woman. But he'd never had as much to lose as he did that night. The distant sounds from the Golden Grill at the edge of Olde Town followed them across the triangle. Not long until even that establishment would be quiet.

"I don't often get to experience this time of night," Cookie said. "Early mornings are pretty quiet though. But different somehow. It's like sound, life, whatever is winding down now. In the morning, it's more like the day is dreading waking up. Or delighting in that time." She paused. "Sorry."

"Sorry for what, sweetheart?"

"I'm a little nervous. Before you say anything, I'm not regretting coming home with you. I've wanted this for... well, awhile." Her lips twitched then she smiled. "I'm glad I don't have to wait any longer. And I've never said this before, but I like when you call me sweetheart. I've never been anybody's sweetheart. And just to let you know, I really dislike babe."

"I'll do my best to remember that." He drew her close and under the watchful eye of the bronze pony express rider, kissed her to seal his passionate promise.

She clung to his shoulders and he deepened their connection, teasing, nipping, dancing his tongue with hers. Fighting to keep his breathing even, he drew back. "We need to get inside."

"My thoughts exactly." Cookie took his hand and with long, rapid strides pulled him across the triangle. She had her keys in hand, taking them through the front door of the bakery, then up the creaky stairs. They paused only when he needed to retrieve his keys and unlock the door.

Now what? How did they move from the door to the bedroom?

Cookie glanced around the living area. "You haven't done much more in here."

"I focused on other areas. Bathroom." He paused a moment then said, "Bedroom."

Dropping her tiny handbag on the coffee table, Cookie stared pointedly at the closed bedroom door. "Show me?"

Before he led the way, Tony drew her into another kiss. Lord love him, he could kiss this woman forever and it would never be enough. He rested his forehead against hers. "You're sure?"

Cookie stepped back and poked his shoulder. "I'm the surest. What do I have to do? Throw you over my shoulder? I may be able to drag a fifty-pound bag of flour around, but I don't think I could carry you."

As though to cancel the sharp poke, she stroked his shoulder. Her voice lowered to a rumbling, sensual whisper. "The night's being wasted, Tony. I want to feel you. Feel your skin against mine. Learn what pleases you."

"You please me."

"I'm gonna try." She took a step back. "Tony?"

"Yes, sweetheart?"

"Let's go to bed."

The heavy, throbbing heat of his arousal agreed, so he took her hands and backed toward the bedroom door. "I hope you like what I've done."

"I'm more interested in what you should be doing right now."

He recognized his truth in those words and continued his backward steps until the bed stopped their progress. Delivered a few days ago while Cookie had been obsessing over the wedding cake, the bed was tall, with an extra thick mattress. He'd considered the style of furniture in Cookie's apartment and although the search had been long and fraught with many missteps, the sleigh bed looked like it could have been gracing this room since the founding of the town. He appreciated the dark curving wood of the carved head and foot boards. None of what he thought mattered. This was all for her.

"Oh my," she said breathlessly and reached around him to test the mattress. "Oh... My." Then she grabbed a handful of the comforter and top sheet and tossed them across the wide mattress.

So far so good. He sat and encouraged her to join him.

But Cookie shook her head and backed away smiling.

What was she up to?

He didn't to wait long. In some feminine movement he didn't understand, she shed her dress and stood before him wearing only a lacey bra and a tiny pair of matching panties. He swallowed and draw a breath. And thigh high stockings topped with lace. That matched the bra. The details imprinted on what was left of his functioning brain. She'd dressed like this for him.

For him.

She kicked off her shoes and sighed. "Oh God, that feels good."

He could make her feel even better. He surged to his feet, fumbling with the buttons of his shirt. Cookie watched him for a moment then added her fingers to the mix.

"Stop messing around, Tony. Let me do this."

Within seconds his shirt joined her dress in a rumpled heap on the floor. He skimmed his hands down her sides and over her hips then caught his fingers in the tops of her stockings to ease the silky fabric to the floor. Nice. Maybe next time he'd ask her to leave them on. One at a time, he lifted her feet and removed the stockings.

"Sore feet?" he whispered in her ear before catching the lobe between his teeth.

"Yes," she sighed, but he wasn't sure if she answered his question or liked how he teased and nuzzled her ear. It didn't matter. She was in his arms and it wouldn't be long until she was in his bed.

Slow down. No reason to hurry.

Except her hands roamed his body with an almost desperate haste. If she kept doing that, he wouldn't even make it to the bed. He captured her hands and brought them to his mouth to kiss both her palms. "We need to slow this down, sweetheart."

She shook her head. "Don't wanna. Tony, please."

Barely controlling the fire of his own passion, he took her mouth in a fierce, demanding kiss. She mated her tongue with his in equal demand. Then she planted her hands against his chest and with a determined shove, pushed him onto the bed. For a moment she stood over him, one eyebrow arched.

Balanced on one hand, she leaned over him. With her free hand she traced the planes of his chest and stomach. His muscles contracted and quivered under her touch. With wicked, deliberate slowness, she tucked a finger under his waistband, sliding it back and forth under the button.

To encourage her, he arched and was rewarded when her fingers scraped along his zipper sending electric jolts through his nerve endings. With a laugh, she drew the zipper down and straightened. "Well now. That's encouraging."

Undressing while lying on the bed wasn't the easiest, but he couldn't lose his clothes fast enough. When nothing restricted him, and her heated gaze caressed his skin, he held out his arms. "Join me?"

With a twinkle in her eye, Cookie tapped her cheek with one finger. "Let me think about it." Showing off her shapely bottom, she crossed the room and turned off the overhead light.

Once Cookie turned out the light, she breathed a sigh of relief. It had been damned difficult standing in the harsh light wearing nothing but the new underwear she'd ordered online, hoping this night would end this way. But it was too dark and she wanted to be able to see Tony bathed in the passion she hoped was bottled up within him. She tugged open the heavy curtains allowing moonlight to stream into the room, the pale glow highlighting the bed

The cool light spilled over the sheets and created delightful shadows on the man waiting for her. "Join me?" he asked again.

Feeling sensual and powerful, she swayed her hips and strolled to the bed. Since he was naked, it was only fair... she released the clasp of her bra and let it fall to the floor. Her panties followed. Conscious of his burning gaze on her, she sat then swung her legs up onto the bed.

Oh yes, the bed was as comfortable as it looked.

Then his hands were on her and comfort fled her mind... except the comfort of his kisses after the sharp nip along her collarbone. He teased and tasted, gave and took in the same glorious moments. She'd never imagined such perfect pleasure. He was perfectly attuned to her needs and responded to her moans and whispers, the encouragement of her hands.

"Tony."

He lifted his head from her breast leaving her nipple cold and bereft. "Yes, my darling?"

"Don't stop."

He response was muffled as he returned to his ministrations. "Wouldn't dream of it."

As he drew her tighter and higher, touching her with a gentle yet insistent intimacy, he whispered against her skin. She didn't know what he said, didn't care, didn't.... Stars exploded behind her eyes and she cried out the name of her love. "Tony."

"That's it, Cookie." His fingers moved, stroking. "Again? For me?"

She tossed her head in denial even as he coaxed her body to do as he asked. "No, with you. With you."

His rough chuckle vibrated longing through her. "With you, always, sweetheart." He continued to move his fingers, added the flick of his thumb and drew her firm nipple into his mouth, scraping the sensitive peak with his teeth. She shuddered and the waves of a second orgasm tumbled over her.

With a lazy grin, Tony sheathed himself with the thin layer of protection, moved between her thighs, and entered her before the glorious sensations faded. She gasped at the rightness of being filled by him. He stroked damp hair from her forehead and pressed his lips against her temple.

"Cookie, I'm sorry."

She blinked and stared into blue eyes filled with a passion so intense it brought tears to her eyes. "No, never sorry," she gasped.

"I should have... we should have done this... before now."

No regrets, his or hers, would dampen the beauty of this moment, of them joined as one. She needed him. Needed him to move. "Don't care about then. Only now. Move, Tone. Please, Tony. Move."

His laugh lifted him within her and the rise of another orgasm made her draw her lower lip between her teeth. No. Too soon.

Tony rotated his hips. "Like this?"

She tightened around him.

"Oh, yeah," he moaned and began a slow retreat and return.

Cookie arched to meet his thrusts, playing the rhythm she needed with her fingers against the taunt muscles of his butt. He matched the pace she set. She planted her feet against the mattress and pushed up, opening further to him.

Shorter, faster, he thrust into her. His breath burst past her cheek. She wrapped her arms around his shoulders and one leg over his hips. With a groan, he pressed her hips deep into the mattress and shuddered with his release. She followed, sighing his name into the moonlit night.

They remained wrapped in each other while their breathing slowed. Tony rested his forehead against her shoulder. "Ah, sweetheart."

"You said it, Tony," she whispered then turned her head to kiss his cheek.

Silent, he looked at her. Something she didn't recognized filled his eyes. The remnants of passion, yes, but something more. Interesting. Confusing. So like her man.

Her man. She liked that. Her man. Her lover. She liked that even more.

"I should move. I must be getting heavy."

The length of him warmed her... from the inside out. She grinned and clenched her inner muscles.

His eyes widened, then he shook his head. "Wicked. Give me a chance to recover." He pressed his lower body to hers. "Shouldn't take too long."

"Do you mind if I get some water?"

He jerked, sending ripples of delight through her. No, it wouldn't take long. "Let me."

"No, I've got it. Do you have any bottled in the fridge?"

"I'll go."

She patted his shoulder. "I need to stretch a bit before we... you know. Again. I'll be right back."

"Promise?"

The plaintive fear in his tone made her pause. She held up her little finger. "Pinky swear."

"You know that's like a blood oath, don't you?" He eased from her body then lay on his side and linked her curled pinky with his.

"A time-honored tradition."

The tension around his eyes eased. "So I've heard. Don't be long?"

"I won't." She slipped from the bed, stumbled over their

discarded clothing then paused by the door. It should feel odd to wander through his apartment wearing nothing but her skin. Instead it was as natural as being with him had been.

She found water and a small covered plate with sliced cheese, cut fruit and was it? Yes, chocolate. He'd planned for this night and done a good job. A bottle of wine chilled in the fridge, but she opted for the water. She didn't want anything to dull her senses or her reactions to her lover.

Her lover. She'd never get tired of calling him that. At least in her head.

She grabbed the plate and two bottles of water and returned to the bedroom. Tony lay curled on his side facing the door. But his eyes were closed and his breathing deep and even.

Grinning, she set the midnight snack on the bedside stand and slipped under the sheet next to her sleeping man.

He wrapped his arm over her waist and snuggled her back against his body. After nuzzling her hair, he sighed. "Stay with me tonight?"

The night was three quarters over already. Why would she leave now? She entwined her fingers with his and held their joined hands between her breasts. "Yes."

"Mmm." His breathing slowed.

Cookie closed her eyes. She'd been running on only a few hours of rest and pure adrenaline since the day before yesterday. A little sleep would work wonders She snuggled deeper into the curl of Tony's body.

"Cookie?"

His mumble made her believe he was asleep. Still, she answered softly. "What?"

"Stay with me forever."

CHAPTER TWENTY-TWO

*T*ony stood at the bedroom window watching the early Sunday morning activity in the Olde Town triangle. Well, not so early, he amended. It was well past nine. He turned and perched his butt on the wide window sill to watch Cookie sleep.

Amazed with the woman in his bed, he studied the soft lines of her face relaxed in slumber. The faint discoloration of his love-bite marred her pale shoulder. She was his. He'd marked her. He shook his head and stared at his bare toes. Didn't that make him sound like some macho shithead. He didn't mind that a bit, if she didn't. As long as she was his.

The vague memory of him asking her to stay with him forever stilled his breath in his throat. Forever was a long time when she hadn't even said she loved him. Shown him more love that he probably deserved but hadn't said 'I love you'.

After that one time at the shack, though, neither had he.

Maybe it was all the romantic shit surrounding Ryder's wedding bringing these thoughts to the surface. Or maybe it was time for him to officially take his relationship with Cookie to another level.

Cookie shifted, curling around her pillow and baring the length of one leg. Tony's body awoke with interest. No way, he told himself. If she was still asleep, she needed rest. Not him pawing her. Wait, nothing so crass. He'd wake her with kisses, touches and the passion of his body.

In order for her to rest, he needed to leave and get his thoughts together. Whether buoyed by wedding excitement or not, he needed her. And her love. The merest hint of the thought she might not return the strength of his feelings forced him into action. Watching her while dressing silently as possible, he formed a plan to show her he was worth more than a good time in bed. He was a keeper.

He sat on the edge of the bed to slip on his shoes. As he'd hoped, Cookie woke with a smile brightening her still sleepy eyes. She rested her palm high on his thigh.

"Going somewhere, buster?"

Her touch, the softly sensual way she said 'buster' were nearly enough to chase his plan from his mind. Lifting her hand, he pressed a kiss to the center of her palm. "Yeah, but just for a little bit. Thought I'd forage for breakfast."

Her expression showed disbelief. Then Cookie grinned. "I'm not hungry. Come back to bed."

Tempting. But no. "Sorry, sweetheart. Sometimes you just have to eat. Renew your energy. I shouldn't be long."

A wide yawn stopped her from speaking and her eyelids drifted closed. "What time is it?"

"Nine twenty-five or so."

Her eyes popped open. "That late? I never sleep this long."

"Enjoy it while you can, sweetheart."

"I'd enjoy it more if you stayed." She stretched; his temptation incarnate.

"Me, too. But you're still tired and if I don't leave soon, the Sunday special at Pearl's will sell out. I haven't had their huevos rancheros since I've been back."

"Oh. That does sound good." Cookie snuggled into her

pillow and pulled the sheet up under her chin. "For me too, please."

Tony kissed her forehead and rose. "Yes, dear."

"That's what I like to hear. Give me one more kiss and I'll let you go."

Tony obliged willingly and one kiss turned into five or six before she pushed on his shoulders. "Don't keep my stomach waiting. It's your fault I'm hungry now. Hurry back."

Leaving her was difficult, but he walked from the bedroom, out the door and down the stairs before stopping to calm the pressure against his zipper. Tugging on the hem of his untucked shirt, he entered the bakery.

Ava glanced up. "Hey, Tony."

"I know you're not open yet, but is it okay if I go out the front?"

She nodded. "It's close enough to ten. Would you leave the door unlocked for me?"

He stepped from the cupcake shop and stood on the top step surveying the triangle. The uncomfortable sense of being watched crawled across the back of his neck. Casually, he studied the area. A loud exclamation drew his attention to the front of the soda shoppe. Great. Two Hartwoods.

The older grabbed his son's upper arm and pulled him toward the street. The kid gave a feeble protest then followed quietly. Tony wished he could be the proverbial fly on the wall, but not enough to get closer. Unfortunately, Junior had been right. His father had gotten him absolved of any wrong doing at Stick Pony.

Although that came with a price the kid obviously wasn't happy about. He was being sent back to live with his mother in Denver.

Tony wished the poor woman luck.

Dismissing the Hartwood drama, he headed to Pearls with a spring in his step. Dessert wasn't common after breakfast, but he had sweet ideas of how to spend the rest of the day in bed.

⚜

Cookie woke to a silent apartment and it took her a few moments to get her bearings and remember Tony would be back with breakfast. Her stomach rumbled. Soon, she hoped.

A check of the clock showed she'd only slept another ten minutes, so she might have time for a quick shower before he returned. Or maybe she'd just wrap herself in the lightweight robe he'd pulled from the closet for her. They could shower together later in that amazing, luxurious shower. He had done a remarkable job remodeling the bathroom.

With that plan in mind, she rose and quickly made herself presentable. The chirp of a phone drew her into the main room. She grinned at where they'd set their phones together on the counter for charging. How romantic. And how silly was she being?

She didn't care. She stood in the center of the room and twirled in a circle. The phone chirped again and she jerked to a stop. Not her phone. Tony's. He'd left without it.

She drew her brows together. Who would be texting him on a Sunday morning? Batting down an unwelcome rise of jealousy, she shrugged to relax her shoulders. No big deal. Probably not too important if they only left a message.

Then her phone rang. She rammed her shin against the edge of the coffee table then limped to the kitchen counter. The screen showed 'Deke'. Why would he be calling her?

She pushed the speaker button. "This is Cookie."

"Sorry to bother you today, but there was a situation yesterday you need to be aware of. You'd left the reception last night by the time I looked for you."

A fission of unease traced down her spine. She pulled her robe tighter around her. "What happened?"

"There was a disturbance at the gate. Cale Hartwood was sloppy drunk, insisting on being allowed in for the wedding." Deke paused and cleared his throat. "After the old newspaper man and city trustee angles didn't work he said he was your date."

"He what?" Laughter burst from her and she hoped she didn't sound hysterical. That bastard had balls to think she'd ever date him now.

"Yeah, that's what we thought. Took a while before he left, even after the authorities were notified. You need to know—"

"Unfortunately, I do know what he's capable of. Thanks for the warning. I'll be careful."

"Cookie, if he tries anything you need to let authorities know. Let Tony know."

She hated how memories could ruin this day. Unwilling to allow the fear and humiliation back into her life, she found the determination to say, "Don't worry, Deke. Thanks for letting me know. I'll watch out for him. Have a great day."

She pressed the disconnect button.

Damn Hartwood. Until the moment Deke mentioned that name, all she'd held in her heart was happiness and joy. All because of how much she loved Tony.

Today she'd tell him. Maybe she'd even answer the question she wasn't sure he knew he'd asked. Yes, she'd stay with him. Forever.

As she returned her phone to the counter, she knocked Tony's to the floor. Grimacing, she said a silent prayer that she hadn't broken the expensive phone. The message chirp sounded. Thank goodness, it worked.

Feeling a twinge of guilt when she tapped the screen to access the message app just to make sure, Cookie held her breath. She'd confess this sin later, and promise never to look through his phone again. Knowing too well how it felt to have her personal space violated, she almost returned the phone to the counter without glancing at the words. No, she'd better make sure.

> *Negotiations concluded successfully yesterday. Agreed to your latest round of terms. Congratulations!*

She frowned at the sender's name. Tony's agent. With precise movements she closed the app and returned the phone to the counter. The sting of impending tears made her catch her bottom lip between her teeth. Hartwood was right. Tony had been offered what must be a lucrative deal to continue filming his show.

He'd be leaving Spencer.

She sank onto the couch. Of course, he would leave. She'd known that all along. But if he left this week to sign contracts, would he ever be back? Would he want to pursue a long-distance relationship? Or had all this been just a convenient and pleasant way to pass the time until he moved on? A playmate at every job site? Who would finish the Stick Pony treehouse?

She fisted her hands. And she'd been ready to proclaim her love. Idiot. Love-sick fool. She shouldn't have thought she meant that much to him.

But at the shack he'd said he thought he was falling in love with her.

He thought.

Had that just been a clever line to get her in his bed? Had he said those words to other women?

Stop. She held her fists at her temples to press away the memory. She was driving herself crazy with the questions. The assumptions. She owed him the opportunity to tell her the truth. But not today. Maybe never. It might be better if he just left before she got any more involved.

Fell any more in love with him.

Today, this minute, the anger and disappointment

rumbled through her. She didn't want explanations. She didn't even want to see him.

It would be better if she left. Give herself time to adjust to the new reality facing her. Give him time to come up with a way to tell her. She returned to the bedroom and picked up her fancy dress. So, it was the morning after walk of shame for her. At least her apartment wasn't far. Tony's fingers had made a mess of her hair and precious minutes passed until she felt presentable.

The bracelet he'd given her the day before lay on the top of his tall chest of drawers. She touched the colorful heart. She'd worn the jewelry when they'd made love, until the clasp had tangled in his hair. With the greatest of care, he'd unfastened the chain, kissed the heart and put it here for safe keeping. She'd thought this meant so much to him. To her. She picked it up, set it down, and picked it up again to press the cool ceramic against her lips. With a final caress, she replaced the jewelry on the dresser and turned away.

Crumpling her clutch purse in her hands, she gave what felt like a last look at the rumpled bed, the tidy living room and kitchen, and stepped from the apartment. Shutting the door seemed so symbolically final, yet part of her still hoped there would be a way for them to stay together. She couldn't shut the door on her love this easily. Pressing her palm to her chest she started down the stairs.

The outer door opened. Tony looked up, saw her. He held up a paper bag from the coffee shop and a wide smile stretched his sensual lips. No, she shouldn't think that way. Falling back on memories would make leaving too difficult. Then he noticed her dress and his brows drew together.

"Cookie?"

"Sorry, Tony. I have... uh... there's something I need to take care of. I... I can't stay."

He took the steps two at a time until he stood on the step below her and reached to take her hand.

She jerked away at the last second. "I've got to go... take care of this."

His scowl deepened. "What's happened? Did Hartwood do any—"

Shaking her head, she refused to meet his eyes. "He's got nothing to do with this. Really, Tony. I've got to go. I'll... we'll talk later."

"Uh, okay, sweetheart. Not much later, though." He offered her a soft, entreating smile. "I've got something I need to tell you."

She bet he did. Especially now that the contract was ready to be signed. The bloom of fresh anger helped her step past him. "I've got to go."

Fighting the weight of his gaze on her back as she descended the stairs, she told herself over and over leaving now was for the best. For both of them. The final separation wouldn't hurt so bad.

Dry-eyed and determined, Cookie strode across the park to her apartment building and up the stairs. But once she'd closed the door to lock out the world, and despite her internal insistence she could deal better with the pain of his leaving now rather than later, her tears fell unchecked.

❧

Tony stared at the closed door for a long minute. What the hell was that all about? Cookie was acting strangely, and it got him worried. She'd claimed it had nothing to do with Hartwood, but that incident still had to be fresh in her memory. But what would have caused her to bolt like that?

And just when he was ready to open his heart and bare his soul to her. "Cookie," he whispered to the quiet air. "I love you."

Feeling the fool standing on the stairs and saying words meant for his love's ears, he stomped up the rest of the stairs and entered the apartment. Nothing looked different. He dropped the food on the kitchen counter and wandered through the apartment. Other than the messy bed and a bathrobe he'd swiped from an expensive hotel, there was no evidence she'd ever been there.

A glint of silver caught his eye. Her bracelet lay centered on the dark wood of his dresser, the chain catching the morning sun. He held the small ceramic heart between his thumb and forefinger and lifted it to eye level. She hadn't wanted to take it off, even when it was the only adornment on her smooth skin. So he'd made love to her with the jewelry the only barrier between them. He'd believed it brought them closer still.

Why would she leave it here? What had he done? He needed to discover the answers himself, the only person he needed to talk to about this was her.

But she hadn't acted like a discussion was on the table. Her demeanor, how she'd turned from his kiss... something was seriously wrong. Sure, the café had been busy and their food took longer than he'd expected. But what the hell happened in the hour he'd been gone?

Wrapping the chain around his fingers and cradling the heart against his palm, he returned to the kitchen. The spicy aroma of the breakfast he'd brought for her soured in his stomach. With more force than was needed, he slammed the take-out bag into the garbage can. He couldn't eat what he'd brought for them. For her.

Shit. What was he supposed to do?

His phone rang and he stuffed his hand in his empty pocket. He turned in a circle. The song he used for a ring tone started a repeat. There. He leaned past the sink and snagged the phone, pulled out the charger chord and answered. "Cookie?"

Laughter greeted him. "No, man. Your long-suffering agent. What'd ya do? Lose your woman?"

The man's laughing question felt too close to the truth. But no one needed to know that. "What do you want? It's Sunday, fool."

"Didn't you read my text?"

"What text?" Damn it, the man needed to get to the point.

"The latest round of negotiations were successful. You're out of your contract. Although I still think you're an idiot for refusing the per show increase they offered. But hey, I'm not you. I would have highly enjoyed my percentage."

Tony listened with half an ear while his agent rambled then interrupted. "I've got something going on here. What's your point?"

"Sorry, Anthony. The point is although they've agreed to your terms concerning literary rights and future programming concepts, they still insist on meeting with you in person. Here. By the end of the week. What day do you want to travel? I'll get flights and a hotel set. Consider it one of my final duties. So, when?"

The network demanded an in-person meeting? Why now? That was why he had his agent and attorney work through the negotiations. And this week? Shit. How could he leave Spencer when he didn't know what was happening between him and Cookie? She would be sure to get the wrong idea.

"Anthony?"

"Uh... now really isn't a good time. Can't you put them off?"

"Sorry, but no. I get the feeling their mentality is that if you don't show up now, you weren't really serious. I didn't think I'd need to say anything, but they've set a time stipulation. If the contracts aren't signed by the close of the working day this coming Friday, they'll be null and void. And you'll be committed to fulfilling the original contract."

"Four more years?" That would be unbearable but breaking the contract would be financially disastrous. He'd started from the bottom before, but not when another person was involved. And he wanted Cookie to be involved. He needed to talk to her. Now.

"Okay, get me the latest possible flight out of Denver to make their deadline. I've got to go. Text me the details."

"You got it. Anthony? I've enjoyed working with you."

"Yeah, great. Me, too. See you Friday." He disconnected and immediately called Cookie. The phone rang, then sent him to voice mail. "Cookie, we need to talk. I don't know what I did, but give me the chance to make it right. Things are changing. I've got to talk to you. Please, sweetheart? Call me as soon as you can. I..." He almost spoke his truth, his love. No. The first time needed to be in person. "Just call me."

After disconnecting, he stared at the phone, willing it to ring. After ten minutes he sighed and pocketed the phone. He flopped onto the couch but immediately rose again.

Great. If she didn't want to talk to him, he wasn't going to push the issue. Whatever. He certainly wasn't going to sit around moping. He'd work on the treehouse. Give her time to do whatever she needed to do.

Give himself time to figure out what he could do to make things right. If he could ever figure out what went wrong.

He changed into work clothes and stomped to his truck. Restraining the urge to rev the engine and speed through town and down the highway, he gripped the steering wheel until his knuckles turned white. By the time he reached the camp and hiked to the treehouse, his temper faded but the hurt and pain remained. Why wouldn't she talk to him?

Framing up the second level platform and walls burned off the remaining anger, but nothing filled the hole in his heart. He'd read the signs incorrectly. Or he hadn't confessed his love soon enough. Maybe she'd gotten tired of waiting for him to commit. Maybe she'd just gotten tired of him.

Hoping his thoughts were born of desperation, Tony packed away his tools and sat at the edge of the platform, the beauty of the landscape before him as lost as the answers he tried desperately to find.

The sun set behind the mountains but the glorious display of colors barely made an impression on his dark thoughts. Stars sparkled overhead but were nothing compared to the twinkle in Cookie's eyes when she called him 'buster'. The chill of the night finally chased him from the trees and back to his lonely apartment.

She wasn't there. She hadn't called. He lifted the bracelet from the counter and pressed the heart to his lips. Then he found a clean bandana and wrapped the cloth around the precious piece of jewelry before hiding the bundle in the bottom of a drawer.

Life went on.

He wasn't sure if he would.

CHAPTER TWENTY-THREE

*A*fter a long night staring at the television, Tony had no idea what had been on the screen. His body ached from remaining motionless in an awkward, uncaring position. He'd remained at the treehouse until the night's chill chased him back to town.

Hadn't mattered. Cold that had nothing to do with the late spring night had settled around his heart.

None of the half-assed situations he'd considered made any sense. He had no clue what triggered Cookie's escape, so he didn't even have a starting point to deal with his emotions.

He needed to talk to someone. But Cookie's phone had stopped sending him to voice mail around three a.m. and he'd given up calling.

He'd become accustomed to the soft, early morning sounds rising from the shop as they readied for the day. This morning he strained to recognize any noise he could attribute to Cookie.

So messed up. He rose and wandered to the bathroom. A long shower did nothing to revive his spirit, but helped him pass the time until the pottery store opened. Even if Mom didn't have any answers, she'd always been there to ease his hurts.

He hurt real bad.

Mom was just unlocking the door when he arrived, and she ushered him into the shop with a hug and a wide smile. He didn't return the embrace and her smile faded, her brow wrinkled, and she took his hand to lead him to the curtained-off portion of the building. She pushed him onto a stool and perched on the low, glaze spattered table facing him.

"What's on your mind, dear?"

"Why should anything be on my mind. Can't I just stop by for a visit?"

"Cut the bull crap." She poked his temple lightly with her finger. "I can always tell when something's bothering you. Let's not make a game out of this. Spill."

"I'm in love with Cookie."

The smile returned. "And you've told her?"

"Yes. Well, sort of. I told her I thought I was falling in love with her. But she didn't say anything back."

"Love doesn't always need an immediate response, sweetie. Wait. You didn't say that just to get her into bed, did you?"

Heat flared up his neck and into his face. "What? Mom? No. Of course not."

His mom didn't give him a chance to recover from her pointed question. "Maybe she's waiting for you to say the words. Without the 'I think' qualifier. Thinking really doesn't mean anything in the long run. Have you told her straight out?"

"Uh, no. I didn't think I needed to."

She spread her hands and stared at the ceiling. "And that's part of what's wrong with a man's brain. Either one of them."

"Mom, please."

"You may be my kid, but we're adults here. Aren't we? Now then, you've been spending time together?"

He managed the energy to nod, earning another smile.

"And you believe you've shown her how much you love her. Am I right?"

Another nod. Despite how sometimes her thoughts rambled, Mom could usually get right to the point. He knew what she'd say next. "Now you're going to tell me that showing isn't always enough. Sometimes you need to tell someone that you love them. I need to say the words."

She touched his nose. "Bingo. I knew I raised an intelligent young man. So, what's your next move?"

He let his shoulders droop. That was the problem. He had no idea. "But what if she doesn't love me? What if all she wants is a friends with benefits kind of relationship?"

"I don't think you need to worry about that, sweetie. I've seen how she looks at you. How you look at each other. You're good together."

The heat returned to color his face and his mother chuckled.

"I didn't necessarily mean in that respect, but that's definitely a benefit. I'll ask again. What's your next move?"

He spoke slowly, questioning each word as he formed them. "Tell her how much I love her?"

"You're asking me? Anthony Burnham. Honey, just tell her. If she doesn't feel the same—which I don't believe—she'll let you know. Either way the two of you can decide what kind of relationship you'll have. Or not. It doesn't do any good to sit and wait and worry about what she might or might not feel toward you. Don't get bogged down in what might be when you should be focusing on what could be."

What could be. Yes. Focus on the possibilities, not the questions. He took his mother's hands. "You're right, of course."

"Then get going. I'll expect a full report later. Shoo."

Chuckling, she walked him back to the door and brushed at his wrinkled shirt. "Janelle and I both approve, sweetie. Cookie will be a loving, welcomed addition to our family."

※

On Wednesday morning Cookie made arrangements with her staff to take off the rest of the week. Explaining she needed some time to relax after the wedding met with disbelieving stares from Ava and a disappointed head shake from Darryl. She supposed she hadn't really hidden anything from the pair. At least they hadn't commented when she'd acted like a scorned teenager and made excuses to be out of the bakery yesterday when Tony left. Or again today when she'd heard his footsteps on the stairs she'd hidden in the walk-in cooler, claiming to take inventory.

While she didn't think her baking had suffered, she hadn't paid attention to her business. Thank goodness Darryl, Ava and the rest of her staff had her back. With her growing feelings for Tony, she'd known there'd be changes. She just hadn't expected this level of pain.

Leaving her store in more capable hands than hers right now, Cookie strolled past the park, barely noticing the wild display of colorful spring blossoms edging the grassy area. The short walk was a blur and she blinked in surprise when she stood in front of the bookstore. The clerk at the checkout counter waved for her to enter.

"Kate's waiting for you in the back," the young woman said.

"Oh. Okay. Thanks."

A trio of customers trooped to the counter as Cookie passed, exclaiming over the hand-crafted journals and cards in their hands. Their excitement brought the hint of a smile to Cookie's face. Both Vianna and Kate would profit from the tourists.

In the homey coffee area, Kate sat in a wingback chair, absently rubbing her huge belly. Vianna greeted Cookie from the coffee bar and held up a plate with a trio of thick crispy rice treats topped with a deep layer of chocolate. "From the Cooling Rack."

Kate groaned. "Between your cinnamon rolls, Cookie's cupcakes and the offerings from the bakery, it's a good thing I'm pregnant. I'd look like I was anyway." She closed one eye and her lips twisted in a grimace.

"Are you okay?" Cookie perched on the seat of a neighboring chair.

"Oh, sure. Just a twinge. I have to have a soccer player in here."

Cookie and Vianna exchanged a worried look. Kate shook her finger at them. "Stop worrying. Where's my treat? I need chocolate."

Vianna set the plate on a low table between the chairs then moved a third chair close to make a tight triangle. Now she and Kate shared a significant look and both turned their attention to Cookie. Before the questions evident in their expressions started, Cookie asked Vianna, "Shouldn't you be on your honeymoon?"

A warm pink blush filled Vianna's cheeks. "This really isn't a good time to go away with so much going on getting the camp ready to open in less than four months. Besides, I had enough of traveling on the art show circuit before I came to Spencer. Our cabin is enough. He's promised a trip later, but I don't care. Besides, I'd hate to be away when Kate has the baby."

Kate took Vianna's hand. "And I'm blessed to have you here." She held out her other hand to Cookie. "Both of you. This experience has been so different than with Madison. Easier."

Cookie had never had friends like these two women.

Both humbled and grateful she hoped they'd be able to help her focus her thoughts.

After squeezing her hand, Kate turned her full attention to Cookie. "So. You called us and left your shop in the middle of the morning. You're not your usual cheery self. And those dark shadows around your eyes aren't a makeup fail."

Staring at her tightly clasped fingers, Cookie continued to wage her internal debate. Talking to her friends about Tony had to help, but now that she was faced with voicing her thoughts, she wasn't sure she wanted to expose how foolish she'd been. How stupid to fall in love with him. She shrugged.

Vianna touched her knee and Cookie lifted her gaze. "Did you and Tony fight?"

That they hadn't done. She hadn't given him the chance. "No."

"Ryder mentioned Tony's been moping around the past couple days, too. What happened? And no, I have no idea. My guides are silent on this."

Her soft smile relieved Cookie. As much as she honored Vianna's ability to communicate with the spirit world, she hadn't realized how she'd dreaded the possibility anyone might already know what happened or have an idea what the outcome might be. Especially if that knowledge gave her no hope.

Vianna's grin widened. "And no, although I have my hopes, I have no clue what the future holds for you. My guides don't work that way. So why the miserable expression?"

Taking a deep breath, Cookie realized the only way through this was straight ahead. "Tony's leaving Spencer."

Brows furrowed. Kate leaned forward. "Really? Jack hasn't said anything."

Cookie nodded. "He's going back to work on his television show. The network offered him everything he wanted.

He'll... He has to sign the contract with them this week. He'll be gone."

She sniffed. She would not cry again. Especially not in front of her friends.

"And he told you this?" Kate asked, then grimaced again.

This was the most difficult to admit. Guilt over how she'd invaded Tony's privacy sat heavily in Cookie's belly. She ducked her head. "No."

"Then how do you know?"

Without lifting her gaze, Cookie spoke softly. "He left his phone on the counter and I read the text."

"So that's why the sad face. What did he say when you told him?"

Hoping for a reprieve she didn't deserve Cookie bit the inside of her cheek. From the incredulous expressions on her friends' faces, she must look guilty as hell. "I didn't. I was angry he hadn't said anything about going back. He's only talked about possibilities if he didn't. I didn't know what was real. I just left. I've been avoiding him, not answering his calls. I thought it would be easier this way. His leaving, I mean. I was wrong." Her voice broke. "So very wrong."

Pressing her hand to the small of her back, Kate leaned forward. "Let me get this straight. You read a text saying he was going back to his television series."

"Well, not in so many words."

Kate's brows arched. "What words?"

"Negotiations were completed. He got everything he wanted."

Kate rolled her gaze to the ceiling. "So the text said nothing specific about the show?" When Cookie shook her head, Kate sighed and continued. "Did you stop to think that him getting everything he wanted might have to do with his other plans? About leaving the show? Honestly, Cookie. You didn't think about that?"

"But, I—"

"Oh, good grief. This is just like a romantic movie on one of those special channels. A simple misunderstanding breaks the couple apart, when all they have to do is sit down and have a conversation. This isn't a movie or a book. It's not make believe. This is what you need to do, girlfriend. Sit down and talk to Tony. Give him the chance to explain. And let him know why you shut him out."

The solution couldn't be that easy, could it? Since she was the one who walked away, she had to find the courage to make the first effort. A glimmer of hope brightened her despair. As long as he'd listen and forgive her.

Kate clutched the arms of her chair. "Uh, Vianna, would you call Chet for me? I'm going to need some help getting to the hospital."

Vianna and Cookie surged to their feet. "It's time?" Vianna asked.

"Oh, yeah. I probably should have had you take me over an hour ago, but we needed to get Cookie sorted out. Ooh. Call Chet."

Cookie dug her phone from her tote. "I'll call Jack."

"Yeah, thanks." Kate moaned. "Good idea. Tell everyone to hurry."

❦

Tony sat on a saw horse with a bottle of warm water cradled between his hands. He stared at the pattern of rocks and torn up grass at his feet. He should be working on the treehouse, but just couldn't find the desire or energy. His agent had called that morning with the details of his flights. He'd only be gone a couple days, but part of him wondered if he should bother to come back if Cookie didn't' care.

Why wouldn't she talk to him? If he could figure out just one 'why', maybe he could get past this.

Nope, he couldn't face a future in Spencer without

Cookie at his side. He scrubbed one hand over his face. He was in such deep shit. And unless she cared, why should he?

Ryder sauntered over and leaned against the cabin wall. "Morning, sunshine."

"Shut up."

"So don't talk. Listen. That kid, Braydon? He's done a remarkable job repairing the vandals' damage. After pulling the nails, he filled all the holes. The walls are clean. Keane Dagleish was so impressed, he's offered the kid a job this summer. You done good there, coz."

With a shrug, Tony stood. "Happy for the kid."

"What the hell is up with you, dude? You've been moping around the past two days. Everyone's afraid you'll bite their head off if they ask a question. This isn't you."

He didn't care if he acted 'normal' or not. Why bother? Until now everyone had left him alone. That worked. "Get lost. You should be on your honeymoon, not badgering me."

"Our official honeymoon can wait. You, on the other hand, need to get your shit together. Vianna tells me Cookie's been acting the damn fool, too."

Tony gave Ryder his back. "So?"

"Don't be giving me that 'I don't give a fuck' attitude. Anyone with eyes can see—"

Spinning to face his cousin, Tony balled his fists. "Give. It. A. Rest."

Ryder lifted his hands in a conciliatory gesture. "Whoa, Tone. Chill."

Attempting to relax the muscles across his shoulders, Tony shook his head. "Sorry, man. She won't talk to me. Just walked out Sunday without an explanation and won't talk to me."

"What did you do?"

He gave a rough chuckle. "Why does everyone think I did something? Everything was fine. I left for about half an hour to grab breakfast. When I got home, she was already half-way down the stairs. She tried to get away without me even knowing. What's up with that?"

"Couldn't tell you. We're guys, and we'll never completely understand a female's mind."

"Big help."

"I can only tell you that most of the arguments Vianna and I have had could have been quickly and easily settled by just sitting down and talking to each other."

Yeah, that's what his mom had inferred as well. "Sure. But not so easy when she won't answer my calls or respond to texts. Hell, I don't know."

Whooping and hollering, Jack rounded the corner of the cabin and skidded to a stop, gripping both Tony and Ryder by their shoulders. "I'm having a baby."

"Yeah we know," Ryder drawled.

"No, I mean yes, I mean right now. Katie's on the way to the hospital. Cookie called me." He paused and stared at Tony. "Sorry, man. But our son is almost here. Come on. Cookie said Katie said both of you need to be there."

Tony tried to resist the tug on his shoulder to remain isolated here. He shook his head.

"You're going," Ryder insisted and jerked his thumb toward Jack's retreating form. "Great time to talk to Cookie. Besides, he's in no shape to get there himself."

"You go."

Ryder pressed one hand between Tony's shoulder blades and forced him forward. "Not without you. The pregnant lady commands our presence."

He couldn't fight that logic. He'd go. Wasn't doing anything constructive out here anyway. He'd see what kind of a reception he'd get from Cookie. If she didn't want to talk, he'd just walk home.

That, at least, would answer at least one of his questions.

CHAPTER TWENTY-FOUR

Once Jack changed into scrubs, Cookie and Vianna left Kate and her husband alone with the nurses and entered the maternity ward waiting area. Vianna rushed into Ryder's embrace. Concerned how Tony would react to her presence, Cookie paused in the doorway.

Tony turned and she took a hesitant step forward. He looked as wrung out as she felt. He hadn't shaved. His blue eyes were dull and lifeless. One corner of his lips twitched before he flattened them and gave her a jerky nod. She couldn't tell if it was a greeting, a simple acknowledgement of her presence, or permission to come closer.

She chose the third option and wound her way through the maze of waiting room chairs and low tables to him. Once there, she didn't know what to say, how to start the painful conversation. She settled on a truthful, neutral statement. "I can't wait to see Kate's baby."

A spark of surprise brightened his eyes before the color dulled again. "I'm happy for them."

"How've you been?" Maybe if they started with some general conversation, they could move into the important things that needed to be said. Although, from the dark glower on Tony's face, her question wasn't the right starting point.

"You really don't want me to answer that right now." He plopped onto one of the chairs, leaned back with his arms crossed and stared up at her. "So, how've you been?"

The snark in his tone shook what little confidence she'd been able to summon. She sat across from him and stared at her clasped hands. The air around her shifted and she lifted her gaze as Tony leaned across the open space between them.

He spread his hands. "Cookie, I'm sorry. I just want to know what happened. Why you left Sunday. Why you won't talk to me."

"And I want to tell you." She glanced at the others in the room. "But not here. Can we—"

A commotion at the door drew everyone's attention. But instead of the doctor bringing news, Jakob Spencer strode into the room, followed closely by Willa. "What's happening. Is my great-grandson born yet? Where's the doctor?"

The older man's uncharacteristically frantic demands broke the tight tension keeping Cookie from saying more. A chuckle from Tony gave her hope that it had done the same for him.

The older man's bright green gaze moved around the room. "Well? What's happening?"

Ryder moved toward Jakob. "They'll let us know, Grand-dad. You've just got to be patient like the rest of us."

Tony's words were soft in Cookie's ear. "He's always been impatient. You'd better not be late around old man Spencer. But I've noticed he's relaxed, become more approachable since he and Willa finally got married. I can't imagine what they've been through, having to be apart from the one they loved." Cookie strained to hear his next words. "I hope to God I never have to. Sweetheart, please talk to me."

They rose together and stood simply looking at each other. This was what Cookie had hoped for, wanted. "Can we go somewhere once the baby arrives? I don't want to miss that."

He agreed with a tired smile. She longed to cup his cheek and feel the prickle of stubble against her palm. Then she'd tell him everything would be fine. She wanted to, but until their conversation actually happened, how could she be sure of her wished for outcome?

"Let's join the others," she said. Until they were actually alone, she needed the safety and relative comfort of other people around them. There was a crack in the ice between them, and she didn't want to expose anyone else to her insecurities. explaining to Kate and Vianna had been difficult enough.

Trivial conversation was much easier with the others and she discovered she liked the formidable Jakob Spencer when he wasn't wearing his successful businessman demeanor. The six of them sat with their heads together discussing future plans for the Stick Pony property, but time still passed much too slowly.

"Excuse me?" At the bright voice, their conversation jolted to silence and they rose as one to face the doctor. She grinned. "Baby boy Spencer and his mother are doing fine. The nurses are finishing up getting everyone presentable then Kate wants all of you to come meet her son. Oh, and Jackson's doing great, too. He only nearly passed out once. Probably from the pain of Kate's grip on his hand."

The doctor chuckled and returned to the hallway. Jakob pulled Willa into a tight embrace. "Our great-grandson will never have to worry about his name or who he is."

Cookie caught Ryder tugging Vianna closer and she heard his whisper, "I can't wait to be a dad, too."

What did Tony think about kids? She'd never seriously considered having a family. Her childhood experiences hadn't been the best, and she'd assumed the expectations her father had put on her mother and her were normal. The scenario had been reaffirmed by the strong-willed chefs who'd taught her baking. Until she'd moved to Spencer.

Tony's family, both his nuclear family—she loved both his moms—and the extended family of aunts, uncles, and cousins, had shown her life with another person could be so much different. Her reactions to that stupid text had stemmed from those insecurities and old beliefs.

Tony's experiences in this huge, loving extended family were far different from hers. Of course, there had been conflict, and there would be again. But in moments of crisis, and moments of overwhelming love, they remained family. Together, supporting, and loving. She wanted this. Ached for this. With Tony.

Tony would be a fantastic father. He'd be able to help her, guide her through the times when her insecurity and doubt surfaced. Would she be a good parent? She glanced at Tony, who watched her with a calm, serious expression. With his support she would. If they still had a chance.

A nurse appeared in the doorway. "The family is ready to welcome guests. Normally we like to keep the number of visitors in the room to a minimum, but both parents insist all of you come in at once. Follow me, please."

Jakob gestured for Willa to exit first, but his tall, anxious figure was right on her heels. Chuckling, Ryder and Vianna followed. Tony offered her a similar gesture and a smile as they stepped into the hallway. Amazed she was included in this special family moment, Cookie caught her lower lip between her teeth. She'd stay at the back of the room, let the family admire the baby. She'd have her chance later.

The bed was centered in the room. Dim lighting cast the edges of the room in peaceful shadows. The tiny boy lay on Kate's chest, skin to skin. Cookie had heard that was important. Sitting on a chair pulled close to the bed, Jack rested his hand on his son's back. His grin brightened the room and he motioned with his free hand. "Come in. Come in."

Then he stood and stroked Kate's cheek. "We're so happy you're all here to share this moment with us. You're our family and we love you." He blinked. "I'm a dad."

Kate shook her head, her grin weary. "I know it doesn't count because you didn't know about Madison. I'm sorry you didn't get to experience my exuberant cussing with her birth, but I was an idiot not telling you about your daughter."

"Let us see the boy," Jakob commanded in an awed voice.

Kate shifted the tiny bundle so he faced them and adjusted the soft blanket covering him. "He's perfect. All the right number fingers and toes. He looks a little squishy right now, but he's been through a lot."

Jack caressed the soft brown fuzz covering the baby's head. "You are the first to meet him, the first to know his name. Kate and I, with Madison's help, decided to name our son Sean, after my father. Michaels for Kate's family. And of course, lucky little man, he's a Spencer from the get go. Please welcome Sean Michaels Spencer to the world."

While the others pressed forward to congratulate the new family and take pictures of the baby with their phones, Cookie eased toward the door. This was family time. She was only here because she'd been with Kate when they'd brought her to the hospital. She caught Kate's eye and lifted her hand to wave but the new mother shook her head.

"You're not leaving yet, Cookie. Come say hello to Sean. You, too, Tony."

Cookie blinked in surprise. Tony wasn't part of the family group surrounding the bed. He'd moved toward the door as well.

Unable to refuse her friend's good-natured demand, Cookie moved into the place at the bedside Vianna vacated. Tony stood at her side. His hand brushed against hers then he interlaced their fingers. Holding her breath, she glanced at him. He made silly noises to the baby, encouraging the tiny fingers to wrap around one of his.

Dear God, she was lost. If she hadn't loved him before, he'd filled her heart for sure now.

"So, what do you think?" Kate asked.

"You done good," Tony answered. "Congratulations to all of you."

Cookie added, "He's such a cutie."

Kate snickered. "You might not think so when we ask you to babysit."

Kate might allow her to babysit? The honor held her speechless for a long moment before she managed to say, "Anytime."

Kate turned her attention fully to her son. Time to leave. Cookie backed away and Tony moved with her. His hand still tight around hers, they paused in the doorway but the occupants of the room were focused on the baby. Good.

Tony walked beside her along the bright, clean hallway and out into the parking area. His expression filled with earnest hope, he faced her. "Come out to the treehouse? I don't have my truck, came in with Jack and Ryder." He paused as if considering his next words. "If you drive, you'll be able to leave whenever you want."

"We'll have to walk home to get my car. I rode over with Vianna. Then, yes, the treehouse. A good place. To talk."

CHAPTER TWENTY-FIVE

$\mathcal{F}$earing she would disappear, Tony held tight to Cookie's hand as they strolled to her apartment. Lost in thought, he remained silent. As did she. A good thing since their attempts at congenial conversation at the hospital had certainly fallen flat. Now he focused on how her fingers felt entwined with his and the way she allowed their hands to swing slightly as they walked. It felt comfortable. Right. And that meant something. Didn't it?

By the time they reached her SUV he still hadn't decided how to bring up the questions he needed answered. Afraid to chase her away—again—he considered allowing her to start the conversation. By leaving, she'd orchestrated the direction of his life over the past few days. She might as well have control of this moment. As long as they made progress working on this dark place in their relationship.

"Did you want to drive?" she asked.

Tony shook his head. "Want stop for sodas or something on the way out of town?"

"Sounds good."

The drive to Stick Pony was a silent as their walk had been. Tony attempted to gauge Cookie's thoughts and moods, but her expression remained a calm mask as she studied the minimal traffic on their stretch of highway. By the time she parked in the designated area near the cabins, his gut was a mass of jittery 'what ifs' and questions.

As they exited the vehicle, one of the construction workers waved. Tony handed Cookie the small cooler with their drinks. "I'd better go tell the guys the news. Jack made a scene when we were leaving."

"Go ahead. I'll wait here." Cookie's smile was natural, but tension showed in the tightness around her eyes and with the tiny lines between her brows. He'd discover how to soothe that tension once they'd passed the roadblock she'd set in their way.

He jogged to the gathering of workers, gave the baby's details and answered a few questions. A cheer rose when he gave the celebrating crew the rest of the day off. Losing a few hours of work was worth assuring he and Cookie wouldn't be disturbed at the treehouse.

Much of the tension had eased from Cookie's face and her now soft smile encouraged him. He offered his hand, and she took it without hesitation.

"They seemed pretty excited about Sean's birth," she said.

He considered the wistfulness in her tone, then set aside the possibilities and answered. "Yep. The crew's gotten to be like a big old family over the past few weeks. And giving them some time off this afternoon didn't hurt."

She chuckled. "I suppose not. But what was with that money exchange?"

"Keane Dagleish won the baby pool with the closest date and time. I held the bets. But he won't keep his winnings long though. Most everyone is heading to the Wild Card and the first round's on him."

"Will you miss going with them?"

"Huh? No. I'm where I want to be. I've got, we've got... we're more important right now."

"Yes, we are." She pulled him to a stop. "Tony, I'm sorry. You'll never know how sorry I am with how I left on Sunday. I owe you a huge explanation."

Yes, she did. But he'd recognized at the hospital she wasn't the only one who needed to clear the air. He hadn't been forthcoming with his plans, with his love. He loved her with a depth of need and longing that put passion to shame. Every cell of his body yearned for her. No matter how she might feel about him, she deserved to know how much she meant to him. How much he loved her. Once he'd spoken the words, he'd face whatever future she decreed for him.

"I have something I need to say to you as well, sweetheart. But not here."

"No, not here. At the treehouse."

They strolled toward the trio of trees at the edge of an expansive pasture. Tony leaned sideways and snapped the stem of a wild flax and handed the pale blue blossoms to Cookie.

"You still don't need to give me flowers, buster."

Buster. It was an odd term of endearment, but he treasured the syllables from her lips. That she'd said it now buoyed his hope and he subtly increased their speed. Words pressed against his brain, insisting to be spoken. The middle of a pasture wasn't the place for confessions. He'd always felt he left a piece of himself, a part of his soul in every build. The show's producers had exploited the 'heart' of his construction. This treehouse held even more. His dreams, hopes, his love. The only place for confessions and declarations.

Soon, but not soon enough, they stood in the shade of the trees looking up at the expansive platforms he'd build among the branches. Silent, he watched the wonder invade Cookie's expression. While he'd seen similar reactions over the years at reveals, this moment could change his future, his world. If she didn't approve of his passion, he wasn't sure what his options might be. For her, he'd find one.

"Spectacular. Oh, Tony, this is fantastic. Amazing."

He drew her to another vantage point and pointed to a section of a broad ramp. "Because of regulations, the ramp will be long and twisting, so this is just a small section. I'm still trying to work out an elevator system. There will also be stairs and for the adventurous, a ladder. So there's a way for every ability to experience the treehouse."

"I've watched your show, seen what you can do, but I never could have imagined anything as spectacular as this."

"You need to come up and see the platforms. And how the world looks from up there. Unfortunately, right now only the ladder is operative. Will you come up?"

Her smile brightened the late afternoon, tree-shaded glade. "Lead on."

Slinging the strap of the soft cooler over his shoulder, he climbed the sturdy wooden ladder bolted to the trunk then peered over the platform as she followed. The builder in him took over. "Over there will be an enclosed room and access to the higher platforms. Every platform will have sturdy safety railings. We'll add safety harnesses of for anyone who wants to climb to the upper platforms. There's two. But no way to get up there yet unless you can scale a tree."

She laughed. "This is high enough for me today. Oh, look at how the branches frame the mountains. Perfect."

"It is when the sun sets. Want to sit there?"

A serious expression dimmed her dark eyes. "Not too close to the edge, though. I don't mind being up high as long as I feel contained somehow. I'll need that railing."

"It will be in place before you come back again. I hope you'll come back."

They sat with her leaning against the rough bark of the old tree trunk. She fiddled with her water bottle, twisting the cap off and on. He gave her time to gather her thoughts. Hell, he wasn't sure how to order his own scattered concerns to put into coherent speech.

Cookie's phone jangled and with a guilty look, she pulled it from her pocket and glanced at the caller ID. "Vianna. I hope everything's okay with Kate. I should—" She held up the phone.

Tony nodded his agreement but before he could lean forward to listen to the conversation, his phone rang. With a muffled curse, he glared at his phone then chuckled. "Ryder."

He moved away a few steps before he answered. "What do you want?"

"Hell of a nice way to say hello, Tone. Are you with Cookie?"

"Yeah."

"Gonna come clean with her?"

"Yeah."

"I hope you've got better words for her than you do for me. Jack says thanks for letting the crew know about Sean. The Dagleish brothers have already been here with flowers." He chuckled. "And a tiny little blue hard hat. Madison's been here and approves of her new brother. Kate and the baby are both sleeping. Jack's just standing over them grinning like a fool. Damn, I hope I'm not such an idiot when Vianna gets pregnant."

Tony remained silent, the image of Cookie with her baking apron tied around where their child grew made him fumble his phone.

"Tone? Just talk to her. Get this settled."

The call disconnected. He lay the phone on the plank flooring, absently stroking the slightly rough wood. Needed sanding.

Cookie held her phone against her thigh for a moment before setting it next to her. She'd just reiterated her promise to her friends to figure out where she stood with Tony. While her friends having her back was a welcome comfort, the hard work was hers.

Tony had finished his call first and now sat with one leg

bent, resting his forearm on his knee. He stared past her shoulder and she angled to look behind her. The bright ball of the sun neared the distant mountain peaks, announcing what was sure to be another spectacular Colorado sunset.

She loved being here in the mountains. But if Tony left, she wasn't sure how long that love would last. Each sunset would be a reminder of her stupidity. Her foolishness. She squared her shoulders. Confession time.

"This treehouse is beautiful."

Tony jerked, then gave her a sheepish grin. "Sorry. Thanks. It'll be more so when completed. And there's people here to enjoy the experience."

"You're building something wonderful with these spectacular treehouses. It's what you should be doing. Need to be doing." She took a deep breath. "I have a confession."

Confusion tempered by a spark of hope filled his expression and he leaned forward. "Confession? Go on."

"Last Sunday, while you were at Pearl's, Deke called me. He said Hartwood had tried to get into the wedding, claiming he was my..." She swallowed the bile rising at the thought and took a quick sip of water. "Claiming he was my date."

Tony surged to his feet, fists and jaw clenched. "Was he?"

The anger didn't surprise her, but she needed to diffuse it quickly. "What? Don't be an idiot. Deke called to tell me to watch out for him. I already know that. Oh, Tony. Stop hovering. Sit down, please. So I don't have to look up at you. This is difficult enough."

He turned and stomped to the other side of the platform. Had she lost him? Surely he couldn't think she had any interest in the other man. The tight set of Tony's shoulders relaxed and he returned, sitting in front of her so their knees nearly touched. "Sorry. Bastard brings out the worst in me."

"I understand. No more about him, okay? I wasn't going to tell you about Deke's call because I knew how you'd react.

But because of that call, when your phone's message tone sounded, I thought Deke was texting you. I didn't want anything or anyone to ruin our day. Then, then I did just that. I ruined that day. And the days since then."

"I don't understand. Why would a phone message make you leave and shut me out? I was coming back to tell you something important."

Confession time. "I can't believe I did it, but I looked at the message. I invaded your privacy, after you'd been so careful with mine. I'm so sorry, Tony. So sorry. No, let me go on before you say anything else."

Tony drew back the hand he'd extended toward her and nodded.

"I opened a message from your agent. About the successful contract negotiations. About you having to sign the contracts this week. And I knew you were leaving."

"Yeah, for some reason the execs have to see me in person to conclude this business."

"I was sad. And I was angry you hadn't told me more about the negotiations. Oh, I've always known you'd leave someday. I just hoped it wasn't so soon."

"Signing a stack of papers filled with legal gobbledygook won't take long."

"Maybe not, but your show will take most of your time. There won't be time for Spencer. For me."

His brows drew together. "What are you talking about?"

"Your show. They agreed to your conditions. Hartwood told me they wanted you back. I'm sure you'll be successful for many more seasons. How could you not be? Just look at this partially completed project. I'm amazed. You're doing what you're meant to do. Maybe you could spend a little of your down time here. With me," she finished in a whisper.

She'd said what she needed to say. Almost.

"Tony, I'm going to miss you. More than I can bear. Because... I should have said this sooner... because I love you."

Tony rose to his hands and knees, leaning forward until his face was inches from hers. "You love me?"

"Yes."

He kissed the tip of her nose. The simple gesture made her smile despite the tears burning to be released. She loved him, but how did he feel?

Sitting back on his heels, he studied her. "And I love you with all my heart and soul. At the shack I said 'I think'. But I know. I'd known then. I love you, sweetheart."

The flash of joy in her heart slammed into a wall of reality. They loved each other, but could they make a long-distance relationship work? Unsure how to broach the subject, Cookie gnawed on her bottom lip. The only way was to face the question straight on. "So, after you sign the contract—"

"About that. It's not what you think. Hartwood was actually right about something. The network did try to get me to honor the rest of the contract. They sweetened the deal for the remaining seasons. But after I'd been home a couple weeks, I knew I couldn't go back. What we've finally agreed to is that they keep the show concept with a different host. The remaining years of my contract were written off. Other than anything that might cast a bad light on the show or be competitive, I can do anything I want. And what I want is to stay here and, I don't know, maybe write a book. Teach a new generation of treehouse builders. Work here at the camp. Hang out at the cupcake store."

She'd lost track of his explanation after he'd said he wasn't going back. Fascinated, she watched the movement of his lips, the smile that grew as he spoke. He wanted to stay in Spencer. He loved her. She loved him. Anything was possible.

Touching her fingertip to his lips, she halted his speech. He kissed her finger, her palm, the back of her hand. "Cookie, come here?"

"What are you thinking, Tone?"

His eyes lit then darkened as the desire she recognized softened his face. "I'm thinking I need to kiss you."

She went willingly into his arms. He teased her lips, nipping and soothing. She captured his face between her palms and demanded the kiss she ached for. Deep, satisfying yet leaving her wanting more, she sank against him.

He lay back, cushioning her against his chest and continued the sweet, sweet torment. Between kisses he whispered of his love against her lips and into her ears.

Breathing heavily, he rested his head against the fragrant pine-plank flooring. "Sweetheart, all of the confusion and pain I felt over that past few days could have been avoided if you just would have asked me Sunday about my plans. I hate to say it, but I think we're both guilty of assuming we know what the other feels. Hell, Cookie. Some of the time I don't know how I feel until I'm forced to put it into words."

The seriousness in his tone raised a flag of worry. She slipped to his side, sat, and waited.

"I don't want that to happen again."

"Me, either. I shouldn't have assumed. Not because of what I thought I knew, or what someone else had said. Especially not from an unreliable source." She rested her hand against his chest. The beating of his heart gave her courage. "I'm sorry. I'll probably fail—because I'm human—but I'll do my damnedest to come to you when I have questions. Stupid shit like I pulled shouldn't keep us apart. We can get through anything if we keep communicating."

"I like communicating." He sat to meet her lips then drew back. "I'm human, too. I know there will be times we get upset with each other. But if we talk about what's bothering us, maybe we won't end up miserable for days. I promise to do that. To talk to you when something's bothering me. To keep communicating."

She communicated her approval with another kiss. "I promise, too."

Tony's broad smile challenged the bright, late afternoon sun. "Sweetheart, I have a couple of questions for you. First, Cookie Lamont... hey, I don't even know your middle name."

This wasn't a question and she didn't have to answer. She'd used her middle initial exclusively for legal documents. But considering keeping even that harmless information from him made her chest ache. Her man wanted to know, so she'd make a second confession.

"You know how you're embarrassed because your middle name came from the movie character."

"Yeah, but at least I didn't end up as Narvarre."

She tweaked his nose. "That would have been cute."

Catching her hand, he kissed the palm. "You're avoiding telling me your middle name, sweetheart."

"Okay, you're right, Tony. My father chose my middle name because of a movie, too."

His eyebrows rose but he remained silent.

"Since our last name is Lamont, he thought it was hilarious to name me Cookie Lena Lamont."

"Lena Lamont? Like from *Singing in the Rain?*"

"Exactly. You know the movie?"

"Duh. My sister's a dancer. She loved the old musicals with Kelly and Astaire. And *Singing* is a family favorite. Wait until I tell Mom."

"Don't you dare." He still hadn't asked his questions. "Your question?"

"Oh, yeah. Think you could take off two weekends in a row and go with me? With you by my side, I'll know I'm doing the right thing when I sign all those damned papers. You'd be surprised how many pages of legalese we'll need to go through. Not exciting, I know. But as a perk, while the hotel's not up to the Aspen Gold Lodge standard, it is first class. We could hunker down and run up a damn high room service bill on the network's tab. Start making more memories."

Her answer took no thought. "Yes. Of course, yes. Sounds like fun. Especially the room service."

He rose and offered her his hand. She allowed him to pull her to her feet and into his arms for a lingering kiss. He turned them toward the west and the golden-orange ball of the setting sun. Overhead blues and purples streaked the cloudless sky announcing the coming night. The moment was more lovely and more intensely beautiful with Tony's arm around her waist, his body warm against hers.

"I have another question for you."

Hoping this would be as easy to answer as the first, she nodded.

"Cookie Lena Lamont..."

Great, she should have never told him her middle name. Maybe she could bribe him to forget it. A couple of delightful bribes came immediately to mind.

"Cookie, look at me, please."

She faced him. A final blaze of sunlight turned his hair to pure gold. Unable to resist, she brushed the back of her fingers against the soft strands.

Tony's eyes darkened to match the night sky. "I love you, Cookie. I want to share my life with you. I asked you once to stay with me forever."

She grinned at the memory and moved her hand to caress the rough stubble covering his jawline. "I thought you were asleep."

"Not quite. And you said yes. Right now, in this moment, I am fully aware of what I'm asking. Cookie Lena Lamont, will you stay with me forever? Will you marry me?"

The world tilted. Froze. The rustle of settling birds and the buzz of night insects fell silent. Marry? Did he say marry? He said marry.

Worry, hope and so much love filled his expression. "Sweetheart?"

She took his hands. "Anthony Navarre Burnham. Yes. Yes,

I'll marry you. Of course, I will Tony. And I'll stay with you forever and for always."

"I love you. Stay here with me tonight?"

"Isn't that over your requested question quota, Tony? All night?"

"Wait here." He scrambled down the ladder. Wondering what he was up to, she crossed as close to the platform edge as she dared to watch him unlock a small shed and pull out a thick roll of fabric. He tossed the sleeping bag to the platform before returning up the ladder.

"I stored this here after I spent those nights hoping to catch the vandals. It's not much and we'll have to share, but it'll offer a little cushioning. We can lay back, talk and look at the stars."

She considered the merits of sharing a sleeping bag. "And other things?"

His bright smile chased the last of the doubt from his expression. "And other things."

Cookie rushed into his embrace. The stars could wait. Talking could definitely wait. She was talked out. Now was the time to show him how deeply she loved him. As her lips met his, she sighed. She'd never before made love in a treehouse.

And now, she was sure it wouldn't be the last.

DEAR READER

With today's world of vast reading choices, word of mouth is the best advertising. So please let others know about this book. Tell your friends, relatives, acquaintances, the book reading stranger on the bus. By sharing a good book, you may discover a new friend.

Reviews help readers discover and connect with new authors. Every review is important to us and is greatly appreciated. Please consider leaving an honest review of this book at your favorite review sites or at any or all of these places: Goodreads or Bookbub

※

Once upon a time a group of writer friends got the grandiose idea to create a continuity series. We threw ourselves into developing characters, fashioning families, dynamics and a setting, which evolved from one member's love of all things Colorado. We created character profiles, detailed maps, brainstormed titles and themes. We collected photos and researched. We proposed our idea to a few publishers and got no traction. So, after a time the contracted books came first, members came and went, and the project was set aside.

Years after the initial idea, we rallied again to write the stories, now hoping readers will feel the same intensity and appreciation for this project as we do. We welcome you to join these families, laugh in their good times and cry in their sad times, follow them as they solve mysteries, expose secrets, recover from their pasts, reach for their goals and, most importantly, as the residents of Spencer Colorado fall in love.

Thank you for reading. Telling stories is one of our greatest delights and we hope you enjoyed your time in Spencer. Readers like you spark the energy needed to tell these tales. Again, thank you.

These Aspen Gold books are independently published by the authors. We thank you for your support, and we take pride in giving you quality books and excellent stories. We're thankful you've chosen to follow us and be part of the AG community.

The Aspen Gold Authors

Want to know more about Spencer, Colorado, and the Aspen Gold Series? Sign up for our email messages which include the monthly *Rocky Mountain Rumors*, new book announcements, and fun surprises. Your email is safe with us, will never be shared, and you can, of course, unsubscribe at any time. You can find the link on the Aspen Gold Series website. www.aspengoldseries.com

Be sure to follow all the Aspen Gold Series updates at:

Aspen Gold Series Website www.aspengoldseries.com

Aspen Gold Twitter https://twitter.com/@gold_aspen

Aspen Gold: The Series on Facebook
https://www.facebook.com/AspenGoldSeries/

Rocky Mountain Rumors, the newsletter
https://www.subscribepage.com/n9n7p3

Aspen Gold YouTube
https://www.youtube.com/
channel/UCQ3aDHsNrzby3e3XdlHgQ1Q

THE ASPEN GOLD BOOKS

Dancing In The Dark Aspen Gold Series 1
(Second Chance Small Town Family Saga Romance)
Cheryl St.John
He had everything a man could want--except her forgiveness...

~

Call Me Mandy Aspen Gold Series 2
(Second Chance Small Town Romance)
Debra Hines
The last man she loved took everything from her...

~

Ryder's Heart Aspen Gold Series 3
(Homecoming Forced Proximity Psychic Small Town
Romance)
*lizzie starr
She can't allow secrets to steal love from her...

~

For Keeps Aspen Gold Series 4
(Secret Baby First Love Family Saga Small Town)
Barbara Gwen & *lizzie starr
Hiding the truth is like denying the sun...

~

Second Chances Aspen Gold Series 5
(Second Chance Small Town Single Mom Romance)
Donna Kaye
She tried the fairy tale and the fairy tale didn't work...

~

Sleepin' Alone Aspen Gold Series 6
(Protective Hero Romantic Suspense Small Town Enemies to Lovers)
Bernadette Jones
Every man is guilty of the good he did not do...

~

Stay A Little Longer Aspen Gold Series 7
(Protective Hero Romantic Suspense Small Town Second Chance)
Bernadette Jones
Death wasn't frightening. Living scared the hell out of him...

~

Speechless Aspen Gold Series 8
(Small Town Wedding Romance Short Story)
*lizzie starr
How many peonies does it take to get married?

~

Close to the Heart Aspen Gold Series 9
(Friends to Lovers Small Town Seasoned Romance)
Debra Hines
He'd raised her child as his own...

~

Finding Hope Aspen Gold Series 10
(Cowboy Former Military Small Town Romance)
Donna Kaye
Is the peace he's found too good to be true?

~

Fortunate Cookie Aspen Gold Series 11
(Friends to Lovers Small Town Bakery Romance)
*lizzie starr
This woman... wearing frosting... and nothing else...

~

Lonely Eyes Aspen Gold Series 12
(Protective Hero Romantic Suspense Small Town Forced
Proximity Age Gap)
Bernadette Jones
She'd come to the right place. He was the monster hunter.

~

Whisper My Name Aspen Gold Series 13
(Secret Identity Small Town Sheriff Next Door Romance)
Cheryl St.John
She was the girl behind the headlines

~

Gorgeous Scars Aspen Gold Series 14
(Contemporary Romantic Suspense Rodeo Cowboy Heroine
in Peril)
M.A. Jewell
The rodeo never prepared this cowboy for bodyguard duty.

~

Another Night Alone Aspen Gold Series 15
(Protective Hero Romantic Suspense Small Town
Older Man)
Bernadette Jones
*She'd had the courage to save her child. Can she do the same for
herself?*

~

Yesterday's Promise Aspen Gold Series 16
(Anthology Short Stories Romance Collection)
Romantic short stories from the Aspen Gold Authors

~

Maybe I'm the One Aspen Gold Series 17
(Friends to Lovers Second Chance Small Town Deputy
Romance)
Cheryl St.John
While adored by millions, her world has become very small

~

Just My Imagination Aspen Gold Series 18
(Friends to lovers Forced Proximity Family Saga Fantasy
Romance)
*lizzie starr
Will his magic heal her reality?

~

A Better Man Aspen Gold Series 19
(Protective Hero Romantic Suspense Forced Proximity
Bounty Hunter)
Bernadette Jones
*Stripped of everything, her life threatened, she's forced to trust a
stranger.*

~

I Sorta Do Aspen Gold Series 20
(Fake Relationship, Single Dad, Small Town Romance)
Her heart is under lock and key...his knock is irresistible
Cheryl St.John

~

Trust Me Aspen Gold Series 21
Donna Kaye

~

Anything For Love
*lizzie starr

~

Serendipity
Debra Hines
*She didn't realize her happiness was on hold...until a chance
encounter*

~

Right Here Waiting
Bernadette Jones

~

Christmas Promise
Aspen Gold Short Story Anthology

Ryder's Heart: *Aspen Gold Series Book 3*

Ryder discovers an intriguing woman in his bed...

Five celibate years in Hollywood didn't ease Ryder Barlow's guilt over his father's death, and now he's coming home to Spencer with a new purpose— to create a camp specializing in equine therapy. When he discovers a beautiful woman in his bed, his plans aren't exactly derailed, but definitely knocked off kilter.

Escaping her past hasn't been easy for Vianna Harrison, but she thinks she's found a welcoming home in Spencer—as long as she can keep her ability as a psychic medium hidden. Not an easy task when spirits need to speak of forgiveness and joy to so many loved ones. Or when the owner of the exquisite cabin she's been allowed to live in comes home unexpectedly.

Neither can start a new chapter in their lives until they

stop rereading the old ones. Will acceptance overcome their secrets and show them their Rocky Mountain path to love?

❧

For Keeps: *Aspen Gold Series Book 4*

Hiding the truth is like denying the sun.

Widow Kate Michaels kept a secret from the man she loves, and from the entire community of Spencer, Colorado. She's content running her bookstore and life is good. But in order to pay for his medical care, she must sell the ranch that was her father's dream, and in doing so disappoint her 8-year-old, horse loving daughter. Madison makes an unlikely friend in someone Kate would rather forget.

Veterinarian Jackson Samuels is intrigued by the charming girl, and occasionally lets her shadow him in his nearby clinic. He's enamored with the child's mother, but her defenses are so sturdy, not even his charm or their shared past can make a dent. When Jack uncovers a family secret, the truth makes him question who he thought he was.

Will two people who once shared a heartfelt love, allow their lonely secrets to consume and define them? Or will they help each other, forgive each other, and build a future together—For Keeps?

(Author's note: Barbara Gwen was one of the original authors who created the Aspen Gold Series. When I joined the group and planned my own story, we discovered our heroes were best friends. When Barb left this world much too soon, how could I not finish the book of her heart. **For Keeps** is by her and for her.)

Speechless: *Aspen Gold Series Book 8*

How many peonies does it take to get married?

It's a beautiful day in Spencer, Colorado, and the peonies are in bloom. A perfect day to gather for a wedding, filled with love, traditions, fun, and maybe even a prank or two.

Vianna Harrison and Ryder Barlow would love the honor of your presence as they celebrate their marriage.

Fortunate Cookie: *Aspen Gold Book 11*

This woman. Wearing Frosting. And nothing else...

Cookie Lamont owns a successful cupcake shop in Spencer's trendy tourist center. Life would be perfect if not for the escalating unwanted attention from a self-important town trustee. She has everything she needs— and a man is the last thing on her mind.

Until he walks into her shop.

Treehouse builder and TV personality Anthony Burnham returns to Spencer and finds focus building cabins for a new camp. His passion for treehouses is rekindled as a sweet, sexy new love blooms.

But the past haunts his steps and threatens his growing relationship with the alluring baker.

Some Days are Diamonds, is a short story included in:
Yesterday's Promise: *Aspen Gold Series Book 16*

A high-stakes poker game, first meets, a dog rescue, loves lost and rekindled, and life-altering choices fill the history of Spencer, Colorado. Discover the challenges faced in these heartwarming stories crafted by the multi-author group who brings you romantic fiction at its finest in The Aspen Gold Series.

This collection includes:
The Card Game~~ M.A.Jewell
Some Days Are Diamonds~~ *lizzie starr
Ah, Venice ~~ Debra Hines
First Chance ~~ Donna Kaye
Racing Hearts~~ Bernadette Jones
Rescue Me ~~ Cheryl St.John

Just My Imagination Aspen Gold Series 18
Can his magic save her reality?

Owner of the Keltic Ranch gift shop in Olde Town, Konnor MacDhuibh is skilled in forging fantasy blades and keeping his Faerie heritage and magical abilities a secret. But when Bonnie Zhang and her two doxies need a place to stay, the empty apartment above his store is the perfect solution. Being so close to the cautious woman with haunted eyes tosses his good intentions to the wind.

Bonnie brings secrets of her own to Spencer. Leaving her broken past behind, she's ready for a new beginning. But if her secret is exposed too soon, she could lose any hope for acceptance--and a family.

Will their truths lead to love or destroy any hope they've forged?

(This book is also a part of the Keltic Multiverse: Children of the Triad 2)

OTHER BOOKS BY *LIZZIE STARR

FANTASY ROMANCE

Double Keltic Triad Collection Box Set

The Double Keltic Triad is a series of interconnected, stand-alone fantasy romance novels. All 6 books, and a bonus 7th story are included in this set.

It ain't easy being fey...

By Keltic Design   Allyn Keely, Celtic artist and friend of Faerie, finally finds a man she can love. But she's older than he is and faces the insurmountable task of helping him realize his destiny in the Faerie Otherworld.

Fires of a Keltic Moon   Lara Zeroun needs something in her life, so she opens a portal in time and travels to the ancient Highlands. But, how can she become involved with a dark, mysterious man who belongs to another time?

Keltic Flight   To the Faerie Gentry of the Otherworld, the fairy wee folk are but a myth and legend. Until the fairy

Korin falls in love with a half-Gentry maid. Forced to bargain with an evil king to woo her, he risks discovery, and his life, to fulfill the conditions.

Wild Keltic Carouselle   Falling in love was easy. But demons of the past and evil-doers intent on destroying the present tear Carrie and Bryce from their newfound love, throwing them into a world of deception, lies and revenge.

Keltic Dreams A spiritual quest throws Bard, naked and alone, from his world to the desert Sahara. Each grueling step through the shifting sands only adds to his questions and confusion. What did the seven Guardians mean for him to learn in this strange place? Will Kaelea help him discover a way home?

A Faire Keltic Renaissance It ain't easy being fey… and the subject of prophecy. Three worlds are in peril. A pieced together ancient prophecy might defeat the separate evils, but will it also bring Jayse and Lucidea love?

Bonus story: Prince of Dark Ness An ill-prepared fey prince struggles to protect two worlds and a newfound love from the evil of an ancient fire elemental.

Here's a little more about the individual books

By Keltic Design: *Double Keltic Triad 1*

It ain't easy to be fey when you don't believe in fairy tales.

In the fey Otherworld, a half-faerie child is born. To protect him from evil's crusade to ensure the purity of the faerie race, he is abandoned in the human world, never to know of his magical heritage.

Now Jaye Zeroun is a successful businessman, rooted in reality. Fantasy is only something from an undisciplined imagination. Until he meets Celtic artist and friend of Faerie, Allyn Keeley.

Allyn has found the man she can love but fears their age difference and the overwhelming task of helping him realize his destiny will tear them apart. But Allyn knots her way around Jaye's heart and fills his life with a fantasy he refuses to believe.

Until danger threatens their love, forcing him to either accept a deadly battle or lose the very things he never planned for in his life' a family and a love beyond his wildest imaginings.

❧

Fires of a Keltic Moon: Double Keltic Triad 2
Can love find a way through time?

Lara Zeroun needs an adventure, so she opens a portal in time and travels to the ancient Scottish Highlands. She meets two mysterious men but dares not trust her heart with either.

Under a matriarchal line of succession, Iain is unable to claim his father's holdings--his home. With no lands or possessions, he fights the temptation of a golden-haired woman who came to the manor on the arm of a wandering storyteller.

The storyteller's deceptions bring danger in Iain's time and threaten the destruction of Lara's present. Will Lara and Iain defeat the power of this growing evil and find their ways through time to the love they both desire?

Keltic Flight: *Double Keltic Triad 3*

What does she need to believe in love?

Even as a mythical faerie, Nanceen doesn't believe in the legends of tiny winged fey. Until a soft voice compels her to search... for love. She doesn't know what she believes but what she discovers changes everything.

Korin Goodfellow has loved the gentry maid from afar. But showing himself to her is forbidden by the fairy king, until using deceptions hidden by dark plans, the king forces Korin into an agreement with seemingly impossible conditions. Fueled by his pure emotions, Korin appears to Nanceen as a wingless man. One she can see. Touch. Believe in.

The evil fairy king keeps Korin's heritage hidden, warping the conditions to force Korin into battle after battle until he discovers his true place in the fairy world. Will Nanceen stand at his side as he risks everything for love?

Wild Keltic Carouselle: *Double Keltic Triad 4*

Falling in love is easy, the possibilities endless.

After months of searching, Bryce accepts he'll never find the masked dancer who captured his heart. Time to get on with life. But when his darlin' daughter climbs onto the lap of a captivating woman in a coffee shop and calls

her Mommy, he certainly wouldn't
mind exploring the possibility.

After a lengthy vacation, Carrie dreads returning to the job she once loved. Especially when a blond-haired cherub insists on calling her Mommy. The tiny girl's father is intriguing, and Carrie believes she's ready for a real relationship. But memories of a horrific attack surface making her doubt and fear a happy future.

Although he's human, Bryce's family ties are to the Faerie Otherworld, so when one of his fathers is kidnapped, no one knows if the abduction was of human or fey origins.

Falling in love was easy. Telling Carrie about the Otherworld risks that love. But demons resurfacing from both their pasts and evil-doers intent of destroying the present are intent on tearing them from their newfound love. Will their love survive a world of deception, lies and revenge?

❧

Keltic Dreams: *Double Keltic Triad 5*

Passion   blazes   hotter   than   the desert sun.

A spiritual quest throws Bard, naked and alone, from his world to the desert Sahara. In search of answers, each grueling step through the shifting sands only adds to his questions and confusion. What did the seven Guardians mean for him to learn in this strange place?

An ever-present evil continues to stalk her family, so Kaelea researches possible protections at the Fey Library of Alexandria. The appearance of a stranger at the oasis is an unwelcome interruption. Her instant fascination with the man, and the overly possessive actions of a fellow researcher are even more distracting.

Time alone might bring solutions to Bard's quest. But will unknown danger and the search for knowledge drive a wedge between him and Kaelea? Will they survive a passion that burns hotter than the desert sun?

✤

(**Author's note:** The action of the book *Prince of Dark Ness* takes place between Triad books 5 and 6. While it's not necessary to read *Prince of Dark Ness* here, it does give background into Lucidea's life prior to meeting Jaysson.)

A Faire Keltic Renaissance: *Double Keltic Triad 6*

It ain't easy being fey... and the subject of prophecy

Lucidea had no idea her father wasn't human—until a chance assignment as a forensic artist leads her to Scotland and a family she never knew. With her uncle imprisoned in the World Between Worlds, she's forced to assume leadership of a parallel, underwater world as his half Alfar-Sindhu heir.

Then she meets Jaysson Zeroun who has Otherworldly issues of his own. Once again evil plagues his clan and protecting a newborn child takes priority over personal dreams. When Lucidea offers to hide the family at her uncle's manor, Jayse accompanies them to Scotland. He's falling for Lucidea, but he fears how she'll react to the fact he's part Faerie.

Three worlds are in peril. A pieced together ancient

prophecy might defeat the separate evils, but will it also bring them love?

❧

Prince of Dark Ness: *Keltic Mulitverse*

(Author's note: This story takes place between books 5 and 6 of the *Double Keltic Triad* and introduces the heroine of book 6.)

An ill-prepared Alfar-Sindhu prince struggles to protect two worlds from an ancient fire elemental.

A romantic fantasy

Torn between duty and love, Morghan stands alone to protect both his Alfar-Sindhu underwater world and humanity from an ancient fire elemental bent on escaping the World Between Worlds. While he's loved Coralie long upon long, he never acted on his desire.

Raised in the royal household, Coralie has remained steadfast at Morghan's side through long human years. She's hidden her true feeling for him, even from herself.

A forensic artist from America, Lucidea Galvagin travels to Scotland to determine the identity of a skull found on Morghan's land. What she discovers changes her life and possibly the fate of two worlds.

Will Morghan's two worlds be lost if he chooses family and Coralie over battle? Or will his actions doom a multi-verse of worlds to fiery destruction?

❧

Blue Keltic Moon: *Children of the Triad 1*

Love and redemption? Only under the blue Keltic moon.

It's been twenty years since Morghan, leader of the Alfar-Sindhu, was trapped in the desolate World Between Worlds. Now blue moons are aligning in a multitude of worlds, signaling a magical opportunity.

Devoting his life to the Fey library hasn't saved Gowthaman from the agonies of his past, and the long moments he spent in the World Between Worlds. Now, the woman he loves stands ready to lead others into that cursed place. Only he holds the knowledge enabling them to enter. And with luck, safely return with the prince. The risk to his mind doesn't matter, as long as he keeps Breanna from harm.

A competent warrior, Breanna sets aside her personal desires to lead the rescue mission, facing the unknown to bring Morghan home. While she's loved Gowthaman forever, he claims their age difference is too great. But she's seen their soulfire and knows he loves her as well.

Together they must face the World Between Worlds. Can a place filled with despair and loss also be a discovery of love and redemption? Perhaps... only under the blue Keltic moon.

⚜

Just My Imagination: *Children of the Triad 2*

Can his magic save her reality?

Owner of the Keltic Ranch gift shop in Olde Town, Konnor MacDhuibh is skilled in forging fantasy blades and keeping his Faerie heritage and magical abilities a secret. But when Bonnie Zhang and her two doxies need a place to

stay, the empty apartment above his store is the perfect solution. Being so close to the cautious woman with haunted eyes tosses his good intentions to the wind.

Bonnie brings secrets of her own to Spencer. Leaving her broken past behind, she's ready for a new beginning. But if her secret is exposed too soon, she could lose any hope for acceptance--and a family.

Will their truths lead to love or destroy any hope they've forged?

(Author's note: This book is also a part of the Aspen Gold Series 18)

❧

Candy Guy and the Chocolate Brownie: *Keltic Mulitverse*

A Keltic Multiverse short story

Who better to assist a struggling chocolatier than a Brownie?

Candy Guy is in trouble. Winning a design contest will prove his abilities as a chocolatier, but creativity eludes him. An enchanting intruder invades Trace's workspace. She may be real, or she might be a dream. It doesn't matter. Desire consumes him at her lingering touch and the deep chocolate flavor of her kiss.

Deleesi hopes to end the ancient fey curse haunting her family, but the handsome wisher defies her sleep-inducing magic. Something about this human calls to her soul, and, unbelievably, to her heart. The sensual distraction proves impossible to ignore, even while granting his unspoken wish.

By the end of the rainy afternoon, Trace has his inspiration. But will he ever again see the tiny woman who captivated his heart and became his muse?

FANTASY ROMANCE

Double Moon Destiny

On the night of the Double Moon a child is born, and the destinies of an acolyte and a rebel are changed forever.

Jermanah, acolyte of the religious Compound, has never been given the opportunity to make her own choices. Although she accepts her way of life and yearns to rise higher in the order, she learns ancient, forbidden healing from the Seer. On the night of the Double Moons, a child is born and given into Jermanah's care until the boy is taken to the king.

Kierigh was born moments before the rising of the Double Moons, but his twin brother wasn't so lucky. Rumors flow from the Stronghold—following an ancient prophecy, the king sacrifices the baby boys to increase his power. But Kierigh senses that even after five cycles, his brother still lives.

When Kierigh's rebels attack the procession, he takes the babe, and Jermanah, to his hidden camp. The captivating acolyte disrupts Kierigh's ordered and simple life. He opposes her religion and all the Compound claims to stand for. She's everything he doesn't need in his life. Yet she is everything he desires.

No longer considering herself one of the Compound,

Jermanah discovers freedom, and truths she finds difficult to believe. But when the babe is taken from the forest, she will do anything to save the child, including face the leader of the Compound—and the king.

Can a rebel and an acolyte set aside pride and differences to find a lost brother, defeat evil, and discover their prophecy fulfilling destinies?

CONTEMPORARY ROMANCE

Birds Do It!

A search for truth, switched babies, and a threat from the past

Macaws as lovebirds?

An avian expert, Birdie Simons is called to help control a cantankerous hyacinth macaw during a young girl's birthday party. Inexorably drawn to each other, she and single father Garr Logan share an afternoon of joy and bittersweet memories, for Garr's wife died the same day as Birdie's newborn child.

Something about Rachelle makes Birdie wonder if the golden-haired girl is her daughter, switched at birth. Then her child's father returns, dogging her search for understanding and throwing her deeper into fear and confusion.

Ready to move on after his wife's death, Garr wants the intriguing woman, but Birdie keeps the search, threats, and hidden relationships to herself, driving a wedge between them.

Will discovering the truth from nine years ago bring them closer, or forever tear them apart?

SHORT STORIES

Written in Stone: *Structs in the City 1*

Undercover agent Stone Mason must find a data-link before a demonstration for underground bidders leads to mass destruction. His search of a posh hotel is risky, but time is up.

Monika Linberg returns to her hotel room after her boss dumps her and assumes the striking, robotic sex-struct is her consolation prize.

Fantasy Romance

Stone is no construct, but a living, breathing man whose touch and need for information and assistance turn her world upside down. Will working with the sexy agent to keep the city safe be too dangerous for her heart?

Dead Lily Blooms: *At Death's Gates 1*

For ages uncounted, Master Death has assisted souls in transition. But what happens when love gets in the way?

Someone wants vampyre Lily dead, and a bargain with Death has been struck. Death sends servant Agaar to bring Lily to him, but the task becomes more complicated than either Death or Agaar anticipated.

Fantasy Romance

This short story originally appeared in the anthology Tales From The Mist. This re-release has had minor corrections from the original edition.

Death and the Dryad: *At Death's Gates 2*

For ages uncounted, Master Death has assisted souls in transition. But what happens when love gets in the way?

What's Death to do when a dryad appears at his gate without her soul? She can't move on, nor go back. Will Death find a place for her--at his side?

Fantasy Romance

This tale appeared originally in the **Martini Madness** *anthology and this re-release has had minor corrections and additions from the original.*

*lizzie also enjoys creating journals and guided workbooks for authors and other creatives. Look for them on her website.

ABOUT THE AUTHOR

*lizzie always made up games and stories to keep her company. So, a cunning witch lived in Grampa's weather research station and was only held at bay by waving a certain weed. An ancient road grader morphed into a boat carrying wild adventurers to islands filled with fierce lions and dangerous cannibals, which really looked a lot like sheep.

Now filled with fantasy, love, and romance with a sparkling twist, the stories of her imagination swirl their way into the mundane world.

*lizzie recently retired from her more routine life of being *the Lunch Lady* at a private school. According to the kids, she was 'the best cooker!' Yes, she misses the students and teachers, but is delighted now to start her days by telling stories rather than opening cases of chicken nuggets and counting milk cartons.

Her tag line of *Author and lunch lady~~what a combination!* no longer holds true (which makes her sad because she really liked that one).

Now you'll know *lizzie by her tales of...
~~*Romance with a sparkling twist*~~

Want to keep up to date with all of *lizzie's worlds?

Sign up for her newsletter
https://landing.mailerlite.com/webforms/landing/o9q4q4

One link to find them all
https://linktr.ee/lizziestarr

Website
www.lizziestarr.com

facebook.com/authorlizziestarr
twitter.com/lizziestarr
instagram.com/lizistarr
amazon.com/*lizzie-starr/e/B003F33Y0W
bookbub.com/profile/lizzie-starr
pinterest.com/lizziestarr
tiktok.com/@authorlizziestarr